INTO THE SUNLIGHT

'I'll do anything. I'll sing, dance, scrub the floor—anything.'

Helen Jarvis was determined to look after her fragile sister Etty and escape the slums of London's Bethnal Green. She had resolved that, somehow, she would marry into the aristocracy and become a lady, via a career in the performing arts. Starting as a serving wench at Swains' Music Hall, Helen rose to dominate the London stage, but the cost of her ultimate goal was high. When she met happy-go-lucky Jack Waters, love and passion had to fight ambition and duty...

INTO THE SUNLIGHT

INTO THE SUNLIGHT

by
Harriet Hudson

Magna Large Print Books
Long Preston, North Yorkshire,
England.

British Library Cataloguing in Publication Data.

Hudson, Harriet
  Into the sunlight.

  A catalogue record for this book is
  available from the British Library

  ISBN 0-7505-1156-7

First published in Great Britain by Severn House Publishers
Ltd., 1996

Published in Large Print 1998 by arrangement with Severn
House Publishers Ltd.

Magna Large Print is an imprint of
Library Magna Books Ltd.
Printed and bound in Great Britain by
T.J. International Ltd., Cornwall, PL28 8RW.

Author's Note

I owe a great debt to my agent Dot
Lumley of the Dorian Literary Agency,
who gave me guidance and encouragement
throughout writing this novel. Thank you,
Dot. The idea for the novel sprang
initially from reading of the career of
the remarkable Dame Marie Tempest,
though the private life and character of
Dame Helen Hill are her own. Dame
Marie celebrated her jubilee of 50 years
on the stage, and I have drawn on the
description in Henry Kendall's memoirs
I remember Romano's, on which to base
Helen Hill's farewell, and on James Agate's
criticism of Dame Marie's acting.

The extract from W.B. Yeats' poem
'When You Are Old' appears with the
kind permission of Messrs A.P. Watt, on
behalf of Michael Yeats.

PART ONE

April's Lady

Chapter One

'I'll do anything. I'll sing, dance, scrub the floor—*anything.*'

Helen wasn't used to pleading, but she was desperate. Swains' Music Hall was her last chance. London's East End was crowded with such halls, but also teeming with those who like herself saw them as a means of escape from the pit of hopelessness in these slums.

Swains, a portly florid-faced man in his fifties, took another puff of his cheap cigar, and looked her up and down speculatively.

'Anything, eh?' His hand reached out perfunctorily to her waist and encircled it. 'And just what can you offer that's so extraordinary?'

Indignantly, she pushed his hand away, and her eyes blazed in excitement. She *knew* what she had to offer...

'A diddiki moucher must have left you for sure,' her mother used to rant, looking in disgust at Helen's dark gypsyish curls and sallow complexion. 'Why can't you be like Etty here?'

Helen would gaze at Etty meekly

scrubbing at the dirty washing with Sunlight soap under the shared cold water tap in the yard, and wonder why she had been born so ugly. If she looked like Etty, Ma would love her too. Henrietta had been born in 1862, three years before Helen, and Helen loved her. She was gentle and kind and all the things Helen wanted to be and *was*, except that somehow she could never show it—save to Etty. If she did, Mother just shouted impatiently at her and she felt bruised, like Father's rotten fruit, only this was deep inside. Instead, she allotted herself the task of protecting her older sister with her fragile pale looks and innocent blue eyes.

Helen had opened a cautious eye as she arrived in this world, as if realizing it might not prove entirely to her liking. She promptly yelled for the attention that she needed but it was grudgingly given. Boys were more use in this world. Then Helen faced her next battle—survival. In mid-Victorian Bethnal Green, teeming with vermin, much of it human, this was not easy, but she managed it, for she quickly discovered that if you stuck out your chin no one would know what you were feeling inside.

She tried to love chubby red-cheeked George who followed her into this world a year later, but Mother discouraged her caresses of the first-born son.

'Keep yer dirty hands off 'im, 'Elen.'

Rejected, Helen saw the children that survived the first year of life merely as a succession of waifs, who presented her with more work and less room in the large ancient bed which housed them all in the one bedroom with the curtained-off recess. Mary and Michael Jarvis were luckier than most costermonger families: they had two rooms, almost three if you counted the kitchen area, a whole floor rented for half a crown a week. But for Helen it became a place of fear, for downstairs lived the monstrosity of Mrs Blades, their landlady.

'Come in, come in, dearie.' The hoarse whisper was more sinister by far than all Father's yelling and shouting. 'Let's see what you have for Auntie today.'

From the age of five, Helen had to take the Monster's shopping in, had to unpack it as the twisted blob of a face, ruined through gin and syphilis from her years as a prostitute at the docks, leered at her. Mrs Blades was so gross she was confined to a chair, yet her evil seemed everywhere in that dank-smelling room, so that whichever way Helen looked there was Mrs Blades looming, grinning with her terrifying lips, breath and body rank.

'I'll do it,' offered Etty bravely, guessing

Helen's nightmare.

But Helen would not let her. She was determined to conquer this thing, this bestiality. Besides, one thing made the visits almost bearable. In the midst of the worm-ridden furniture and smelly bric-à-brac, was a tattered but brightly-clad doll in an exotic dress of red satin, a doll with flowing black hair and a lace shawl, perhaps thrust into Mrs Blades's hands by some drunken sailor.

'Touch her, dearie.'

Helen always ignored the rasped command. To touch it might remove its magic. The doll puzzled Helen, partly because she had never possessed such a thing, and partly because this shining object surely had no place in Mrs Blades's world. Somewhere, Helen reasoned, there must be a world where such beautiful things existed.

But it was a long way from Bethnal Green. Behind their street of shabby terraced houses, lay the notorious rookery called the Nichol, a complex of narrow streets through which the sunlight never filtered, and the dregs of society created a swarming hive of viciousness. Here too lived the families of the decaying Spitalfields silk trade, toiling sweat shops in what had once been a proud and thriving industry. Honest workers who struggled eighteen hours a day to make ninepence jostled side by side with those who had long since given up the unequal struggle to respectability and existed by prostitution, begging, stealing, murdering. They lived five or six to a room in cheap lodging houses in the warren of alleys with open cesspits. Men, women and boys were all crammed together, the great unnumbered of the metropolis.

'Out of the Nichol most like,' Mary Jarvis grunted, when longing for gratitude Helen gave her mother a present. It was a scarf she had picked up in the street, and Mary threw it on the fire.

Any hopes of love from her mother that Helen might have harboured died, as she watched the flames lick, then burn it up. From her father, she knew it was impossible for he ruled by different means. Helen would never show her fear of him for that meant giving in. When he regularly pulled her drawers down and thrashed her for whatever the misdemeanour of the day had been, she would force herself to her feet and glare at him pugnaciously. If she cried, she reasoned, he'd think he'd won and do it all the harder next time. He never touched Etty though, whatever she had done, for Mother would always defend her. Then Father would swear and disappear down to the pub, not returning till too drunk to find his way to the curtained recess without a push from the children, the smell of liquor spreading around him in an evil-smelling blanket.

'I'd 'ave risen to parlourmaid if I 'adn't married you,' Mary would hurl at her husband in constant complaint.

Risen? What did she mean, Helen wondered. It sounded good, like that man Jesus whose picture she had seen at her Board School. The picture showed him up in the air in the clouds, spreading out his hands. She liked it. At the school she learned to read and write after a fashion, and grasped a firmer idea of that far-off world which might offer more than Bethnal Green.

'Turn again, Dick Whittington, thrice Lord Mayor of London.'

She would say this over and over again to herself, for the story made a deep impression on her. Dick hadn't liked his home either, so he ran away and became Lord Mayor. Could she do that? She decided to keep it as a thought for the future for it didn't seem practical at the moment. What did was more immediately at hand. At the school were some of the children of the Nichol where she was strictly forbidden to go, and they had less savoury companions who never bothered with school but were hardened criminals by eight or nine. If she couldn't be like Etty and please Mother, perhaps *they* would love her? Helen investigated. Some, she discovered, specialized in stealing from barrows, others in stealing laundry, some were highly professional beggars. Most, however, were dippers, apprentices for the adult élite swell mob who chose their victims with care and dressed accordingly.

Won over by their praise of her quick eye, Helen was soon adept in the art of dipping and took pride in her skill, convinced she was beloved by the mob. Even if she was ugly, she was clever at something. On her second dip at King's Cross Station, however, trouble arrived, though not of her making.

She would have been content merely to have stood and watched this fascinating grey smoky place, full of huge iron snakes. Where were they going, these green-painted monsters, belching smoke and fumes? Who were all these people so beautifully dressed and important-looking? Then Archie Thomas, with quick eye and face already wizened at eleven, made his mistake. He chose a victim with a cold, who gave an overpowering sneeze which jerked his arms up—and found his wallet half-way out of his pocket in the hand of a small wiry boy.

'Stop that boy. *Police!*'

Archie was quicker than the staring crowd and so were his accomplices. 'Crushers, mizzle,' he yelled at Helen, as three hefty policemen materialized in his path. Blind with panic, Helen headed straight for them, sobbing with fright. Then she felt something grip her arm, yanking her so that she stumbled in a heap by the wall. It was the crook of a walking stick, and its other end was held by a strange figure.

'Sit down, dear child. Stop panting, do.'

Two of the police rushed on, but the last paused, looking suspiciously at the still sobbing Helen.

'Who's that?'

'My niece—er, Sergeant,' her rescuer supplied promptly.

Thwarted, the policeman departed, and Helen looked warily at her saviour. He was very, very old, she decided, for his face was heavily lined, but his mild blue eyes were gentle, reminding her of Etty's. He wore a battered old gibus hat, tattered frock coat, something that might once have been a bright ascot and baggy grey trousers. His toes were poking out of his shoes.

'Might I enquire your name, niece?'

Helen had never heard anyone speak so grandly before. ''Elen, sir.' Self-consciousness made her truculent. ''Elen Jarvis.'

'Well now, Ellen Jarvis, so you're a thief.'

'No, I ain't, and I'm 'Elen not Ellen.'

'We are two of a kind, Miss Jarvis. You ain't a thief and I ain't a matchseller.' Surprised, she glanced at the pathetic array of Bryant & May's goods laid out on his tray. 'You may think,' he continued, 'I am a matchseller because you see these matches. But it's what's inside yourself that counts, and inside, Miss Helen Jarvis, I am a *poet.*' He banged his chest proudly. 'Frederick Hewson, poet, at your service.'

'What's a poet?'

He looked shocked at this ignorance. 'A poet, my dear young lady, is a person who can transform this dull world of ours into a place of splendour, of mystery, of beauty.'

Helen was bewildered, but sensed it was a good thing to be a poet.

'I have come down in the world, Miss Jarvis,' he continued. 'I began my career as a balladeer. I compose my own poetry. Alas, this cruel world had no time to listen to poetry, though spoken from the heart, and so I became a patterer, Miss Jarvis. Do you know what a patterer is?'

She shook her head.

'He speaks the news. He is the voice unto the people. He brings knowledge to those that cry out for a sign. He

21

tells of Ghastly Murders in Scunthorpe, of Beauteous Brides Betrayed by Brutal Beasts, of Fiercesome Fires in Fife. But alas, education brings words to those who cannot comprehend them. The soul of the news is no longer heard. It is simply read, Miss Jarvis. In common *newspapers.*'

He took out a dirty white handkerchief from his pocket and wiped his eyes. 'And so, Miss Jarvis, I am now a matchseller. By striking matches, you see, I may still bring light into a dark world.' He smiled, but the joke was lost on Helen. 'But never do I forget, Miss Jarvis, that inside I am a poet. And now, dear lady, permit me to escort you home. I think perhaps an omnibus. The gods have been kind today.'

He gravely offered Helen his arm. She had to stand on tiptoe to reach it and walk on her toes, but she managed it. As they drew nearer her home after getting off the omnibus (in itself a rare and treasured experience) she grew quiet. Suppose he told her father? Fear made her run from him, long before they reached home, but she heard his voice floating after her. 'Any time, Miss Jarvis. You'll find me at home. King's Cross Station, remember.'

She need not have feared her father's discovery of her criminal activities, for he had already heard about them through the costermonger fraternity. But retribution did not follow the course she expected, for he eyed her with a new interest.

'You're coming with me, me girl, on the barrer.'

She hated the barrow. She disliked the donkey which always seemed to be waiting its chance to kick her in the shins, and the smell of the bad fruit carefully concealed beneath the good made her feel sick. This time, however, it was different, for today Father bought only the best at Spitalfields. Even the donkey had a ribbon round its neck and Father was wearing his best Sunday scarf. He abandoned his usual pitch in Cable Street and they went further afield to a quiet Islington square where the houses looked very grand.

'Down there, girl, and quick about it. *Now.*' He pointed down into one basement.

'What fruit do I take?'

'Yer brings stuff back, not takes it down. Git moving.'

It was her introduction to area-diving, choosing a time when the servants were upstairs, and lifting anything lying around in the basement. Helen dreaded it. As she crept into the dark dungeon of a kitchen, she felt trapped. It was not like dipping pockets, for you were free to run then. She did it for a week, and was never caught, because her mother found her in

23

possession of a beautiful watch which she had concealed from Father, intending to stow it in her 'Dick Whittington Fund', for running away. In a trice Mother had the whole story out of her, and her fury broke, partly over Helen, but chiefly over her husband's head.

'Not content with pulling me down in the world, you have to start on the kids too. You and your common ways...'

Helen and Etty clung together, waiting for the storm to end.

'It's only bloody 'Elen. It's not as if it's your precious Etty,' Father blustered.

The storm went on for hours, until at length all was quiet behind the curtain, save for those noises that made Helen shiver...sounds she couldn't put a name to.

Etty, always Etty. Dearly as she loved her, Helen couldn't see why only Etty should have a special outing once a year, when she would unwillingly be pushed and pummelled into her Sunday dress, and she and Mother would take a real omnibus. Mother looked quite different on those days. She would put on her best dress of dark blue serge with the lace collar and did something to her hair so that she looked quite pretty. An omnibus in itself was unusual for that meant spending money, but Father never lifted a finger to

24

stop them going. The trotting horses would sweep them out of sight, perhaps for ever. Helen's stomach always knotted up lest she lose Etty, and she took station by the window until hours later she would see them walking up the road. All Etty would say in answer to Helen's eager questioning was: 'We went to the big house, and we saw *him*.'

'Who's *'im*?' asked Helen, agog.

'A big man, with a moustache and beard. Mother said she used to work for him before she married Father.'

Helen digested this information and decided she wanted to go to the big house. Perhaps the big man would love her as he must love Etty. She gave her mother no peace, until on her ninth birthday her mother gave in.

The omnibus itself was fun enough, to sit there swinging her legs and looking at the people opposite. Helen longed to be allowed to clamber up the ladder outside, and sit on the top deck with the young men, and only fear of being sent home made her give up pestering her mother.

'But why not?'

'Because it ain't decent. That's why not. There ain't no boards.'

'But why ain't that decent?' A sharp slap was her only answer.

They took the first omnibus to somewhere called the Black Horse. Helen watched excitedly to see this animal, but was disappointed to find it was only a building. There they had to change, and this time the omnibus had a richer clientele, almost as grand as the one at King's Cross. Full of excitement, she knelt on the seat looking out at the crowded pavements and shop windows. Eventually after walking along a lengthy stretch of grass, they were in a street of *really* grand houses, much larger than those in Islington, and her mother tugged at them to follow her down a flight of area steps. Helen hung back, in case Mother was going to make her do what Father had forced her into.

'Come on, 'Elen. What a little devil you are. Why can't you walk nice and proper like Etty here?'

Inside they were greeted by a large round rose-cheeked cook presiding over a kitchen where the most delicious smells were emanating from a range. On the table cooling was the most enormous pie Helen had ever seen and plate after plate of cakes.

'I want one.' Helen's hand went out, but it was slapped smartly down.

Then they were summoned by a smart gentleman to follow him up a narrow flight of stairs, and then up and up again on carpet so thick Helen's feet seemed to sink in. Surreptitiously she wiped some muck from the street off her boot.

'Hendricks, sir.'

Etty hid behind Mother as they went into the room, but Helen marched forward, wide-eyed and inquiring. It was the most beautiful place she had ever seen: large windows with enormous gold velvet curtains overlooked that green grass they'd walked along and on the ceiling there was a huge painting of boys and girls without any clothes on running about. The walls too were painted with gold. It was just like Sleeping Beauty's palace.

A man rose to meet them. He did indeed seem enormous. He had huge black eyebrows, black hair, black coat, black-striped trousers—perhaps he was the Lord Mayor, like Dick Whittington, Helen thought in excitement, edging forward. The stranger bent down to kiss Etty on the cheek, and Helen saw her shrink away. Now was her chance. He turned to her, but he looked forbidding, not welcoming.

'And what's your name, little girl?'

''Elen.' She tried to look bright and lovable.

'Sir,' hissed her mother.

'Sir,' Helen added, heart sinking. Now she'd ruined her chances.

'Helen, child. Not 'Elen. There was a

man who once said,' he boomed, "drop your friends before you drop your aitches." Remember that, child.'

Helen did, although she didn't understand what he was talking about. All she realized was that she had done wrong again, and this man too would never love her. Well, she didn't care. In any case, the memory of the big man was soon blotted out by what happened next.

As they came out of the house onto the pavement, blinking at the sudden sunshine, a princess passed them. Helen knew only a princess could look so lovely, even if she didn't have a crown. Instead there was the most lovely hat perched on the back of her hair, which in front cascaded in ringlets to her shoulders. On the hat were flowers and ribbons and feathers, all in the same shade of blue as her satin dress. The dress was drawn in very tightly in front with a close-fitting bodice, and in a darker shade of blue an overskirt stuck out behind and fell in folds to the ground, giving the princess the most elegant shape imaginable. Everywhere were frills and flounces and draperies and the opening at the front of the dress was filled with filmy lace. The princess had a tiny waist and a haughty look. Underneath the dress, as she undulated up the steps, Helen could just glimpse dainty white shoes with funny little heels which stuck her foot up in the air.

Helen drew in her breath sharply. 'I want to look like her.'

'You can't, child.' Mary impatiently tugged at her to come away.

But Helen would not budge until the lady had entered the house and the large door had clanged behind her. 'Won't I ever look like her?'

'No, you won't.'

'Why not?'

'You've got to know your place, that's why. She's not our sort.'

Helen said nothing more aloud, but under her breath she muttered, 'I *will.*' Some day, even if she had to steal, beg, lie and fight, she would look like that lady. *Then* people would love her, they would have to, and she'd be able to be as gentle as Etty. Helen carried this resolve with her and it sustained her as a beacon through her remaining childhood and the harder years of her adolescence.

As she grew older, two other things sustained her as well as the memory of The Lady: her love for Etty and Mr Frederick Hewson. She had made her way back to King's Cross, and an odd friendship had sprung up between the two of them, partly because she had decided that if she were to look like The Lady she needed to be educated, and only Mr Hewson could tell her how not to drop aitches. He had much advice to offer on education, not all of it practical.

'Poetry, my dear Miss Jarvis, is the way to the stars,' he waved his arm roughly in the direction of the Great Bear. 'Why, a man who has poetry in his soul can eat with princes and dine with kings. Words, my dear Miss Jarvis, are the key to whatever kingdom one cares to enter.'

'Yes, yes, Mr Hewson.' Helen grew impatient, for the years were passing and no such vistas were opening in front of her. 'But *how* do I do it?'

'Soul, Miss Jarvis. *Words*. They give one power over people. My songs, now.' He placed hand on breast and in his cracked uncertain warble began to half sing, half recite:

'"The steed jumped the fence, with one bound he was there."
He smote at the bonds bound the infant so fair.
With a wave of his hat, the knight cried out, "Sire, Tell them Sir Jasper saved the babe from the fire."'

'Beautiful, beautiful,' he murmured.

He showed her books she devoured; she constantly asked questions: where was York, what was asparagus, who was Helen of Troy?

'The most beautiful woman in the world, Miss Jarvis. She lived many years ago, and far away. A gentleman called Schliemann recently set off to find Troy and her resting place.'

'Did he find it?'

'He found Troy, and he found the jewels of Priam. Helen's gold. Doubtless you were named for her.'

Helen flushed. She knew she must be ugly, but that didn't matter. Being beautiful got you nowhere useful in Bethnal Green. 'I ain't—am not—beautiful.'

He looked reproachful. 'You have beauty of the soul, Miss Jarvis.'

Helen considered this and was gratified. All the same, there were other more important things. She had to bury inside her that other Helen who was awaiting the moment when she would meet someone to answer her need for love. That would happen at the *end* of the path she'd chosen. She couldn't keep diving off it, or she'd never get there.

When Etty was thirteen, she was apprenticed to a milliner near Piccadilly, a position obtained for her by the Big Man. Etty hated it. She worked seventy-four hours a week and that was less than some of the others. What little money she earned was commandeered

31

by Father, and the milliner herself, a painted coarse Frenchwoman, was rude, overbearing and a hard taskmistress. Helen raged at seeing Etty return home tired and drawn, exhausted by the long hours and developing a chronic cough. She resolved that when she too was thirteen she would not be an apprentice. It would be time to use her Dick Whittington money to help her run away, and she would take Etty with her. She knew that many girls of her age were something called prostitutes and that the choice might lie between that and the sweat shop. Living as they did, no one could be ignorant of the facts of life, but as yet Helen associated them with the constant pregnancies of her mother, and with a vague feeling of repugnance which she pushed to the back of her mind. It was not important for she had a path to follow—somewhere and sometime.

Then the time came: the night of the penny gaff. Helen had never been to any kind of theatre. Father sometimes went off to the music hall, but a penny gaff aspired nowhere near to that status. On Etty's monthly day off, Helen was attracted by a notice-board on which was chalked:

The Dreadful Story of Maria Marten
The Harleequinnade
Shaksperes Roameo and Jooliet.'

Helen had heard of Shakespeare, for Mr Hewson often spoke of him, rolled off speech after speech, none of which made any sense to Helen. Perhaps if she saw the whole play, it would. She persuaded a trembling Etty to come into this strange world with her. The disused storeroom boasted a rough and ready stage erected out of wooden boxes and beer barrels, and makeshift seating all round. The audience was young, and pressed body to body were taking full advantage of proximity. Helen impatiently brushed off her neighbour's grasping hand, for she was staring at the backcloth. It was tawdry, but she didn't notice. All she saw was the scene it depicted—a bridge over a stream. This was not the smelly sinister-looking water of the city streets, but a sparkling clear bright ribbon, and it seemed to her an omen. It was her path to escape.

Romeo and Juliet lasted a whole twenty minutes and concluded the performance. Shakespeare did not impress her, however, for sandwiched between the melodrama and the play Harlequin and Columbine had come floating into Helen's life, he in a costume all colours of the rainbow, spangles a-glittering, and she in a pure white dress.

Helen felt as if Dame Fortune had

touched her shoulder with Harlequin's magic wand, and said: 'Come alive, Helen. You *shall* be loving and beautiful.' She remembered Mr Hewson telling her poetry was a pathway, words were power. *That* was what she could do. She would act like Harlequin, dance like Columbine, and sing her way to freedom.

She took Etty's hand and half danced her all the way home with excitement—only to find Mother was beside herself with rage for word had got back.

'I don't blame you, Etty; it's this diddiki sister of yours. Daughters of mine going into one of them places! Nothing better than whore-houses.'

'What are whore-houses?'

'It's where women of the street go.'

'What are women of the street?'

'Prostitutes,' Mary screamed at Helen. Etty had shrunk back, overcome by her mother's violence. 'I didn't bring you up to be one of them. You're never to go to one of them places again. Or is it too late? Are you ruined already? Did they do anything to you?'

'Do anything?' Helen repeated. 'Who?'

'Anyone. Men. Filthy beasts. Come on, girls, answer me.'

The look in Mary's eyes was wild. Well it might be, for she was remembering her own girlhood. She'd been older than Etty and Helen, but just as stupid. Sir had taken advantage of her, for all he was a gentleman, and Etty had been the result. She'd done better than many, of course. He'd seen to it that she was fitted up with a husband and some money, even if it was only Michael Jarvis.

'Well, did they touch you?' she demanded.

'No,' Helen shouted. What was this awful thing? Why shouldn't men touch you?

Mary went slack with relief. 'Men are beasts,' she said, calming down. 'Remember that, girls. All of them. Beasts.'

Helen did remember, though she could not quite believe it. Surely there was love somewhere like in books, if only she were rich and famous enough. Then they wouldn't dare be beasts.

She knew where her escape path lay now, but the time was not yet, so she acquiesced in going to the match factory to work while she waited. Two years to learn. Two years of hard work and small wages. Two years enduring the conditions at home, which worsened as the children grew older. Mother wailed and wept with successive miscarriages, and sickly children died. Two years enduring smutty talk from her fellow factory workers, and ignoring blandishments to join them for extra money on the streets, two years of keeping herself free from the local boys and two years of visiting music halls all over London, paid for not out of her wages which were handed over to her parents, but her carefully budgeted Dick Whittington money.

And finally the time came:

Now!

It was her battlecry, as Helen sloughed off the verminous skin of her childhood, to emerge as a chrysalis onto the world's stage: Swains' Music Hall.

Chapter Two

'Hard work, Mr Swains, that's what I've got to offer.'

'Well. Miss Eighteen-year-old Rose Shelley,' Swains leered at the obvious false name and age she'd given, 'how d'yer like to prove it? Start tonight—as a serving wench.' Even Swains could see she had more to offer than hard work. The large dark eyes bristled with strength and her face was alive with sharpness and intelligence. That often spelled trouble, but he'd soon see.

From that first moment when the doors were opened and a mass of humanity swarmed in, descending on the tables, grabbing chairs and shouting with anticipation at the evening ahead, the noise overwhelmed Helen. She squeezed between tables full of raucous, writhing men and women out to enjoy themselves, often at the expense of the serving maids. Swains' was old-fashioned in still placing tables in the auditorium, for by now most music halls were relegating drinking to the back of the hall, but mindful of the profit from the sale of drinks and the predilections of his customers, Swains kept to the old tradition.

She seemed to pass muster with Swains except that he had sighed with exasperation as he saw her high-necked grey dress. The other two serving maids had tight-skirted, gaudy dresses cut so low that their breasts almost fell out as they bent over their customers.

'Lower, Miss Shelley, lower,' Swains said, shaking his head in resignation. 'Not that dress. Not grey. And lower.' He put his hand on her chest to indicate how low.

Helen endured it without throwing off his hand, though she wanted to scream at his touch. After all, she thought, what did it matter. She valued this job, after the weeks of struggle before she found it, weeks when her precious store of money had disappeared at an alarming rate despite the cheapness of their lodgings, and she and Etty had been forced to accept Mr Hewson's financial assistance in order to eat at all. Their lodgings were in a ramshackle old house near the canal. Mrs Hicks, the landlady, was a fearsome sixty-year-old former actress—always in a formidable poke bonnet, she blew hot and cold on her tenants, mostly encouraging what she largely termed the travelling life, which seemed to encompass even

Mr Hewson, but in times of depression berating them soundly for their choice of profession.

'Regard me as your manager, dear Miss Jarvis,' Mr Hewson had offered grandly, as Helen had returned bedraggled, hungry and dispirited after yet another rejection. Tired as she was, she looked with affection at his shabby coat, the still faithful gibus hat, and the shoes, brightly polished, but worn thin and cracked with age. 'And Miss Etty here,' he continued gently, looking at the thin delicate girl, with her hopeful eyes, 'shall be our salaried staff.'

Etty had been firmly forbidden by Helen to seek work herself, but it was her task to scour the markets in search of their food, keeping well clear of any neighbourhoods that Michael Jarvis might be likely to visit. For four weeks Helen had trailed from tavern to music hall, some pretentious, some unassuming, some little more than penny gaffs; the managers after a while seemed to blend in her mind into a composite whole—one bloated, self-satisfied, coarse, leering monster that only seemed capable of one word—no. She was not even allowed the usual courtesy of a trial turn, to take her chance on stage with an audience to see how she fared. Music hall entertainers were two a penny now, and all of them had talent, it seemed, and, even more depressing, experience.

She was fearful that Mr Hewson might not help over the dress, and how was she to buy one before she got paid? She must tell him that she'd specially chosen the name Rose Shelley to please him, because of his blessed old poem.

'Look on my works ye mighty and despair.'

Ozimanduss—something like that. She hadn't understood exactly what it was about when Mr Hewson read the poem, but she got the general meaning. It meant be proud, alone, fight for yourself for what you want and not show people you cared too much, otherwise you got hurt. That's what she had done when she left home. It had seemed so easy at first, taking her precious hoard of money, arranging to meet Etty after work—and then never going back home. Just disappearing. No more bluster and shouting from Father, no more dirty horrible chores because that slut Gladys, whom Father had brought in after Mother had died six months ago, couldn't be bothered to keep house. It had been time to leave Bethnal Green, leave Father—and leave Mrs Blades, that monstrous canker on her life.

As Mr Hewson escorted her back to her lodgings that evening, she tried flattery, coaxing, outright appeal, all in vain.

'You are going to be a lady, Miss Jarvis. A lady. So act like one, even though you are only fifteen.'

'But I mustn't lose this job—and I told them I'm eighteen,' she pleaded, summoning tears to her eyes. 'It's not for myself Mr Hewson. I don't care about the job. I'd starve... It's for Etty...' She gulped.

Mr Hewson stopped short. 'Ah yes, Miss Henrietta. She must be considered. She needs nutriment. We must see what we can do. I myself possess no wench's garb, but...'

Early next morning Mr Hewson knocked on their door, before setting off to King's Cross. Held up in front of him, incongruous under his white hair and mild face, was a bright blue, spangled satin dress, fashioned for far-off crinoline days, too long and too wide to complement Helen's full figure. But it had a low neck, and frills. Helen stared at it in wonder, seeing not the tawdriness but the sparkle and colour. It was the dress of a lady, she was sure of that.

'Mr Hewson,' she announced, 'I shall kiss you.'

He went pink, and muttered under his breath, but she could see that he was pleased. It transpired that it belonged to Mrs Hicks, who back in the days when

41

the queen was young, and music hall not yet thought of, had strolled the countryside as a travelling player in a stock touring company, making a sparse living when and where she could.

Etty looked at the blue creation: 'You know,' she said thoughtfully, 'I could make that fit you.'

If she was going to pander to those men, Helen decided, they should have full value. The neckline was lowered so that it stretched tight across her breast. Mr Hewson's eyes nearly popped out of his head, but Mr Swains merely cast an approving look and a careless, 'That's better.'

Helen spent a year at Swains' as a serving wench becoming used to the job, youth and energy keeping her on her feet, and she quickly became used to the regulars. You bent over them, tipping the contents of the floury white baked potatoes, for which Swains' had a reputation, onto their plates with practised dexterity; you teased them, you lifted their glasses and pretended to drink from them so that your breasts would swing up, then you swirled round quickly with a tantalizing rustle of silk, presenting a bustled backside that might be well nigh irresistible to pat if you didn't move too fast for that. What idiots men were.

Kate and Josie, the other serving maids,

had learned to be wary of her. She'd tried to impress them to gain their admiration, telling them that her father was a manager who had sent her out to get experience of 'other halls.' They believed her at first because of her grand manner and the way she spoke after Mr Hewson's tuition. But gradually the truth dawned.

'You're nothing but a coster,' said Josie scornfully. 'Only them as could steal the way you do.'

Helen reddened. So her small acquisitions of scraps or odd things left behind by the performers dashing to and from one hall to the next had not gone unnoticed.

But she could not admit this. There had followed a fight that would have done justice to any street market brawl. Helen had emerged victorious, albeit with bruises that could be ill-concealed by her dress, and were eyed interestedly by the patrons. After that the girls left her alone.

Helen was restless now. Time was passing and it seemed she would never escape from the bar to the boards. Her dreams of getting somewhere in the world seemed to progress no further. There seemed no point in even trying to save a little of her hard-earned money, because she had no idea of what she would do with it. But she went on doing so. Unknown to her Etty too was squirrelling pennies away, for Etty's nightmare, as was Helen's, was that she might be forced to return to Bethnal Green. It was never far from their minds, and one day the nightmare came true.

There'd been a catch at her arm. Nothing unusual in that. Men were always hauling her back, to hand her a glass, pass a joke with her, try to slide their arms around her waist. But even as she turned, she knew this time it was different.

'Nice to see yer again, 'Elen. Me dahling daughter.'

He hadn't changed. His coarsened face with its bloodshot eyes was smirking with triumph.

Helen stared at her father, sick to her stomach. 'How did you—'

'Mate told me. Your 'Elen, done up like a barrowload of monkeys all la-di-da, down in that dive Swains'. So being naturally anxious to see my loving daughter again, I comes along.'

'Well now you've seen me. So go away. I'm not coming back.' She faced him belligerently.

His face lost its smile. 'No, dahling daughter. Not you. You can do what you bloody well like. You were heading for the streets since the age of three and now I reckon you've got there.' He looked her up and down appraisingly. Helen fought her fear. She would not let him see she was afraid.

'No,' he went on softly, 'it's Etty I want. Etty. Where is she?' He pushed his face up close to hers threateningly.

'Where you'll never find her,' she replied coolly, beating down her panic.

'Oh, but you'll tell me all right, 'Elen. Sooner or later. Dahling daughter. She's under age you know. You both are...' His voice drifted off insinuatingly. 'I could 'ave you up for abduction.'

She laughed in his face. 'Abduction. You try, you just try, that's all. We'll see who they believe, you drunken—'

The roars from the other tables grew more insistent, and she pulled herself away. When next she looked in that direction, the table was empty. He was gone. Slack with relief, she went about her duties mechanically for the rest of the evening. She found herself shivering at the thought of the encounter. He could do nothing to her—but Etty! What if he should find her?

For several weeks she and Mr Hewson took precautions in going home from Swains'. When nothing happened the sense of threat receded and they reverted to their usual route. A week after that they returned home to find Etty gone.

Helen cried all night but got up with

45

resolve the next morning. But she found she had no allies. Mr Hewson was no help at all.

'We can do nothing, Miss Jarvis. We are powerless. The law is on his side.'

'The law. Phooey for the law,' shouted Helen.

'As the poet says—'

'I don't care what the poet says,' Helen flung back at him, as she set off briskly to the omnibus stop. 'I'm going to get Etty back.'

The barrow was not outside the house. So far so good. Only Gladys to deal with. She knocked on the door repressing a shiver of her old childhood terror at being back and conscious of what lay behind the downstairs window. A window shot up upstairs and Gladys leaned out in mob cap, dirty ginger curls straggling out under it.

'Oh it's you, is it? And what do you want, my fine madam?'

'Etty,' shouted Helen.

Gladys cackled. 'Etty stays here, Miss La-di-da. Where she'll learn some manners. Not whoring. I've heard about you down at Swains'.'

People were beginning to gather on doorsteps now to listen to the fray. In the background upstairs Helen could hear Etty sobbing, enraging her.

46

'You can't keep her there all the time locked up. She'll run away again. When she goes to work. Won't you, Etty?'

'My, my,' mocked Gladys. 'So she wants to send poor little Etty out to work. She's far too delicate. Little Etty's going to look after home for Mother.' Etty was trying to say something behind her but Gladys's big frame shut her out and she shouted to Helen: 'Get back to your beat, girl, and leave us alone.'

'Not while you've got Etty.'

This time for answer Gladys leaned out of the window and emptied a chamber pot over Helen's head. She stood still as the liquid poured over her head and shoulders. Then she turned and walked away, ignoring the neighbours laughing at her discomfiture. She waited till she had turned the corner before she wiped herself down. And she waited till she got back to her empty rooms before she cried, great hot tears of rage, beating the cushions in her fury.

'I'll get even,' she vowed. 'By God I will.'

For some weeks she was listless at work. There was no one to work for any more. The struggle seemed pointless. Even Mr Hewson failed to rouse her.

'Come, Miss Jarvis, what of your

47

ambition? To climb to the heights of Mount Olympus. Join the immortals. Surely you still hear the tones of Melpomene and Thalia? Do the muses of tragedy and comedy not still beckon?'

She tried hard to smile. 'If anyone's calling, Mr Hewson, it can't be very loudly. Mr Swains doesn't seem to hear.' As the weeks went by, however, her old fighting spirit began to return. After all, it was true what Mr Hewson said. Time was passing. She was nearly seventeen now, and hadn't even had a whiff of an opportunity.

'How can I ever be a lady,' she cried despairingly, 'if I can't even get my foot on the stage?'

'There is more to being a lady,' said Mr Hewson portentously, and mistaking her meaning, 'than being married to a lord. Being a lady, Miss Jarvis, begins in the heart, in the soul, not at one's boots. A lady, Miss Jarvis—'

But Helen wasn't listening—darling Mr Hewson had unwittingly opened up a whole train of thought. Why had it never occurred to her before? Marriage to a lord. That was the thing. Why, lots of actresses did it nowadays. Hitherto she had connected marriage only with the costermonger louts, and the beery, coarse patrons at Swains'. The mere thought of one of them kissing her, really kissing her...even closer—she shuddered. But a lord. Marriage might be possible after all. Lords were gentlemen—they would never...

'...and always gentle...' Mr Hewson rambled on.

Helen turned a beatific smile in his direction.

After that, she pestered Mr Swains continually to be given a chance on stage. But he was both adamant and annoyed. 'Hell and Tommy, woman, you're a serving girl. Be satisfied with that. I was a fool to take you on at all. You've a fine little figure, make the most of it, find yourself a husband.'

When Helen's opportunity finally did arrive, it was luck and not Mr Swains that provided it.

The second house was always rowdier than the first, and this was Friday night. The audience refused to settle down and even during their favourites' performances were querulous and noisy. And those that did not please them were given an even harder time than usual. Tonight it was Stan Barrett. He was a hard-working lion-comique, singing humorous songs in the style of the Great Vance, conscientious but without particular talent. His chief merit lay in picking songs that appealed to the audience, which usually won him a hearing however indifferent the rendering. Not tonight. They laughed, they shouted, they hurled potatoes which burst with a sludgy shower of mash all over him and the stage; even a bottle or two found its way towards the unlucky man.

Swains reluctantly vacated his chairman's seat and strode onto the stage. A potato hit him squarely in the stomach and temporarily winded him. Just as complete bedlam began to prevail, a voice from the back of the hall suddenly and raucously floated over the babel:

'What cheer, me old cock sparrers.'

Helen Jarvis's time had come at last—but not easily.

Caught by surprise, the audience were temporarily silent as she belted out the lines of the currently favourite music hall song being whistled on every street corner:

'You ain't so good? Well, hop up on me barrer
I'll push yer all together with me apples and pears—'

She sensed a shuffle in the audience. Only the power of her voice was holding them. There was no music. Stunned, Swains was watching from the stage, the piano player silent as he listened to the unfamiliar voice coming from an unfamiliar direction. She quelled the shuffle. Fight them. Don't let them beat you. The same technique as with the glasses—catch their eye, give them a wink, get them on her side... The ripple of unease subsided. That man there, him in the front—choose him, the dirty old—charm him, that's right, hand on hip, toss of her backside. Make him think it was all for him... That's right, she'd got him now...

'So I met this bloke...
...a little like you, sir'
(spoken, eyeing her victim...)
'handsome, if you know what I mean...'
(broad wink)...

Now she'd got them. They swung with gusto into the chorus:

What cheer, me old cock sparrer
Just jump up on me barrer...'

At a frantic sign from Swains, the orchestra had come up in with the tune and by the time Helen had gathered several more incumbents for her barrow, the audience approved of her. In vain did Swains try to announce the next act. They would have none of it, and seizing her opportunity Helen marched confidently up to the stage and stood next to the hypocritically grinning Swains.

'Right, me girl, keep 'em quiet and you're in. If they start up again, that's your last five minutes at Swains'!' he hissed in her ear. She shrugged, defiantly.

She started the song again—they roared with approval and her movements grew more expansive. She developed a wriggle on 'apples and pears' which appealed to them. That was better—she began to feel the audience respond to her; she exulted in the power, greeting the intangible wave of warmth flooding towards her over the meagre batten of footlights. Warmth was love, and oh, how she craved it.

The next night she marched in through the stage door, head held high. She was a performer now. She didn't have to hob-nob with the likes of Josie. Mind you, it hadn't been all easy going with old Swains. He didn't like it, she could see that.

'I won't ask for no money for tonight, Mr Swains,' she had told him graciously as she swept offstage the night before. 'But you'll let me on tomorrow night, won't you?'

He'd been silent for a moment, for he still had an inkling she was trouble.

'All right, Miss Shelley,' he had growled. 'You can go on tomorrow night. And if you don't make a success of it, you're out.'

She had not taken offence. For there was no doubt in her mind. She was on the road to fame and fortune. Already her thoughts were dancing ahead—get Etty back, get better lodgings...why she'd even get Mr Hewson a new hat to show her gratitude. But first there'd been the question of a dress. She had to have a dress worthy of her act. She emptied her carefully hoarded savings out of the cracked old teapot, and recklessly put it all in her cloth purse. Then she sallied forth to the market, at a time when Mr Hewson was out. She was going to choose what she wanted, and be blowed to his fussing. She found what she wanted—bright pink, low cut and lots of frills and ribbons, a second-hand slightly dirty cast-off. But to Helen it was again the most tasteful dress on earth.

'And now,' she breathed, twirling round in front of the mirror, 'goodbye Helen Jarvis—for ever.' She was on her way along that sparkling ribbon of a path to riches and love. 'Hallo—hallo Rose Shelley, your own, your very own Rose Shelley.'

Her own Rose Shelley continued her triumphant progress down the tatty damp corridor to the large room that served as changing room to the lady artists, some there all evening, others dashing in at intervals from engagements at other halls. Helen was used to it now: the hot sweaty atmosphere, the sweet cloying smell of cheap perfume, the heavy smell of costumes worn too often and cleaned too rarely, the fetid atmosphere of group excitement, the anxious faces, with lines prematurely etched in, the sagging bosoms, the figures restrained with such difficulty by the voluminous skirts, but faces that once up on a stage would light up kindled by the contact with their audience, lines of anger transformed to gaiety, crow's feet into bewitching smiling eyes, personality conquering age. Tonight she was part of it, she was one of them. She was going straight to the top, another Jenny Hill, The Vital Spark, who had rocketed to the Londoners' hearts when only a little older than Helen herself.

'Come here, dearie,' said one, a veteran of perhaps thirty-five years, old age in music hall terms. 'Who yer trying to look like? Grimaldi?' referring to Helen's efforts with her greasepaint.

Helen flushed. Somehow it had looked all right at home, and she resented being patronized. All the same, she had to learn. So she meekly submitted to having her face cleaned, then pushed this way and

54

that, and having studied her face in a mirror was pleased with the result. The dress raised a few eyebrows, however.

'Keep away from old Swains in that, love,' her champion laughed.

Impatiently she stood in the wings, on tenterhooks waiting for her turn. Still three to go. Ethel Love was warbling away about True Love. Why couldn't she get a move on? Then there was a double act, then old Stan, then her before the interval. She knew why old Swains had put her there, because everyone knew that's when the attention wandered, concentrating on filling up their glasses, grabbing the potatoes that were already beginning to come round.

'The boy I love is up in the gallery,' carolled Ethel Love.

'Rot yer gullet, me'dear,' hissed a voice pleasantly in her ear. She jumped and turned to find the pale inimical eyes of Stan Barrett gazing at her. 'Can't wish you good luck—'gainst tradition, ain't it?' He leered at her.

She stared after him as he galloped onto the stage. He didn't seem very friendly, and after she had saved him from a barracking last night too.

If anything her song went better than the night before. Men she'd been serving beer to only last night were now yelling for her in respectful affection: 'Come on then, Rosie, give us another one.'

She hung around hopefully till the end of the show, waiting for Swains to summon her to his office and with tears in his eyes beg her to accept a permanent engagement: 'Name your own price, Miss Shelley. Only stay.'

Nothing happened.

She had scarcely taken ten steps outside before it did. A hand was round her mouth, an arm sweeping, pulling her backwards into an alley so roughly she was almost off her feet. Gasping for breath, she saw there were three of them, two men, one woman. Then the hand round her mouth wrenched her head back, pulling till she was choking, her neck aching with the strain.

Dear God, it was the garotters. She'd heard of them. You were dead in seconds, before you could cry out. She began to kick out with her feet behind her, but she made no contact. Her head pulled back was reeling, she grew red in the face, and eyes began to bulge.

'All right, Bill,' said the woman dispassionately. 'Let the little darling have it.'

A fist sent a blow straight into her stomach. She could not even double up from the pain as the pressure on her throat continued, and blow followed blow, on her abdomen, her breasts. Then suddenly they stopped and a large ugly face presented itself before Helen's swimming eyes.

Mrs Blades, it's Mrs Blades, was her first terrified hazy thought. Then as the waves of pain died down she saw it wasn't. It was someone she recognized, only not like this—wasn't it Maisie Wright, that lovely tantalizing good-hearted queen of the halls?

'That's right. Maisie Wright,' said the woman unemotionally. 'You won't sing my song again, will you dear? I wouldn't like that, wouldn't like it at all. When Stan told me what you did, I was very unhappy, weren't I, Bill? And Bill here got quite upset...'

The second man, a huge black shape in the evening gloom, thrust a razor in front of her face. 'See that, dearie?' went on Maisie. 'Thinks a lot of me does Bill. He'd see you didn't ever flaunt yourself again. And for why? Well they wouldn't be shouting for you after Bill had finished with you. Not if you sing my song again, dearie.'

The man behind her released her and coughing and spluttering Helen managed to say, 'Your song? But I—'

'My song, dearie. As you know full well. Song I paid for, good and fair. Mine and no one else sings it. See?'

Helen stared at her open-mouthed. She

had had no idea that songs were bought and belonged to people. Why, everyone was singing it. They were just songs.

She coughed painfully. 'I didn't know.'

Maisie Wright simply said with scorn, 'Didn't know.' Then she seized Helen's collar and brought her face close to hers. 'Gawlimey, you're young. How old?'

'Nineteen,' Helen said automatically.

'Garn, you're not seventeen yet, or I'm a dutchman. Maybe you didn't know at that. But now you know, don't you, dearie,' she added softly. 'You know now.'

It was four days before Helen was well enough to return to a triumphant Swains.

'I knew it,' he said. 'You're trouble. I knew it that first moment I set eyes on you. How was I to know you hadn't paid for it? Stupid bitch. Now I've Maisie threatening to sue me. I don't need no trouble. *Out.*'

'How was I to know?' Helen wailed. 'And how do you get songs anyway? And where am I to go now? They're jealous, that's what it is.'

Mr Hewson ran his fingers over the tinny keys of Mrs Hicks's old piano.

'I see no problem, Miss Jarvis,' he remarked mildly.

'Perhaps you don't. But it ain't you got to go traipsing round all these leery old

58

managers again. No it ain't no problem for you. You can go on selling your silly old matches till St Peter comes along and says light us a fag.'

Mr Hewson flushed and rose to his feet with dignity, snapping the lid shut with unaccustomed severity. 'I shall adjourn, Miss Jarvis, till you are more yourself.'

Helen ran to him, penitent. 'Oh now, don't go, Mr Hewson. I'm sorry. But you don't understand. After all my hard work—nothing. Out on the street. And there's nothing I can do. I ain't got the money to go round buying songs.'

Mr Hewson coughed. 'As I remarked before, I see no problem. I, Miss Jarvis, am a poet. And a poet writes poems, Miss Jarvis, that may be set to music. And as I also once remarked, I am a balladeer. It would be my pleasure and honour, Miss Jarvis to write some ballads for your new career.'

'Mr Hewson, I shall kiss you again.'

Unfortunately Mr Hewson and his strong supporter Mrs Hicks were about thirty years out of date. The days of 'The Ratcatcher's Daughter' were long since gone. One needed new catchy tunes, with—well a bit of life in it, thought Helen despairingly after evenings of soulful ballads of love. But she battled on. The long trudge round the halls was longer than even Helen had anticipated. On her seventeenth birthday she woke up with a sense of desperation. Life was passing her. What happened to that Helen of old who was going to beg, steal, and fight to become a lady? What had happened to the Helen who had sworn to look after Etty at all costs? What had happened to Etty now? She was twenty. Was she married to some coster lout? Helen shuddered at the thought, mentally putting herself in Etty's place. Then she steeled herself. It was time for action...

'No, Miss Jarvis. No I shall not.' Mr Hewson stiffened. 'I am a man of honour.'

He was still a man of honour thirty minutes later, but fifteen minutes after that, faced with the full battery of Helen's forceful charm his honour was laid temporarily aside. A few hours later he returned still haughty, but the occupier of a cleaning job at Swains' theatre, a position he had no intention of taking up, and two sheets of Swains' personal headed notepaper.

'Now,' said Helen disarmingly.

'No, Miss Jarvis,' pleaded Mr Hewson. 'Decidedly not. I, Miss Jarvis, am a poet. Not a master forger.'

'But this is the only way you will get your ballads performed.'

There was a moment's pause. Then he

pulled the piece of paper towards him...

The Marylebone had been an old coaching inn. Situated off Baker Street, it was in another league to Swains'. Its very entrance was imposing, and would not have disgraced the Lyceum itself. The Marylebone had a name for 'finding' new talent and several household names in music hall owed their beginnings to this nursery. Nor did they forget it, and came back to grace it with their blazing presence.

Having infiltrated her way through its portals by fraud, Helen took care that she should not be ejected through lack of expertise. Coster language was all very well, but it had to be refined, and the odd quaint word thrown into a carefully diluted cockney accent would work wonders. Goodbye Rosie. Miss Mary May was going to be a different kettle of fish. She'd quite taken to the proprietor of the Marylebone. Decent sort of cove, old Olly Waters. Looked her up and down, but not the way old Swains did. She didn't feel dirty when he'd finished interviewing her, with Swains' letter of recommendation in front of him.

And now here she was for her trial turn. Worst spot of course. If you could control the audience just after the interval you could do anything.

61

The welcome was perfunctory and Helen suddenly found herself nervous. It had sounded wonderful when she and Mr Hewson sang it to the tinny old piano—but here it was so different. There was that posh geezer at that huge flat piano down there a mile away and a real orchestra. She longed momentarily for the raucous intimacy of Swains'. She pulled herself together and began to sing.

Alas Mr Hewson's beautiful ballad fell on deaf ears.

'Don't go on, lov,' yelled a wag from the gallery. 'You're bringing tears to my eyes.'

There was a quick shush from the stalls, but the damage was done.

As she began to sing again, another voice shouted up from the audience.

The chairman intervened at this point. 'Now give her a chance, gentlemen, do.'

Helen was not going to take this calmly. She marched towards the footlights and shouted at her tormentor, 'I don't know why he calls you gentlemen.'

She got no further. The house disapproved. Noisily. Even the stalls murmured. It had a right to show its disapproval of an artiste. The curtain was smartly dropped, and Mr Waters' arm was frogmarching her off. He regarded her in silence in the wings as an old favourite leapt onto the stage to restore order.

'I know,' said Helen wearily. 'You want me to go.'

'Yes,' barked Waters. 'When you've been on the stage twenty years you'll have the right to behave as you did tonight. Not before.'

'Happens to everyone, dearie.' Someone bustled past with a sympathetic eye. 'Don't take it to heart.' Helen recognized Annie Kay, an established favourite of many years' standing. 'Need the work, do you?'

'Yes,' said Helen hiccoughing with her tears. 'It's—it's for my little sister. She's only got me—she's ill. I need the money for medicine...'

It seemed this was going down well, for there were cluckings of sympathy, and a thoughtful look.

'Got any different songs, 'ave you?'

'Yes,' said Helen eagerly, and watched her champion hurry off to Waters' office. She let out a long sigh and relaxed, slumped against the wall. A little smile crossed her lips. It would be all right. She knew it would be. She was fleetingly aware of eyes on her and she looked up to see a young man peering down from the steps to the flies. All she could see was curly brown hair and square set shoulders.

'All right, dear. One more chance. Better spot—but have a different song.' Annie had returned.

'Oh, thank, thank you,' said Helen sincerely. 'You're very, very kind.'

'Had the bird myself from time to time,' said Annie wryly.

'But you're top of the bill.' Helen was amazed.

'Only so long as the audience want it that way. And they're fickle little bleeders. You can wear yourself out working the halls, trying to please them. Just so long as you're laughing out there—that's all that matters to them. Well, here's to you ducky, and your little sister.'

'What? Oh, yes.'

It was a risk to sing the same song, she knew that. She wouldn't have long before old Waters would throw her off the stage again. She'd got to win them first...'

Crash. The sound of breaking crockery in the wings, and a strident female voice shouting: 'You daft old happorth...'

She came backward onto the stage, wiping her hands on a grimy apron, turned, saw the audience with surprise, put her hankie to her eye.

'I called him dear old pal,' she began confidentially. Out of the corner of her eye she could see Waters suddenly swell with fury in the wings. *'For that's what he was to me.'* (spoken)

Then the orchestra changed tempo,

fortissimo, while her penetrating voice soared over it:

'*But a meaner old devil never walked this earth*' (stamping her foot)
'*You should 'ear the things 'e said*' (spoken with indignation)

She had them now:

'*If you knew—if you only knew—what I 'ad to put up with*
You'd cry, ladies and gentlemen, just cry' (spoken)
'*But*' (into melody again)
'*I called him dear old pal...*'

All Waters said as she came off the stage pink with triumph was, 'Very clever, Miss May. Do you wish to stay with us?'

Mr Hewson, however, was less than pleased. 'It was a travesty, Miss Jarvis. A travesty of my beautiful ballad. You have mocked me, Miss Jarvis. Mocked me.'

She was conscious that she had done just that, and shame wrestled with pride.

'You might congratulate me,' she pleaded. 'I've got a regular engagement at last, in a real decent hall, and you're cross because of one old poem—no, I didn't mean that, Mr Hewson.'

Indeed she didn't mean it. She might need more.

Mr Hewson performed yet one more important act for Helen—he brought Etty to her. Established now in new lodgings, in the Edgware Road, far from Mrs Hicks's, and established under a new identity, it was safe to risk it. Heart in mouth Helen sat in her small parlour, restlessly fidgeting. They should be here by now. It had all been so carefully planned. Perhaps they'd been followed. Perhaps Father had found out, waylaid them, attacked them...there was a tap at the door.

She flew to it, opened it, and Etty was in her arms.

She was half laughing, half crying. 'Etty, Etty darling. Tell me, how are you? You're not married? Did they ill treat you? Are you glad to come? Oh darling, I'll never let you go again. Never, never...'

'Helen, you're squeezing me so tight I can't talk.' Etty was laughing too. She was pale, very pale, and thin, thought Helen anxiously. But that was going to change now. Those awful days were behind them. From now on they would never be parted.

Mr Hewson was especially fond of his new ballad about the coster donkey Nelly, and her loving owner. It would bring tears to the eyes of all that heard it. Maybe it would have done, but not with Helen's rendering. It began all right, but suddenly there was a little wriggle here and a little pout there, a flirt of the eyes: 'Whoops, Nelly, don't you go too far...' *(wriggle and wink)*

The audience loved it. Every innuendo Helen rendered a thing of grace and subtlety, never too bland, never too provocative. She had been at the Marylebone for a month now, and was beginning to feel confident of her position. She had introduced 'Nelly's Song' to everybody's delight except Mr Hewson's.

'We've got to live, haven't we?' Helen was genuinely hurt. 'And the money's keeping you as well, ain't it? Don't need to go matchselling.'

'I am wounded beyond measure, Miss Jarvis,' replied Mr Hewson gravely. 'My poet's true soul—'

'All right,' Helen shouted, 'I'll write my own songs, see if I can't.'

'I shall return,' said Mr Hewson with dignity, 'to Hoxton and the honourable estate of matchselling. At least I shall not sell my soul.'

'And bleeding few matches,' muttered Helen, instantly contrite but as usual unable to tell him so. He would understand in the end. She couldn't lose him. He must know how much she loved him.

'Good-night, Miss Etty. Good-night Miss Jarvis.' He lifted his new hat, turned his shabby frock coat back and marched out the door.

'He'll be back, darling,' Helen comforted Etty. 'Just see if he isn't.'

But he wasn't.

If Mr Hewson was displeased by Nelly's Song, Waters was not. He was a man of business, and could smell a winner when he saw one. That song was one right enough—yet it lacked something still.

'I'll give you a feeder,' he told her next day.

'Pardon?' Helen looked blank.

'A feeder,' Waters repeated patiently. 'Someone to help you in your act, and we'll get a proper barrow for you. He can push the barrow. Play up to you. You'll see. Come in an hour early tomorrow. I'll arrange something.'

She came to find the theatre empty, as she first thought. But as she walked on to the stage, lit by a solitary working tee light a figure detached itself from the shadows and ambled up to her. It was the young man with square shoulders.

'Hallo,' he said. 'I'm Jack. Jack Waters.'

Chapter Three

'Waters?'

'That's right. I'm his son.' He grinned at her. 'I like the way you look at me as if I were Albert Edward Prince of Wales.'

Helen glared at him. So old Waters thought he'd keep her in her place by sending his son along as a watchdog, did he? She'd soon show this young Piccadilly Johnnie what she thought of that. She stuck her chin out pugnaciously. He wasn't tall, but it came well below the level of his own. Then she hastily pulled it in again. Soft soap makes for an easy wash, she belatedly remembered. She smiled her sweetest smile, put out her hand and said in her grandest manner and with her best new Baker Street accent: 'Miss Mary May. So pleased to have you join me, Mr Waters. I shall work you hard, mind.'

'You're not pleased. You're as cross as a monkey at the seaside. But you won't have to put up with me for too long. I'm off back up in two months.'

'Up?' queried Helen, puzzled.

He glanced at her quickly. 'Back to

Cambridge University. I'm going into the law.'

She flushed, vexed to be caught out. She should have known that. But he wouldn't catch her again. She'd teach this swell what being a professional artiste really meant. She disciplined herself quickly. No more thinking back to Spitalfields barrows. From now on, it was *up*. And not to some stuck-up Cambridge either. And just let him try to lay a finger on her. Just because he was the manager's son he needn't think she was there to be pinched and poked.

'Very well, Mr Waters,' she said, remembering to keep her vowels pure, as Mr Hewson had impressed on her. ('None of this "Me 'art leaps up when Iy be'old a rainbah", dear Miss Jarvis.' She wondered with a pang where Mr Hewson was now...) 'I'll give you a try,' she concluded grandly.

'Thank you very much.'

'Now then,' bringing her lips together carefully for the 'w', 'what can you do?'

'Nothing at all, Miss May.'

'But you must be able to do *something*,' she said impatiently.

'I can juggle a bit.'

'*Juggle?* What the bloomin' use is—' just for a moment her accent slipped. Then she sighed. 'Go on then,' she said resignedly.

He scouted round the wings for a few minutes and came back bearing an assortment of objects, then took up a centre stage position, stood with legs apart and proceeded to throw three or four objects into the air. And then drop them. Helen's mouth fell open. He tried again, this time managing to keep four in the air for at least three seconds before a saucer crashed to the floor, the noise of its breaking the only thing to interrupt the stony silence.

He looked at Helen and shrugged his shoulders. 'Show you a conjuring trick?'

He ran into the wings and returned bearing an empty box.

'Now imagine,' he began theatrically, 'that I am the Great Wizard of Baker Street. First I will borrow thy handkerchief, which I shall then proceed to burn, ladies and gentlemen, to hashes. Hashes, I said. I the Wizard will scatter the hashes in this box, close the lid, speak the wise words of the wizened old wizard and wave his—that is, *my*—wand. And miraculously, miraculously I say, your handkerchief madam will be restored to full and vibrant life. After which I shall command the handkerchief to speak.'

'Pardon?' said Helen startled.

'To speak, Miss May. Do you doubt the Great Wizard?'

Frankly she did, but he was the

71

proprietor's son. She handed over her handkerchief, somewhat reluctantly as despite all Etty's loving care with the flat iron it was far from impeccable. She watched with some trepidation while the Great Wizard proceeded to burn her handkerchief to ashes, for she did not possess very many.

'Abracadabra, monkey's paw. Go up to Cambridge, study law. Lion's tail and mandragora juice. Up with the box lid—what the deuce?' The charred remains of Helen's handkerchief still remained beneath.

'That's my bloody handkerchief,' shrieked Helen, pretensions to elegance temporarily forgotten.

His face was a picture of dismay. 'I must have mixed them up. I can't apologize enough, Miss May. Get you another one. Get you a dozen. Pure silk.'

'Gawlimy, can't you do nothing right?'

'No, I told you I couldn't.'

Enraged, she marched over to him, grabbed him by the arm and frogmarched him off the stage. In the wings she pointed to her new handcart.

'Do you think,' she said in withering tones, 'that you might manage to push that across the stage, *Mr Waters?*'

'I'm sure I can.'

'Then push, Mr Going Up to Cambridge. Push.'

She launched into a rehearsal of Nelly's Song, playing to an imaginary donkey in the wings. Her strong true voice rose over the empty seats, playing to a gallery peopled with admiring enthusiasts in her mind's eye. She'd show this young swell that he was there just to push the barrow, and nothing else. He was not going to stand in her way to the top of the bill. Not just here, but in the big ones, the Oxford, the Alhambra itself.

As she neared the end of the verse, she turned her back on the 'audience', towards the barrow, threw an imaginary carrot to Nelly in the wings, and leapt up to sit on the barrow and swing her legs as she swung into the chorus.

Unfortunately she had reckoned without her barrow-pusher, who added his own personal, creative touch. As she jumped on, he lifted the barrow from its resting place, tilting it so that it sloped down towards him, throwing her off balance and rolling her onto him, which brought them both to the ground in a tangled heap. Words that Helen could not remember even learning in Bethnal Green emerged from her lips as, incoherent with rage, she tried to disentangle herself. But somehow this proved a complicated job as her skirt, trailing at the back, seemed to have lodged under one wheel, exposing a considerable

73

amount of black cotton clad leg, which in its turn was lodged under Jack Waters.

'What the flaming heck do you think you're doing?' she hissed, tugging in vain at her skirt.

'Getting you off your high donkey.' He put his hands behind his head and reclined at his ease on the floor while Helen struggled to free herself. Suddenly the absurdity of the situation struck her, and she began to laugh. She had been a bit sharpish with him, after all.

'All right, me old cock sparrer,' she said amiably. 'Call it a draw, eh?' She twisted her head round from her precarious position, extricated her hand from under her hip and extended it.

Jack Waters took it. 'Friends—and I'll let you go.'

'All right,' agreed Helen cautiously. 'Friends.'

In a flash he had disentangled himself, then Helen's skirt and was pulling her up gazing unashamedly as he did so. He was not one to pretend not to notice.

'You've got nice legs.'

'In the circles I was brought up in, a gentleman never mentioned a lady's leg. And he wouldn't have looked, neither.'

'What circles were those?'

Helen looked at him belligerently. 'In...' she cast round— 'Queen Anne's Gate.'

74

This was where, she had since discovered, the Big Man lived. 'Enormous house we had. Masses of servants down below. My father—he was a lord you know. He had a butler and everything. I mean, *we* had.' She almost believed it herself as the memory of The Lady came flooding back.

'I can't match that. I come from Holloway myself, till father took the Marylebone and we moved to Mayfair. You'll just have to put up with me.'

She looked at his face suspiciously for a sign of mockery but there was none. She'd done all right.

'Now about those legs,' he went on thoughtfully.

'What about me legs,' Helen said defensively. 'They're all right. You leave 'em alone.' She drew back quickly, the old irrational fear of being touched against her wishes confusing her for a moment.

'Of course, of course,' he said hastily. 'But it does seem a shame. You could go into burlesque.'

'What's that?'

'It's like pantomime for grown-ups. It's what the Gala thrives on, songs, drama, satire, topical jokes, spectacle—'

'And what's that got to do with my legs?' She was suspicious but she had heard of the Gala Theatre. Who hadn't? Under its famous manager Frederick Glaser it was the mecca for all actresses and singers when they wanted to aspire to high society. You had to be really talented as well as beautiful to get taken on at the Gala. Why, some of them had married lords... The thought sprouted in her mind.

'The male lead is always played by a woman. Like Vesta Tilley, a male impersonator. You can strut about in tights and coats.'

'Wear trousers like Vesta Tilley? Top hat?'

'No. Tights, and short coats.'

'Show me legs? To everyone?' Helen was horrified. 'Not on your life I won't. I know what happens. You swells are all the same.' She remembered too late, she was supposed to be swell herself, but he didn't seem to have noticed anything unusual. Burlesque. She put the thought carefully at the back of her mind to take out when the time was ripe.

Their partnership continued reasonably amicably, even when she discovered that it wasn't quite true that Jack could do nothing. He could sing and he could dance. She was taken aback when she first made this discovery, jealous lest the limelight be taken off her, but as he seemed content to let her have all the solos and simply to join in the choruses, she gradually relaxed. She had to admit that his voice added something to her act. And when Mr Hewson's songs ran out, Jack produced one of his own, which was every bit as good and didn't even need 'Helenizing' like Mr Hewson's. Nor was she slow to appreciate that having an act with the owner's son did her some good with the rest of the performers, who treated her with a more grudging respect than before. And moreover he didn't lay a finger on her. He wasn't going to try and get her alone in the property room like some of the others—there wasn't that look in his eye that she'd got to know so well at Swains'. He just fitted in.

Yes, by the time his lordship went *Up* she would be nicely set. She wasn't doing badly now, she thought happily. She'd got a little niche in the theatre for herself, and Etty was working on costume alterations. Although the artistes had to provide their own costumes there were always bits and pieces that needed doing, alterations, repairs, props to be made, and Etty's nimble fingers came in useful. Yes, Helen's first foot was planted on the ladder. She had seen enough of the stage life already to realize it was right to laugh with men, joke with them, even let them kiss you if necessary, but you mustn't get mixed up with them. They would stop her getting to the top. Then once she was top of the bill here, she'd have to move on if she was to become a lady.

But working with Jack was different. It was like having a friendly puppy around. Etty had been nervous of him at first, and envious of Helen's free and easy manner with him. But seeing this, Jack had toned down his manner and was always so gentle with her that she was quite won over.

There were limits to their friendship with Jack, however. Once the theatre closed, their life was their own. Neither of them spoke of where they resided. Etty still lived in fear and Helen had no doubt that if their father found out where they were, there would be trouble. The very thought brought up all her horrors again—Mrs Blades, Father, the barrow—she could not face it again. Bethnal Green must be blotted out. For ever. And for Etty too. But one night:

'I've booked a table at Rules tomorrow night. For dinner after the show. You and me. Will you come?' Jack asked her casually.

'I don't go out after the show. I go home,' she said truculently. 'And what's this Rules?'

'Just a restaurant. Where people go after the theatre—you'll be perfectly safe. We'll take old Mrs Wilson along.'

'What d'yer want her for? She's as deaf

78

as a post,' said Helen.

'Perfect chaperone.' Then as she looked doubtful: 'It'll be the last time. I'm off back to Cambridge next week. There'll be rich people dining there,' he added in a throwaway line.

'All right then,' Helen shrugged, trying to conceal her sudden excitement. But what did one wear for going to Rules, she wondered? She hadn't got it, that was for certain. Luckily she had some money now. She could buy something new. She'd take Etty with her, Etty had good taste.

Etty had, but it was a hard battle against Helen's peacock instincts. In the end they compromised—Helen got the low neck she wanted. Etty succeeded in persuading her to take the duller red, not the scarlet she had her eye on...

Helen knew she was wrong the moment she walked into Rules. She had been silent in the cab on the way there, pretending to be occupied in gazing at the pavement, but she was very aware of Jack next to her, paying his attention to Mrs Wilson, the stage doorkeeper's wife, who was blushing like a twenty-year-old. It was funny to be out with him instead of larking around in the theatre. She didn't know what to say to him in these unfamiliar surroundings, and she was determined not to put a foot wrong. She let herself be handed down from the cab like any lady. He had been very complimentary about her dress but when she took off her paletot in Rules, she was painfully aware that she was exposing more breast than all the other women put together. Dresses cut off the shoulder were clearly not in fashion for dining out. Not that there were many women anyway, mostly men, whose eyes followed her as she marched forward, chin in the air. When they were established in their own little corner she relaxed a little. She hoped after all that there weren't any lords here this evening.

She had glanced somewhat nervously at the huge menus in front of other late diners as they entered and was relieved when Jack told her simply that dinner was already ordered. A bottle of champagne arrived first.

'To celebrate the end of our partnership.'

She had never tasted the stuff before and was relieved to find it not that much different in taste from lemonade, and drank some more eagerly. Even Mrs Wilson came to sudden life, and commanded in the loud tones of the deaf: 'I'll trouble you for some more of that, young man.'

After two glasses the array of cutlery no longer presented such a fear to her. What was it that Etty had told her? Fish the middle one? Or the outside one? What did it matter anyway? She struggled with her glove buttons as the waiter arrived bearing a large tray. She tried to remove her gloves unostentatiously below table level and eventually succeeded in undoing the seemingly endless buttons, though by now flushed with embarrassment.

'I've ordered lobster to begin with,' Jack informed her. 'Have you tried it?'

''Course I have,' cried Helen defiantly. 'We had it all the time at home in—'

'Queen Anne's Gate. Yes of course.'

'It's like a big whelk, ain't it?' The champagne was making her accent slip slightly.

'Both are supposed to inspire love anyway.'

'The only thing that's good for is a pile of money,' Helen laughed. Then seeing his startled expression and realizing that she could be misunderstood, she added hastily, 'I mean—I've heard—there isn't much love about in a one-room tenement.'

'But for Mary May, it's different surely. Hasn't she ever been in love?'

'Me? That'll be the day. I'll fall in love when a lord comes with it, and not before.' She eyed the lobster cautiously, waiting to see how he would tackle it, and when he waited for her, picked up a knife and tried to extract the claw meat. It didn't work, and so, she hastily blew her nose to gain time. Even Mrs Wilson seemed to know better than her how to handle lobster, black bombazine rustling as she dug in with eagerness. Helen immediately copied her and found it wasn't too bad, especially washed down with a large gulp of champagne.

She began to feel confident again.

'Well, how about you, then?' she asked brightly.

'Oh, I believe in love whole-heartedly. I want my own little hearthside in Holloway, a little wife sitting by it, just waiting for me to come home, with my slippers by the fire, a pipe ready filled and a whisky and soda.'

'Sounds dull to me.'

'I've no great ambitions.'

'But you're going to be a lawyer,' said Helen amazed. 'That's la-di-da—grand. You'll make lots of money.'

'I don't want to be that sort of lawyer. I'm one of life's amblers.'

'You've got to have ambition,' said Helen robustly, as she started on a large plate of steak and kidney pie. 'It's the most important thing in the world.'

'Is it?'

'Yes, you've got to fight, do the best you can. Make everyone else see you're better than they are.' The champagne had been followed by red wine and the evening had taken on a pleasant glow indeed.

'Suppose I'm not.'

'Then you've got to pretend you are. And then you really are.' She knew it sounded muddled, but she was clear that she was saying something really important. Her head was beginning to swim though and by the time she had finished a large slice of Bombe Surprise, Jack's face was beginning to become hazy, and it seemed a good idea to lean on Mrs Wilson.

She was aware of Jack coming round the table and of being firmly led out between him and Mrs Wilson, into the cold air outside. She gulped in breathfuls of air gratefully as they escorted Mrs Wilson to her nearby home. She protested at leaving them, but Jack was adamant. Then he frogmarched Helen along the pavement, forcing her to walk until she began to feel slightly better.

'Really,' her voice was artificially high, 'I don't know what came over me.'

'My fault,' he said, contrite, 'I shouldn't have given you so much champagne when you weren't used—I mean, so late at night. Mind you, if you're going to marry a lord it will be good practice.'

She looked at him indignantly, and opened her mouth to speak. But he got in first, goading her, shooting questions at her. 'The thing that puzzles me, Mary, is why you're not used to the late night drinking of champagne. I thought it happened all the time in the aristocratic circles you were brought up in. And surely you've had your fill of lords by now, so why set out to marry one too?'

She thought as quickly as her befuddled mind would allow. 'Temperance,' she said at last. 'Illegitimate. Wouldn't recognize us. Wards.'

Jack burst out laughing. 'Come, Mary. What is your real name; where do you live?'

Suddenly it was all too much. She turned on him, tears of rage pouring down her face. She waved her hand at the scene in front of them—in the early hours of the morning Covent Garden was already buzzing with life, figures rushing hither and thither intent on their business. The familiar smells, potatoes, oranges and apples pervaded the night air. Flower-sellers were haggling over prices, their sharp knowing faces a contrast to the delicacy of the blooms they held. The smell of autumn, of harvest was everywhere.

'Jarvis,' she yelled at him. 'Jarvis. 'Elen Jarvis. Daughter of Michael Jarvis, costermonger—and a rotten one at that. Not even so grand as these fellows here in the Garden. Spitalfields, that's where we're from. Straight from Bethnal Green.

And let me tell you, Mr I'm-going-up-to-Cambridge Waters, that if you'd been dragged up there, where dipping and cheating your neighbours are the only ways of getting a penny over starvation level, where kids are thieves and whores before they're ten years old, you'd want to marry a lord too. You wouldn't be satisfied with no slippers in front of no fire then. It's a lord, I want. So as I'll never have no need of money again. 'Cos I'm not going back. Ever. And nor's Etty. Not while I can earn a penny to keep her and make her strong again.' She found herself trumpeting hoarsely into a handkerchief suddenly produced under her nose.

'I always pay my debts,' he said gently.

She honked again, and glared at him. 'I'll go home now,' she said stiffly.

Too late she realized that would mean he would see where she lived. Oh, well, what did it matter anyway? He was leaving in a day or two.

He stared up at the tall dilapidated building in Edgware Road where she had found lodgings.

'Thank you for dinner,' she said awkwardly, putting out her hand.

He took it in his, and kept it there. 'Ellen,' he said thoughtfully. 'Yes, I like it.'

'Not Ellen. *Helen's* what I said,' she said crossly.

'I've never had a friend called Helen before.' Once he had seen her inside the front door he leapt back on the cab and was gone.

Friends. That's what friends are for, thought Helen bitterly, as she stumbled inside. To trick you, make you feel a fool. She could do without friends in future thank you very much. It was just as well he was leaving. She stumbled into the communal privy and was very, very sick.

Etty gazed into the butcher's window, trying to make up her mind. Even though they had enough money to live now, with their two wages put together, she could not forget the old days when every farthing had to be invested carefully into the maximum amount of food. She would weigh the cost of mutton cutlets against beef steaks very carefully, bearing in mind all Francatelli's injunctions to the frugal housewife.

'You never know,' she said to Helen, surprisingly firmly, 'when we may need the little bit I save. You may be out of a job, and that would mean I would be too.'

There was no one else to help them. Jack was leaving and Helen still refused to seek out Mr Hewson. Etty thought guiltily of her own secret visits to see him at Hoxton. She sighed. Helen was so wonderful, so kind, so warm-hearted, so protective—and yet she seemed to have forgotten all about poor Mr Hewson. She lived entirely in the present—and her dreams of the future.

She would miss Jack. Jack was so kind, and made her laugh. She wished Helen would invite him back to supper, or on a Sunday. But she supposed that he wouldn't want to come. After all he lived in Mayfair. He was Mr Waters' son, although there was something about him that made her forget all that when he was with them. She liked the way his eyes crinkled when he smiled or laughed. He was the first person they had ever laughed—really laughed—with.

She turned her thoughts back to the display of fowl and joints that always made her shudder a little remembering the flies on old Figgis's barrow next to Father's. With an effort she forced herself into the shop and purchased the cutlets, and having procured some vegetables from a nearby barrow, proceeded to the haberdasher for some requirements for her work at the Marylebone.

'Would you deliver them to the Marylebone Music Hall please and charge them to the account?' she asked shyly.

The business transacted, she turned to go out. There, grinning at her ferociously from the doorway was Michael Jarvis. The nightmare had come. Out of the blue on this autumn day. She turned to go back into the shop but it was too late. He grabbed her arm.

'Now you wouldn't want the police, my little Etty? Would you, little daughter?' Mutely, her senses pounding, heart hammering with fear, she walked outside, his hand still gripping her arm.

'That's right. Quite a little expedition you've had this morning, ain't you? 'Ad quite a time to wait afore yer turned up at the barrer—'e said you always came along Thursdays. Spitalfields man, you see. Friend o' mine. Now Etty, darlin', you come straight home along a me. Little George been missing you, 'e 'as. Not to mention your stepmother. Sobbing her heart out.'

'No,' Etty gasped. 'No, I never will.'

'I don't see, Etty, quite what you're going to do about it. You're not twenty-one yet, are yer? And I'm your father.'

'Not for much longer,' Etty replied spiritedly.

'Well, if you want to be difficult, Etty—p'raps we'd better have a word with that nice-lookin' policeman, there—he might be interested in our 'Elen too. Kidnapping's a big charge.'

Etty was terrified. He'd never do it, of course. But might he? Suppose he tracked down Helen at the Marylebone? Suppose she lost her job and was dragged back to

Bethnal Green—and Mrs Blades too?

Suddenly there was salvation, as an omnibus drew slowly away from the stop. Pushing Jarvis with all her might into the path of oncoming shoppers, she leapt on to the bus, as the horses picked up speed. The last thing she saw was her father's face, red and distorted with fury, glaring after the omnibus with the frustrated helplessness of a lumbering animal—baulked of its prey.

When she arrived home frantic with worry and crying, Helen was still lying in bed suffering the after-effects of the champagne the night before. But one look at Etty and she was on her feet.

'He heard you? He knows where we are? We're leaving now.'

Etty stared. 'Leaving? But how? Where?'

Helen looked at her impatiently. Etty was a dear, but she was a ninny at times. 'We can't go to the theatre again, don't you see? He'll turn up there. We'll find somewhere else. We must leave London. Lucky we've got that money we saved.'

Etty gazed at her. 'But the cutlets,' she wailed.

It was all she could focus on. The cutlets seemed to symbolize all the security of the life she was being asked to give up once again.

'But where will we go?' she asked again tremulously.

'Anywhere,' said Helen, more confidently than she felt. 'Up north. They've lots of music halls up there. We'll get a job quick as a flash. You'll see...'

Anything to get away...

Leeds. It looked a long way away as they stood before the departure board for the Great Northern Railway at King's Cross Station. When you could go anywhere it was difficult to know where to go. But Helen had heard of Leeds. She remembered Annie Kay talking about it. How big, how warmhearted a town it was. Do anything for anyone would Leeds.

'We'll try it,' said Helen confidently.

While Helen bought tickets at the booking office, Etty looked around anxiously.

'Helen,' she asked, as she came back, 'would you do something for me before we go?'

'What?' said Helen impatiently.

'Mr Hewson is still selling his matches here.'

A frown crossed Helen's face. 'You want me to say goodbye to him?' How could she? How could she not? If she saw him she'd break down. She could never ask him to come with them—he would refuse and then she would be hurt all over again. No, she'd get rich and famous first, then send for him to join them.

But to please Etty she went. It was four months since she'd last seen him, the proud old devil. He seemed to have aged a lot, she thought critically. And, Hell, Hull and Halifax, there he was, wearing the same old hat.

'What happened to the new hat I gave you,' she joked, to hide her pleasure. 'Not good enough for you?'

Mr Hewson blinked. 'At home, my dear Miss Jarvis. My best hat. Of course.'

He took the news of their departure with only a murmured, 'Not a poetical place, Leeds.'

'Daft old 'apporth,' choked Helen, as they walked away to the train.

'Oh, Helen,' said Etty dolefully. 'You're so hard sometimes.'

Helen glanced at her in surprise. Did Etty know her as little as all that? Her own sister? Didn't Etty realize she was fighting to keep her tears back? That's what happened if you tried to look back. You had to keep going forward. She pursed her lips grimly to keep her eyes from filling with tears as large as Etty's. One of them had to be strong. It had to be her.

The countryside through the grimy train windows was depressing. She'd heard about the country. Great paradise it was built up to be, all green, and cows and lovely milkmaids sitting on stools. Haystacks and little cottages. Garn. It wasn't a bit like that. It was bleak and unfriendly in the dying light, no happy lights anywhere looking welcoming, just a blur of grey and dirty green. The further they went the worse it got. Great factory chimneys belching smoke, great tall black conical mountains. She stared out at them, and remembered the little about the north of England she had learned at school. Coal that's what it was. Coal. The towns seemed blanketed with smoke, not the comforting sooty smoke of the train, but a dirty depressing blanket that hid the fitful autumn sun from their eyes.

Bleak towns, bleak life for the next two months. Warmhearted city? Do anything for anyone? For their own perhaps. But not for Londoners. It seemed every door was shut. True, there were plenty of music halls. But all of them had their own performers, with strange northern accents and did not take kindly to newcomers. The London music halls were welcoming with open arms performers from the north, but the same did not appear to be true in reverse. They trudged from theatre to theatre, from town to town, from lodging to lodging through grey northern towns. Etty began to look thin and worried once again, Helen pinched and hard. Their store of money dwindled fast and doors remained firmly closed.

Not long before Christmas, Helen stood disconsolate on Wakefield Bridge. It was a beautiful bridge but Helen had no eyes to see it. It was just one more town, one more hope. They had been there two days, waiting for a chance to see the music hall manager. It was a small hall for the size of the town and its bill looked depressingly full. Now dressed as formidably as she could manage, she had half blarneyed, half bulldozed her way into the manager's office. But yet once more her hopes were dashed when the manager informed her, apparently with some regret, that his bill was full. He was a big bluff north countryman with red cheeks and waistcoat that stuck out importantly. Helen had come to tell a great deal about managers by their waistcoats: the colour, the cut, how many buttons were undone, the angle they held their stomachs. Nevertheless she was wrong about this man. He had a heart as well as a stomach.

'Miss May—'

She turned back from the door.

'I'll tell you what, Miss May. Ever done burlesque? There's a vacancy over at the Empire.'

As Helen looked blank, he waved his

hand impatiently. 'Westgate. Big fancy place. Touring company. You might suit. Give it a try.'

Burlesque. Suddenly Helen was excited, remembering Jack's words. 'But I've no experience.'

The fat man shrugged. 'Don't tell 'em. Take my tip. Get out of the halls. You'll just be dead before you're forty.'

The Empire was not so imposing as its name, but it was the first time Helen had been inside a 'straight' theatre and had little to compare it with. She was disappointed at first; it was not so ornate as the Marylebone, though there was a certain grandeur about its faded red plush and flaking gilt woodwork. A small tired worried man in early middle age came wearily out of the wings when the stage doorkeeper summoned him.

'Yes, what is it?'

'I heard you had a vacancy—sir. And I want—'

'You want to be an actress. Hugh? You hear that?' yelling to some invisible gentleman in the flies. 'This wretched, wretched life we lead and you want to be an actress. Well come along, don't stand there.'

Somewhat startled at her reception, Helen was led along to his office, at the half walk, half trot she later came to

94

know was Stephen Woolley's usual method of propulsion.

'I heard you had an opening in burlesque.'

He threw his hands in the air. 'No, no, quite wrong, all wrong.'

Helen bit her lip and rose to her feet.

'Sit down, sit down,' he said somewhat less shrilly and more amiably. 'What's your name?'

'Miss May,' said Helen wearily.

'Ah.' There was a long pause while he considered the inkwell on his desk. Then suddenly, 'No opening in burlesque, Miss May. Harlequinade. Ever done a Columbine?

Harlequinade. In a flash Helen was transported back. The penny gaff. The Harlequin. The magic of his wand, the *Columbine!* Could she dance like Columbine?

'Yes,' she said firmly.

'Got a dress?'

'No,' she admitted.

'No matter, no matter. Opening in two days. Christmas week. Got to have one. Dance around a bit, flutter your skirt. Look pretty.' He looked a little doubtfully at Helen's firm handsome face, and striking hair and eyes.

'I've got a blonde wig.' Helen quickly followed his train of thought. 'I'll manage.'

95

'Hell, Hull and Halifax.' She looked at herself later in the mirror in awed wonder. Pink tights, a white dress that only reached the centre of her legs, organdie headdress, spangles, and a wand. She looked like the fairy on top of the Christmas tree she'd seen in the big shop window the other day. She was enchanted with herself.

'Don't I look a sight?' she giggled to Etty, who had appointed herself dresser (unpaid).

Despite her fears Helen was impressed when she entered the Empire for her first rehearsal. This was real theatre. She was a *player*. Or would be, if she could survive this test. The manage had simply fluted at her, 'Clown, dear, he'll show you. Simply trust old Clown,' and rushed off.

Luckily she was light on her feet and had an ear for rhythm, for the dance was complicated. She watched in a haze as Clown went into the complete pirouette of steps and it was all she could do not to giggle as he delicately bent his large body into a Columbine stance, resting his cheek lightly on one hand. He looked at her dolefully. 'Well,' he said, sighing, after he had watched her efforts, 'Harlequin will have to help you. Just look pretty, dear, and twirl around if you can't think of anything else. Can you trip?'

'Pardon?'

'Trip dear.' And he minced, pattering across the stage. 'Now just remember. I'm your friend on stage and Pantaloon's your enemy. Try looking frightened.'

Helen flung up her hands, threw her body back and opened her eyes wide.

'Mouth shut, dear, or Clown will pop an egg in. Wouldn't look nice, not for Columbine.'

And after such brief preparation she found herself part of an on-stage rehearsal of a play whose plot seemed largely made up as they went along. Pantaloon the cruel father, Clown the naughty servant, playing around her, behind her, pushing her here, pulling her there, all the while keeping up continuous fast action. She was in a complete daze. But that was nothing compared with the shock she received when Harlequin appeared for the first time, shot up in the air like a cork out of a bottle from the star trap.

It was Jack Waters, covered in twenty spangles to the inch in a body hugging costume of patched red, yellow, blue and black, cap on head, slapstick wand in hand. *Harlequin!*

'Don't worry about a thing,' he assured her after the rehearsal, 'I've got another day to teach you to dance.'

Helen was awash with conflicting emotions

—she was angry, mystified, ashamed at her poor performance, head whirling as to what he was doing here; the other half of Helen was spellbound, still part of a scene that, confused and uncertain as she was, had cast its spell over her as surely as it had all those years before.

For Harlequin had danced for her, plain Helen Jarvis. In those few brief minutes she was Harlequin's love, with all its wonder and glory. Harlequin with his cap of invisibility. Harlequin poised and graceful in front of her striking one of his traditional poses symbolizing admiration, defiance, determination, flirtation and thought.

Only it was Jack Waters, mask in hand.

'What makes you think I need teaching anything about anything?' said Helen crossly. 'And who asked you to come here?'

'I thought we were friends. You left. So I thought I'd find out why. Took me a dickens of a long time to find you. Lucky Mr Hewson gave me a clue where to start.'

She might have known. 'But you're supposed to be in Cambridge.' Helen was still bewildered and still annoyed. 'What happened to the law?'

'Too much like hard work.'

'And you've given all that up to play Harlequin in a touring troupe?'

'Not much ambition, as I told you. Easy life. No examinations. No judges, no responsibility.'

Even Helen was forced to admit she was not the world's best Columbine. But by hard work she became a passable one, subduing her own vibrant personality into the shy reserve and coquetry of Columbine. She found rather to her own surprise that she could react quickly to other people on the stage, speedily falling instinctively into the necessary poses, her native wit helping her to play up to Clown.

Because it was too much trouble and difficult to find another Columbine the manager kept her on. It might also have been something to do with Jack, whose father was well known to the northern theatres. Every two weeks they moved on to a different town. After the novelty of the first two or three, however, each town began to look the same. So did the hunt for lodgings, the best always gone already to old hands, and she and Etty would be left to the bombazine-clad martinets, where boiled cabbage and mutton were only eatable through their lack of quantity. But they had a job, and they had money, even if pitiable in its meagreness. *And* she was Columbine.

Strange how life can change so quickly. For the first time Helen felt happily secure, away from Father and no direct challenges facing her. Life was presenting itself with no problems. Until one day.

Helen never read *The Times*, but Jack did. Just in case, he explained deprecatingly, he ever needed to take up law again. Thus it was that he saw the advertisement. It was nearly Christmas again.

'*Henrietta Jarvis: Would Henrietta Jarvis, of Cable Street, Bethnal Green please contact Messrs. Scrumpton and Patrick of Cliffords Inn.*'

'It's a trick of Father's.' Helen was suspicious.

'He wouldn't know *The Times* existed,' said Etty scornfully.

'No, they're respectable solicitors,' Jack replied. 'You must go.'

Etty look frightened. 'Can't I just write? I don't want to go alone.'

Jack shook his head. 'You must go yourself. I'll come with you if you like.'

Helen looked at him gratefully. She felt it was her job, but she thought it would be better to have a man go. And they couldn't both go.

'Anyway,' she said, 'it's probably a lot of fuss about nothing.'

Helen had felt lost when they had gone, without anybody to look after, fuss over, not even Jack to laugh with. Suppose Etty and Jack fell in love? After all he was a slippers and pipe man and Etty needed someone to look after her... Yes, but she didn't want Jack to look after Etty. It was her job. Helen's. Not his. She felt Etty was slipping away out of her grasp and began to fret. Of course she was glad for Etty's sake if it was something nice, but where would it leave her? Suppose Etty didn't come back?

It wasn't a fuss about nothing! It was £6,000 left to her by the old gentleman in black, her real father, Lord Bassett, the solicitors explained to her delicately. Had she still been living at home when he died Michael Jarvis would have continued to get the small allowance made to him, and no doubt would have continued to take the much larger allowance to which Etty had been entitled all these years.

Her half-sister. Helen tried to take it in, when Etty returned to tell her the news. Etty was only a half-sister. And the daughter of a lord. Never mind if she was a bastard. It wasn't fair. Why Etty and not her? Helen gulped. Her world seemed to swim around her. Then she took hold of herself. Etty was Etty, her dearly loved sister, and always would be. She embraced her quickly, joyfully and warmly.

'Oh, Helen!' Etty burst into tears. 'I don't want anything to change. I want to stay here with you. Always.'

'No,' said Helen firmly, though it broke her heart to say it. 'No Etty, it's too hard a life for you.'

After much discussion, it was decided that Etty should buy a house for herself and for Helen, if she returned to London. 'But you can't live on your own.' Jack was worried. 'Don't you have a friend who could live there with you?'

'I don't think I have any friends, not in London.' Etty's voice faltered.

He took her hands and kissed them gently. 'Dear Etty,' he said, 'dear, dear Etty. Surely there is someone?'

'Yes,' Etty cried suddenly. 'Of course I have someone. One friend.'

And so it was that Mr Frederick Hewson, now sixty-seven years of age, came to live with Etty and her elderly housekeeper, in a small house in Putney. How Helen longed to be with them—laughing round the piano as they had at Hoxton, with his ridiculous songs. After all, Mr Hewson had been her friend first, not Etty's, and now Etty had come in and taken him over. And she had plenty of money too. She'd asked Helen to come to live with her, to retire, but she must have known she couldn't do it. She was Helen Jarvis. She didn't want Etty's money. She was going to be an actress. A real one. And when she was, she'd join them and then marry a lord. She couldn't give it up just as she was started on the path. They'd miss her though—Etty and Mr Hewson. Or would they?

Helen looked round the shabby room. Her possessions suddenly seemed full of pathos, the photo of Etty and her when they had a day at the seaside at Scarborough, the wind having blown Etty's long fine hair all over her face, and both of them laughing; the playbill from the Marylebone; the woolly dog Jack had given her when they went to the fair one Sunday, full of bustling, good-humoured northerners. Nothing to remind her of Bethnal Green. She looked at them all carefully, and at the old shabby trunk which held all her belongings when she travelled. Even her Columbine's costume suddenly looked tawdry, bereft of stage lighting and glitter.

She looked at them all, and suddenly her eyes filled with tears.

Chapter Four

'Gawlimy.' Helen clapped her hand over her mouth and cast an anxious glance to see if Jack had heard this social indiscretion. It appeared not, for he too was riveted by the spectacle of the transformation scene in front of them. Gauzes were lifting one by one to display a fairyland the richness of which even Jack had never seen excelled on the stage. The opulence of the East, the setting for the pantomime of *Aladdin* was swept away to reveal 'The Realms of Bliss', a scene of feathery clouds and floral banks, with fairies gracefully posed in gauzy muslins of blue, green and pink, and others floating in mid-air.

The music crashed out, fumes of different coloured fires rose into the air, a shrill whistle, and the vision was swiftly blotted out by scenery descending from the flies—a railway station, complete with weighing machine, signals, and ticket office proclaiming prominently 'Tickets for the Orient'. The Harlequinade had begun.

Helen slowly expelled her breath. Trust her to have opened her mouth, thought she, just when she was trying so hard to behave like a lady. She felt like one in the new oyster satin dress with its not too tight skirt, and not too low square neck, and as many frills and flounces as any lady born, not to mention the small imitation robin attached to the frills at the side of her dress. This had caused Jack much amusement until Helen, hurt, had told him that it was all the rage.

She looked with satisfaction down at her white-gloved hands meekly folded in her lap, buttons neatly done up, all eighteen of them. No, no one could say she wasn't worthy of a box at the Theatre Royal, Halifax. None of the swells here knew that she was a Columbine in a tuppenny touring company. This was a different crowd altogether, and a fashionable one. She'd never been inside a theatre as big as this one; you didn't get much chance when you were on the halls yourself.

It was pantomime, he'd explained, they'd be seeing. Like a burlesque but with a different audience. *Aladdin* might be pantomime but in its splendour it bore little resemblance to the performance of *Dick Whittington* Helen had seen before, one Christmas with Mr Hewson and Etty in the Grand, Hoxton. But here, why, the stage must be six times as big, with people in wonderful coloured costumes filling every corner of it. The play was full of excitement: transformations, people leaping out of vampire traps, claps of thunder, crimson fire; it was a joy to behold.

When the pantomime's Harlequin and Columbine appeared for their dance, hands crossed, gracefully poised, it was not the disorganized gallop to which Helen was used, but an elegant *pas de deux,* which caught at her breath. Helen felt completely spellbound, and knew that she had to perform on this wonderful stage. She turned to Jack. 'How can we get work here?' It did not occur to her to wonder if he wanted to come here, or indeed, anywhere with her.

He tucked her arm under his as they went downstairs, but did not reply.

'Don't laugh at me, Jack,' she said impatiently. 'You know I've got to act here. That's why you brought me, isn't it? Isn't it?' Yet he waited until they were seated at the tea table between the palm fronds in the respectable Queen's Hotel that normally would have Helen gasping with wonder. Not today though. He waited until the tea arrived before telling her that it was all arranged.

Her eyes blazed. 'Columbine?'

'Er, no, not exactly.' He avoided her eyes.

'What then?' she asked, disappointed.

'One of those lovely ladies floating in the air, in the transformation scene.'

'What? Me just be a fairy, while you're a Harlequin? Not likely. And what do you mean, you've arranged it?'

'Steady, Helen, steady. I'm not Harlequin or even Clown. I'm working backstage.'

'Backstage? That's not much, is it?'

'But your clown, Helen,' he murmured, 'your clown alone. Now listen to me. You're to have real ballet lessons, and I'm sure with your talent you'll be Columbine in no time at all.' His words were soothing, but Helen was not convinced.

'And what if I don't choose to come?' How dare he arrange her career? She could look after her own affairs.

'You'll have to now, I told Woolley we were leaving two days ago. He's already replaced us.' He laughed as he saw her stormy face.

'Come, Helen. It takes time to rise to the top, but you're off to a good start as a floating lady.'

Accustomed as Helen was to the realities of backstage life, nothing had ever been comparable to the discomfort she was going to endure as a *femme suspendue*, as they were known at the Theatre Royal. Strapped to a thick iron band for an hour at a time, for the transformation scene took long to prepare, the fairies sweltered aloft from their nearness to the hot gaslights, sweat running down their faces. She realized now why the manager had taken her on so easily and without seeing her first—it was hard to get sufficient ladies willing to put up with this nightly torment. Jack blandly ignored the invective she threw at him.

Working at the Theatre Royal, she had realized, was by no means the same as working in a small touring company on the halls. Here she was a very small cog in a well oiled wheel. She struggled to learn.

'It's no use,' she wailed after a week's hard work and only aching muscles to show for it. 'I'll never learn. Not like those fine madams there.'

'Nonsense, I thought you were ambitious, Helen. Never say can't when you can say might.'

'You sound like Mr Hewson,' she said sullenly.

He placed his hand on his heart, stood still gazing heavenward and sighed. 'How right you are, Helen. Inside I have the soul of a poet.'

She fell silent, painfully aware that she had not yet been to London to see Etty or Mr Hewson. Despite her love for Etty, she was envious that Etty was now writing happily of her doings in Putney and of her visits to London. Oh to be back among those familiar streets, thought Helen, who was hurt at the evidence that her fierce love was no longer necessary to Etty, and this contrarily made her all the more non-committal whenever Jack asked her what her plans were for returning to London. He paid regular short visits to London, to see his father, Helen presumed, but she felt diffident about accompanying him. She might bump into old Waters and she did not relish explaining her sudden disappearance from the Marylebone. Nor did she trust herself to see Etty...she might be tempted not to return, to accept the easy way out instead.

However inadequate her ballet technique, she grew sufficiently agile within ten days to master the trick of simply staying aloft suspended by the irons. But her career as a floating lady was destined to be brief. Tired of seeing Helen hanging ungracefully on the iron or surreptitiously clinging to the branch of a fragile paper tree as an extra support, the stage manager allotted her to a place on the *parallele*. This was the vast magic upside down umbrella that was slowly winched up on to the stage, with fairies disporting themselves in graceful poses.

Unfortunately, on her fifth appearance on the *parallele* she mistimed the moment

110

when she should let go her spoke—they had not yet finished unfolding. Realizing her mistake too late, she clung to the nearest object which happened to be the less-than-stalwart fairy next to her. As she collapsed on to the fairy behind her, it took but a moment for twelve of the fairies to be struggling on the floor, legs kicking wildly in the air, rivalling all that Paris could offer, and volubly cursing the instigator of their misfortune.

In the wings Jack choked his laughter into the curtain. He quickly put out a hand to stop the stage manager, who was all for bringing down the curtain there and then, preferring to see what Helen would do next.

Helen looked in despair at the carnage round her; she detached herself carefully from the heap, smoothed down her skirts, advanced to the footlights, raised her eyebrows and her arms and shrugged expressively at the audience. 'Eh, we fairies are nowt but human.'

As the jeers turned to laughter, she quickly improvised a parody of the fairy dance, and since the ladies had still not resorted themselves into formation and were milling about chaotically, launched orchestraless into one of her old music hall songs, a respectable one in view of the audience of children.

The final curtain fell to more enthusiastic cheers than the pantomime had roused for many a long day, but this did not strengthen Helen's nerves as she marched defiantly along to the ill-ventilated smelly dressing room she shared with her sister fairies. What would they do to her? Oh well she'd be out on her ear again. In the end she was not to discover what they would do left to their own desires, for as she entered a vindictive voice shrilled: 'Manager wants tha!'

Twenty-three self-satisfied grins watched her hasty retreat. Back to the halls, she thought despondently, as she knocked on old Rodgers' door. That fat old waddler didn't know a good performer when he saw one.

Apparently he did however, he was a shrewd man, and he knew that the ability to sway the audience, as had Helen, was rare indeed. After a few strictures on company discipline, he gave her the understudy to the lead in a new burlesque to be produced in two weeks' time. It was no more money, but she was sensible enough to know it was an opportunity for learning.

She watched, she absorbed. She was well aware of her own unpopularity in the theatre, though she did not understand why. She was headed for the top, and decided these northerners were an unfriendly lot. The songs were easy to master, because most of the tunes she knew anyway. And the words, though they didn't seem to make much sense, she was confident she could grasp, once she'd mastered the technique for putting over the jokes.

'Acting,' she said to Jack confidently. 'Nothing to it. You just say the words and strut up and down so the men can see your legs, that's all.'

'Poor old Shakespeare must be turning in his grave.'

'He can toss and turn as much as he likes, but I can see what's needed in this little game.'

Maybe she could but she was never called on to put it to the test. For the principal 'boy', a doughty forty-year-old by the name of Gwendolen Friar, obstinately refused to fall sick, despite all Helen's imprecations. Something had to be done, and Helen did it.

'I've got it,' she told Jack importantly one day. 'I told you I would and now I have.'

'What?'

'Principal boy in the next play—Yule-seeze or something. I remember Mr Hewson telling me about him. He was a sort of Greek Dick Whittington.'

'How on earth—' began Jack, genuinely amazed that she had succeeded in circumventing the formidable Gwendolen.

'I got round old Rodgers. Easy if you know how.' Helen was pleased with herself.

'And how is how?'

Helen failed to notice Jack's compressed lips. 'Oh, you know, a flash of leg, and a promise for tomorrow,' she told him jauntily until she caught sight of his face. 'What are you looking upset for? 'E won't get it, whatever 'e thinks.'

'The thought of you letting old men like that touch you.'

''E won't touch me. But no harm in letting 'im think, is there?' She laughed. 'You needn't worry, I'm saving myself for a lord, like I told you. Not going to throw myself away on a tuppenny ha'penny manager. It won't be long now before managers are coming to me, begging on their knees for me to grace their stages.'

It took quite a long time, in fact. In the meantime it was harder than she had thought, she admitted to herself. The words in themselves were no problem, but it took more than a flirt of her bottom to keep the attention of the audience and being northerners they were out for a good time. If the show did not please them, they did not hesitate to use every means in their power to show their displeasure. Like being back at old Swains', thought Helen in disgust one night, when the Friday night audience had been particularly unruly.

Gradually she began to discover that there was another technique she possessed in putting over a song, more subtle, yet more effective—her comic talent. It was untutored. It was rough. But slowly she became aware of the response to her slightest movement, and that intonation and timing of voice could achieve effects just as magical as striding out to the footlights and letting them have it loud and clear. That a slow lingering glance towards the audience with a raised eyebrow when Ulysses first sees Circe was worth ten false embraces. Thus after a somewhat shaky start her position in the company became assured—and without having to fulfil promises spoken or unspoken to old Rodgers.

There were men in plenty to choose from besides him. Not the fellows in the company. They weren't going anywhere. But in the audience were many sons of rich mill owners, out for a good time—perhaps for a wife from the exciting world of the stage. She chose carefully. The other girls laughed at her behind her back. She guessed what they were saying: 'Who's she waiting for? Prince Eddy?'

Her hopes were rewarded one evening

a month or two into the run of *Ulysses'*
Wobble, so called after the marathon walks
so popular nowadays.

'His name's George,' she crowed to Jack
impressively. 'He's a sort of lord. Son of
Sir George Amton. Now, Jack, you've got
to help me. Tell me how to behave like a
lady. What to wear and all that.'

Jack perched thoughtfully on a bench in
the property room, his own special domain,
so crowded with paraphernalia of every
description that few ventured in there.
Large animal property heads hung from
the ceiling, intermingled with grotesque
fairy-tale heads for pantomime. A stuffed
crocodile leered over one edge of the table,
where he had been carelessly dumped.
On the shelves, daggers, swords, spears,
goblets looking sadly unreal deprived of
the glamour of the gaslight to transmute
them into gold and silver, waited to be
called into action. Harlequin's bat lay
patiently by his mask, and a string of
sausages awaited repair after the last vicious
Clown/Policeman fight.

'Where is he taking you?'

'To dinner after the show,' said Helen
eagerly. 'The Grand.'

Jack shook his head disapprovingly.

'What's the matter with the Grand?' said
Helen truculently. 'It's the biggest place in
Halifax.'

'But it has the reputation—well—insist that he takes you to a private room. If you dine outside unchaperoned in the public rooms you'll be classified as one of *those.*'

She giggled. 'All right. What else?'

'Wear a low cut dress off the shoulder.'

She looked at him suspiciously since she remembered all too well her own first dinner engagement with him. 'But I thought it was a fashionable to have square necks and on the shoulder?'

'Yes that's correct. But the real aristocracy feel their own women are so well bred they should wear what suits them. Fashion is for the middle classes. Oh—and a little bit of paint.'

'But I thought—'

'It's absolutely *de rigueur* after eleven o'clock at night. Any lady looks undressed without it.'

Retribution descended on Jack's head earlier than he had expected. At eight-thirty the following morning an indignant landlady was requesting his presence downstairs immediately as a 'lady'—though the sniff that accompanied the word made it clear that no lady would call on a gentleman in his lodgings in the morning or indeed at any other time—was demanding to see him. He found a storm-cloud pacing up and down in the small stuffy parlour.

'I want to talk to you.'

'Do sit down.'

'I blooming well won't. We're going out where I can shout at you.'

'But I haven't had my breakfast.'

'You won't need no breakfast by the time I'm finished with you.'

He sighed, donned ulster and hat, and followed her down the street. 'How did your evening with the pending Sir George go?'

'You know how it went,' she stormed.

'I wasn't hiding in the soup tureen.'

'Well I'll tell you. He started breathing down me neck with the soup, after the pork cutlets he put an arm round me waist and before I could get to the pudding it was on me leg and trying to get up me skirt. And it's all your fault. He told me I couldn't expect nothing else what with paint on me face like a street walker, and asking for a private room an' all—you did it on purpose, didn't you?' Admit it. '

'I admit it. And I'm truly sorry.'

'No, you're not. You think it's bleeding funny, me wanting to marry a lord.' She was half crying now. 'Just because I'm not a lady. You make fun of me. What's bad about wanting to marry above yourself? Wanting to better yourself? And you've ruined it all. He'll never look at me again, and he'll tell all his swell friends—I'll never live it down.' She snorted into the handkerchief that Jack penitently produced. 'Anyway, you're so worried about my virtue. Suppose I'd lost it?'

'I'd back you against twenty unfledged Sir Georges. I knew you'd be all right. How did you manage it by the way?'

Despite herself she began to chuckle. 'I 'it 'im with the chocolate Suffles or whatever they call it—he did look funny with it all running down his face.'

Then they were laughing together. 'He had a chocolate blob left on the end of his nose after he'd wiped the rest away,' Helen spluttered. 'Oh well,' she said, wiping her eyes at last. 'Where there's one lord there'll be another, I dare say. Though how I'll ever learn to be a lady I don't know. Not up 'ere, that's for sure.'

'If you really want it—I'll teach you to be a lady.'

She stared at him, not taking him seriously.

'No, by Dick Whittington's cat, I swear I'll play fair. I'll teach you to be the grandest, most charming lady that ever walked on or off a stage so that you can hold your own with the best in the land.'

'You wouldn't pull my leg, would you, Jack?'

'We'll start now if you like—no wait a

bit—I'll have some breakfast first.'

It took a year of hard teaching to train Helen to be a lady, and another year while she endeavoured with mixed results to put it into practice. Jack did not find her an easy pupil any more than had Mr Hewson, but she was so willing, so penitent when her temper made her throw the whole thing up, and in the evening so transparently delighted when she conquered some new technique that he always forgave her.

'Now say it after me, Helen: "Is Lady Bloggs at home?"'

'Like a swan, Helen, glide like a swan, not a puppy gambolling along.'

'Place your right foot first, in the carriage, Helen.'

'Not such large portions, Helen—ladies have small appetites, not like Gargantua.'

'Twenty minutes only for a formal call.'

They had a series of mock afternoon tea parties, sitting on the remote hillside above the town, with Jack perched on a tree trunk, daintily putting acorn cup to lips, reaching for invisible cucumber sandwiches, coaching her in polite conversation. At first she laughed at seeing the sturdy, masculine Jack engaged in such frivolities, but once accustomed to it, entered into the spirit of the occasion with gusto. To her surprise she found that the sessions helped her stage technique as well, that awareness of her body and how it would respond to control helped in her delivery and posture. What she lost in unconscious direct appeal was more than compensated for by subtlety of performance. Jack kept a bag of coconut candy which she adored and, which he would feed to her like a donkey with carrots and often with the same careless pat.

She could not understand Jack at all. He seemed content just to work behind the scenes, managing properties, designing costumes, arranging scenes, being here, there and everywhere at everybody's beck and call. And he could have been a lawyer. Did he really have no ambition? Funny sort of chap. Knew so much, about Greek and all that, and content just to spend his life betwixt flymen and cellarmen. She asked him why, and he explained readily enough.

'You told me yourself that most music hall performers are dead or dying by the time they're forty. And look at old Fatty Jones there up in the flies, seventy-five if he's a day.'

'I don't want to hang around till I'm seventy-five. I want life to be like—like a star trap. Open, up it flies and up I pop, saying, "Hello Life".'

'Ah but think of the people down below

whom you need to work the star trap for you, Helen. Don't forget them. Anyway what's your lord going to say to popping in and out of star traps all the time; he may want a quiet life. How's the search going, by the way?'

She ignored this sally. It wasn't going very well in fact. She had only met one real lord in these two years, and he was a discharged soldier with a wooden leg and well over fifty. She had dined with him once or twice though she had not confessed this to Jack for fear he would laugh at her, although this time she had been properly chaperoned. Why she minded his opinion so much she didn't know, but his regard was valuable to her.

They met for her 'ladyship lessons', as Jack called them, there on their hillside now it was spring, so they might be free of the theatre and all its claustrophobia, mental and physical. It was a place for confidences, though the majority of them tended to be Helen's. It was as though by telling him of her follies she could cleanse herself of the slight guilt she had about 'The Search.' They would laugh as she recounted experiences of handling immature swells, of bestowing kisses like the Kohinoor diamond. She developed powers of mimicry that stood her in good stead on the stage, and Jack would lie back on the grass, hands behind his head and watch her.

She'd miss him if he left. He was part of her life now that Etty had gone. Letters didn't help, not really. It was people you needed, but she was reluctant to admit how much.

Of her life in London, Etty said little; there was mention of the solicitor who looked after her affairs, Paul someone. There was talk of Mr Hewson; how she wouldn't let him go out any more to sell matches because he was so frail and couldn't shake off this cough.

Helen put Etty's latest letter down with a sigh, feeling much alone. The stage was a marvellous place while you were on it, but once the stage door banged behind you at night—what then? It was all very well waiting for a lord but she had just had her birthday, and now she was in her twenties. All she had to show for it was a small following in a northern town. A queen of burlesque. Where next?

She found Jack waiting for her on the hill, as eager to tell her the latest news, as she was to read him Etty's letter. 'Rodgers told me that Frederick Glaser is coming to tour the northern shows in a week or two. And he's coming to the Theatre Royal.'

Frederick Glaser! The Gala. The house of entertainment, the light frothy shows cultivated by the intelligentsia and the rich alike; the chorus girls who frequently married into society. Married lords...

'Jack!' Her eyes blazed. 'He's really coming to the Theatre Royal?'

'Yes.'

She gave a sigh. 'I think I'm on the way up.'

He pulled her down beside him. 'Not yet, you're on the way down. Relax and have a chocolate almond.'

Some minutes later, licking the chocolate off her fingers, she bethought of what she was going to tell Jack—the latest escapade. 'A real gentleman he was, I behaved *terribly* well. I did just as you told me, used the cutlery in the right order, smiled ever so sweetly and didn't say what I really thought when he was saying such stupid things.'

'Sounds a paragon of a gentleman.'

'Oh, he was. All talk and free hands.'

'What did you do to this one? Crown him with the Stilton?'

'Nothing.' She was indignant. 'Just reminded him quietly that I was a lady and not used to this behaviour.'

Jack roared with laughter. 'I should think you've repelled more advances than General Gordon.'

'Well what do you expect me to do? I'm not going to have their hands all over me till a lord comes along.'

'And what if he doesn't, Helen? Are you going to use that as an excuse for evading life for ever?'

'Evading life. What do yer mean? I've seen more of life than you've had hot muffins.'

'You don't really want to marry a lord, that's just an excuse. You're afraid of love, aren't you? That's why you don't like people touching you. That's why you laugh at them.'

She sprang to her feet in panic. Afraid of love? But she was going to marry a lord. It would be all right if it were a lord. It must be. It wouldn't be like Father and Mother behind that curtain, like old Swains leering at her, hands reaching out... A lord was a gentleman—it would be different. Breathing hard she stared at him, regaining control of herself, and forced herself to laugh. 'You might have second thoughts about love too, if you'd seen what it counted for back where I come from. No, I'll marry a lord first, then I'll take lovers like all the swell folk do. "Hah now, me dear,"' she said in guttural tones, '"wort do you intend to do today. Ho, I intend to meet my lover, in the summerhouse, that's if you don't want your peacock's eggs peeled, or your lordship's—"'

When Jack laughed, she relaxed. For a moment he'd caught her on the raw. She must go on making him laugh. Her small figure danced up and down, mocking and imitating the latest escort. 'Afraid of love?' She laughed. 'That sort don't know what love is.'

'What is it, Helen?' He wasn't laughing now.

'What do you mean, what's love?'

He strolled to the edge of the copse and stood looking out over the hillside to the town beneath. Then he turned round to face her. 'What do you want from love? What is it to you, Helen? Diamonds? Rolling in a haystack? A genteel kiss on the forehead? Two naked bodies in a bed?'

'Why, Jack!' she exclaimed, coming up to him, 'what's the matter. And why are you looking at me like that?'

'Like what?'

'I don't know.' She backed away. The game's rules seemed to have changed. 'Different.'

His cheeks were red and on his face the look was one she was well accustomed to. But not from Jack. He wasn't like those old lechers at Swains'. He was her friend. She caught hold of his arm to tug him back beside her on the grass. But he resisted her and walked out on the hillside.

'We're all alone up here, Helen. We've never seen a soul.'

'What of it?'

'Don't you ever worry about it? Coming here alone with me. A man. Afraid I might seize you, try and make love to you, and not be put off by chocolate mousses and tricks like your swells and mashers? That you might *have* to let me make love to you?'

'You make love to me?' Jack and she had been romping together up here for years. The idea of suddenly having to restrict his pawing hands, have him groping up her skirt was very funny. But then she looked at his face again; he wasn't smiling, wasn't laughing.

'But you wouldn't—'

'Oh yes, I would, Helen. Believe you me, I would. Don't you think I ever get tired of listening to your prattling on about other men kissing you, trying to touch you, seduce you, wondering if you're telling me the truth, wondering if you're deliberately omitting to mention some of them, wondering if you're still a virgin—'

She gasped, her cheeks pink with fury. She caught hold of his shoulder and shook him. 'You bloody well know I am. I'm saving myself for a lord.'

'You're not going to marry a lord,

Helen. You're going to marry me. There's never been any question about that. But I'm tired of waiting for you to realize that for yourself. So now I'm going to make quite sure of it.'

Marry Jack! What an idea! She began to laugh and laugh. He was joking.

'Go on,' she mocked. 'Can you see me fetching your slippers and pipe like a good little country wifie?'

'No,' he said quietly. 'But I'm going to marry you all the same.'

'And how do you propose to do that?' she said, hands on her hips, mocking him. This must be some new game.

'Deprive you of your dowry. Now!' Seeing she still did not understand, he said matter-of-factly, 'In the copse over there. We'll undress and make love there. The rain should hold off long enough.'

She looked at him blankly, then as she took in his words, backed away from him in horror. This couldn't be gentle, happy-go-lucky indecisive Jack? She was the one that led, not he. Take her clothes off—in front of him—and let him—touch her? She shivered.

He was watching her carefully. 'You'll see,' he said unemotionally. 'It won't be too bad. We might even enjoy it. Both of us. Then we can start getting to know each other.'

'Are you going to...' Helen swallowed. She couldn't frame the word. 'Do I have any choice?'

'Oh yes,' he said. 'I forgot to mention that. Of course you do. I wouldn't force myself on you. You're free to walk down that hill now and I won't mention this ever again.'

She looked at him suspiciously, then as he made no move to stop her, quickly picked up her shawl and marched past him.

'The reason that I won't mention it again,' he called after her, 'is that I won't be here. If you walk down that hill now, you will not see me again, ever.'

'Huh,' she said defiantly. 'That's no loss.' And she began to march down the hill, leaving him outlined a solitary figure at the top, watching her with detachment.

As she walked down, she began to think. What he had said, began to sink in. Not see Jack again. Not have him back there to talk to, confide in, laugh with, shout at, argue with. He'd go. Like Etty and she'd be alone. Everyone would have gone. She wouldn't have his support at the theatre, not see him winking at her in the wings, not have his curly head beside her as she was whisked up through the trap onto the stage, not be able to joke with him, not have anyone who cared about her, who *knew* her, Helen Jarvis. Her pace slackened. But then she couldn't do *that* —not like Mother and Father—not like all those jokes backstage at Swains', not what the girls all giggled and laughed about. Why, it was rude. With a gentleman, with a lord, when she was successful, yes. Then she'd find love. But now? This would mean a different life—marrying into the stage life for ever, just as she had sworn not to do. There was no love there. And what would *it* be like with someone you *knew,* with Jack...? Suppose they became like Mother and Father, hating each other, and they couldn't escape—tied together, married. Every day. Suppose she hated it, this making love and then Jack made her marry him. Suppose—but then one overriding thought wiped all these supposes out: he'd said she wouldn't see him again. She wouldn't see Jack again!

She began slowly to walk back up the hill.

She opened her eyes and there was the sun shining through the trees. Then there was Jack, head between her and the sun, his dear, dear head. She put a hand up and put her hand through the curls. She'd always wanted to do that. Somewhere in the background a railway engine was hooting as it rumbled into the distance.

She drew her hand over his face and found it wet with tears.

'Why, Jack,' she said in wonder. 'You're crying.'

He smiled at her, then suddenly he was closer to her again kissing her neck, her lips, her eyes, murmuring passionate words that afterwards she could not remember, only the sounds of the breeze wafting through the trees and the hazy wonderment of the afternoon.

She tightened her arms around him, suddenly, possessively. 'Never let me go, my lover,' she said fiercely. 'Promise me, you'll never let me go.'

The month of May had come forth like a queen that year, bathed in sunlight and regal in her gifts. Not that Helen would have noticed if it had rained every day. For her, that hillside would be in sunshine no matter what. Each day she watched the hands of the clock drag themselves slowly round to twelve o'clock, end of rehearsal and practice session times. Then she would escape, gather some food at the pie shop and make her way up the hillside to where Jack was always waiting.

Goodness knows how he managed to slide out of the theatre, leaving the endless discussions of costumes, battens, counterweights, but he did. When they turned to him with their usual thousand and one questions Jack simply wasn't there. He would be on the hill, waiting for her. She knew he would be. He was woven into her life; there he would be, hair glinting in the sunshine, sprawled on the grass, reading a book. As he saw her he'd smile, close the book and come to her, taking her hand in his, that look in his eyes that excluded the whole world save him and her.

'Is this love?' she asked one day, as she bit into an orange, juice squelching down her chin.

Jack took a handkerchief and wiped her chin. He looked at her eager eyes, dark and ardent, her alive, mobile face, framed in the dark curls. He saw her whole heart, given unreservedly to him. Some men might have been frightened by the intensity they saw in her eyes. But not Jack. For him it was not the sudden flame that had lit up Helen, for he had known since he first saw her standing belligerently on the stage, fighting her tears as she came off...that this was what he wanted, and it did not surprise him that he now possessed it.

'Oh yes,' he said gravely. 'It's love. And you are April's lady, and I am lord in May. Even if you do eat pickled onions,' he added, glancing at the array she had spread on the grass.

'But don't you ever think about your pipe and slippers wife?' she asked anxiously. 'I don't think I'd be very good at that.'

'She went off in a puff of smoke like Aladdin's genie,' he said lazily. 'Unless you fancy living in Upper Holloway?'

Helen shook her head decisively. 'Too far from the theatres. And I'm going to be the best actress you ever saw.'

'No half measures for you,' he said resignedly, pulling down her waving arms. 'Can't you be satisfied as you are?'

'No,' said Helen, matter-of-factly. 'I've got to be the best, you see. Oh, don't you feel it too, Jack? You must. The feeling that you can be out there on that stage controlling people, making them laugh, cry—and not in some provincial theatre like the Royal, but down there in London. I'm going to do it, Jack. So I've got to be at my best when Frederick Glaser comes next week.'

'None of your tricks with him, mind.'

'I don't need tricks any more. Not now there's you. I'm good enough on my own. Oh,' she went on impatiently, 'what a nuisance it is you're not ambitious, Jack. We could do a double act like Henry Irving and Ellen Terry.'

'Fine Henry Irving I'd make. Can you see me staggering across the stage crying, "The bells, the bells! He comes!" I'd have the house howling for mercy in two minutes. No, if you're ambitious for a husband you'd better find your lord...'

She hit him with a mutton pie, and then forced him back on the grass, leaning over him so that her curls tickled his chin. 'Never say that again. Even in jest. I'm yours, yours, yours for ever. Now repeat that after me.'

'Yours for ever, Helen,' he whispered, as his arms closed round her. 'For ever and a day.'

Helen was determined to look her best for Frederick Glaser. She was going to London to be a leading lady and Jack would come with her. He would always be at her side, as her husband. As she went to bed she applied a mixture of honey, lemon and apple juice smoothing it into her face. Not that she looked raddled and tired. Far from it. Her face was glowing, with sun—and with Jack. But it was best to be on the safe side. And so she prayed hastily to God, as Mr Hewson had taught her, just in case He existed. She never had stage nerves so she had no qualms about the performance itself. Nothing could go wrong.

But it did.

After the performance on the Tuesday night, Jack hurried towards her with a telegram in his hands. 'It came an hour ago. I didn't want to give it to you during the performance.'

She eyed it with alarm. She'd never had a telegram before and knew only that they were fearful things with serious news; it had to be if it cost five shillings. It must be Etty. There was no one else.

'Open it, my lovely.'

She tore it open, read it and lifted her eyes to his. 'It's Mr Hewson,' she said with anguish. 'Etty says he's dying. I've got to go at once, she says.'

He took her in his arms and held her close. 'We can get the first train tomorrow. I'll come with you. They'll understand here. We'll be in time, you'll see.'

'But I can't go tomorrow. How can I?' Panic welled up as she saw his face. How could she explain that she could not go back until she could make Mr Hewson proud of his pupil. *And* after tomorrow she would be able to.

Jack dropped his arms. 'Can't go? Why not, Helen?'

'Tomorrow is the night Frederick Glaser will be here.'

He stared at her blankly. 'Helen, you can't be serious.'

'You know how important it is,' she blurted out. Why couldn't she explain *properly?* 'I'll go to see Mr Hewson the next day.' And as Jack still looked blank, she rushed on, 'I've got to meet Frederick Glaser. Oh, darling I've got to. You see, don't you?'

But he did not see, and when she arrived at the theatre the next day he had already left for London.

Frederick Glaser was a large man, with a large paunch and a cigar. But he wasn't like Swains. Not a bit. His geniality was genuine, even though the business sense evident in his face was equally so. As Helen tapped at the door, and went in, buoyed up with after show tension and nervous at what he had to say to her, he swung round from the window out of which he had been gazing on the bleak northern buildings. He stuck the cigar into a tray on the table and gazed at her ruminatively, not saying anything.

It seemed she passed the test for suddenly a large smile lit his face from side to side. 'Fancy the Gala, m'dear?'

Helen nodded, not trusting herself to speak.

'Won't be queen of the hive,' he explained. 'Not yet awhile. Too much to learn.'

The disappointment must have shown in her eyes, for he patted her on the shoulder, and added: 'But someday, m'dear. Oh I should think someday, all right.'

God had let her down in one respect, however. When Helen finally arrived at Putney the following day, Mr Hewson was dead. A weeping Etty met her at the door, falling into Helen's arms.

'He was in such pain, Helen, such pain. He wouldn't let me send for you earlier. He kept saying, "No, she's got her job to do. She'll come when I need her, my little Miss Jarvis."' Etty broke off, for Helen had not come.

Helen's heart was numb, Mr Hewson dead. Her first protector, the first person who'd been kind to her, dead. It wasn't fair. She needed him. How could he die, and leave her? And before she arrived? She forgot her own late arrival, and the reason for it, in the blinding tears that filled her eyes. She blinked them back. She must be strong, for Etty's sake. It wouldn't do for them both to collapse. There would be things to be done, looked after; Etty couldn't manage, she was as helpless as a kitten. And who was to look after Etty now that Mr Hewson was dead? No sooner had this thought crossed her mind than she realized.

'Don't worry, Etty darling,' she whispered. 'I'm coming back. I'll take care of you. Always. We won't be parted again.'

Etty looked gratefully into Helen's eyes,

and blew her nose. 'He gave me a message for you, Helen,' she said shyly. 'I didn't understand it, but perhaps you will. He said to tell you to beware of Ozymandias—that the right name?'

Helen went cold. She understood, but he was wrong, wrong, *wrong*.

She could see herself now, an impatient, grubby nine-year-old, poring over the book: 'Look on my works, ye mighty, and despair.'

''E was a great big man, warn't 'e, Mr 'Ewson?'

'He had no soul, Miss Jarvis. No soul. And thus did he come to dust.'

'Come to dust what, Mr 'Ewson?'

'Two vast and trunkless legs of stone, standing in the desert,' he had intoned. 'Beware, Miss Jarvis. Beware the fall from on high. Those who have eyes and see not.'

Helen swallowed hard, and fought to fight the fear that was entering her heart.

'Etty,' she asked slowly. 'Have you seen Jack?'

'Not since yesterday. I expect he'll come later.' But he did not, nor did he come to the funeral. And when Helen returned to Halifax to work out her notice he had not returned to the theatre.

Chapter Five

The Gala Theatre in the Strand had the reputation of being a happy theatre to work in. Welded into a cohesive unit by its manager, Frederick Glaser, after he had taken it over fifteen years before as a somewhat disreputable music hall, it was the recognized home of burlesque and light operetta, a magnet for London society out to enjoy themselves. To Piccadilly Johnnies, the aristocracy and lads out to cut a dash, the Gala was a second home, yet a Gala chorus girl's reputation was unsullied from the moment she stepped within its portals, and the shows as innocent of sexual innuendo as the Drury Lane pantomime. The theatre exuded luxury.

Glaser was at pains to appear a genial father figure, but his charm hid his shrewd business sense. He expected high standards and he tolerated no falling off; an actress suspected of transgressing the code he set for the standard of his cast was taken aside and the immortal words 'Marriage m'dear that's the ticket' murmured in her ear.

As Helen entered the auditorium for the first time her eye went immediately to the proscenium arch, and she caught her breath. There above it, instead of the usual heavy sculpted muses of nymphs and goddesses so beloved of the London theatre, was a light and colourful frieze of Harlequin and Columbine.

'Like it, m'dear?' beamed Glaser. She had been accorded the rare honour of a personal tour. He was going to keep his eye on her. No great beauty, and too short, but she had something, this little maid.

'Oh yes.' Helen did like it. It seemed to her an omen that Harlequin—Jack—would be with her always.

'Real piece of old theatre, that.' Glaser stared up at it. 'Had it painted meself when we opened up. Without his mask he's just a human being like the rest of us plain folks. But with his mask he's a piece of theatre magic. He's the king of the world; with a wave of his bat he can transform misery to happiness, conjure up laughter and tears together.' He paused and looked at Helen. 'Do you think you can do that, girlie? Laughter *and* tears?'

'Yes Mr Glaser.' Helen had not the slightest idea what he was talking about. It seemed to be the right answer for he patted her shoulder and murmured, 'Good, good.'

During her first weeks at the Gala she saw little of the front of house. She knew only the stage door, and the narrow airless passageways smelling of damp and gas. Used as she was to battling independently through her theatre life, she found the atmosphere at the Gala totally strange. It did not take her long to realize that here she was expected to be one of the company, not an independent spirit, and that whereas at the Theatre Royal her independence had won her her place at the top, here it was unlikely to do so.

On top of the daily lessons which made her legs ache, and her whole body gripped with weariness, there were the endless rehearsals. Her part, although a principal one, was not large. *Romeo and Juliet Up to Date* was going to be unusual for a burlesque in that it was to have not one but two principal boys. She was the second one. By the time the first night approached, however, she was beginning to find her feet at the Gala and life at the theatre became a pleasure offstage as well as on.

Outside the theatre, when she hurried home to Etty's small comfortable house in Putney it was a different matter. The familiar pain would roll over her. Nearly a month now, and no sign of Jack. At first she couldn't believe it. He must come. Perhaps he hadn't heard her news...but he could have found out from Etty. Perhaps he was leaving it till the first night was over, not wanting to distract her? But he must come. He must come. He'd said he'd never leave her. And yet he'd disappeared. Suppose, she could hardly bear to encompass the thought, suppose he never came? She pushed the fear away. He would come. He was hers. She loved him, and he loved her. The thought of never feeling his arms round her again was unbearable. Just for a stupid misunderstanding.

At last desolately she had to face the fact that he was not coming. The first night was but a few days now, and she was determined he should be there. But how was she to find him?

There was only one way, but she needed Etty's help. Courted by her solicitor friend, Paul Monckton, her sister had a calm assurance and glow about her that made Helen nervous of approaching her. She had put on weight and seemed to have all the gentleness of deportment and of manner that Helen yearned for and which even teaching had not been able to instil. But she summoned up her courage.

Etty was doubtful and clearly embarrassed. 'But what am I to say to Mr Waters, Helen?' she asked plaintively. 'Won't he think it very odd, my wanting to get in touch with his son, after the way we treated him running off from the

Marylebone like that?'

'Make up some story,' said Helen impatiently. 'Say, oh say, old Rodgers wants to contact him about some problem or other.'

Etty went off unwillingly, and Helen felt a tight pang of compunction as she watched her forlorn figure don its coat and hat and set off down the road. But she was too wretched about Jack to worry about Etty's feelings for long and by the time Etty returned she was in a fever of impatience.

She rushed to open the door, beating the one maid-of-all-work to it.

'Well,' she demanded. 'Did you do it?'

'I have the address, Helen.' Etty was near to tears. 'But it wasn't very pleasant. He just looked at me like an iceberg, lecturing me for running off so suddenly. I tried to explain about Father but he just didn't understand.'

'Oh never mind Etty. You take things too hard. What does it matter so long as you have Jack's address. You're a dear, Etty, for doing it.' She kissed her joyfully, but Etty was not mollified.

'And then I saw Jack as well,' she added in a low voice. 'He's working at the Marylebone again.'

Helen started. 'Back working there again? Behind the scenes or on stage?'

143

'Stage manager.'

'Did you speak to him? Did he ask after me?' Helen's mouth was suddenly dry.

'I said you wanted to see him, and asked him to come. But, Helen, he wouldn't. Just said no thank you. Why Helen?'

Only her pride stopped Helen from breaking down and weeping in front of Etty. Their hill, only a few brief weeks ago. He couldn't have forgotten so quickly. He couldn't. He said he'd never let her go, be with her always. How could he have changed so quickly?

'Jack!' she called in a low voice.

Although it was summer it was a cold night, and Helen had been waiting for nearly an hour, her dolman drawn up closely round her neck, partly against the night air and partly at the chill inside her. So dull was the ache within her that she hardly noticed the ribaldries from late night revellers hurrying by, ignoring them because she did not see them. Now at last, he had emerged, and, thanks be, on his own. She rushed forward and clutched at his arm.

He swung round in astonishment, and she saw the face that was so dear to her change, almost as if Harlequin's mask had come down over it. He disengaged her

144

arm. 'Helen, there's no point to this. I'll call you a cab.'

'No point?' she echoed in amazement. She stared at the familiar features, the grey eyes, the curly hair, and longed to put out her hand to touch them as she had so often in love. 'But, Jack,' she continued desperately, 'I have to talk to you.'

He did not reply and went to the roadside impatiently waiting for a cab. She ran up to him, urgently, pleadingly: 'Jack, you said you'd never leave me.'

He gave a short laugh. 'Drop your friends before you drop your aitches,' he said lightly. 'That's what you told me was the best bit of advice given to you in your childhood. Mind you, Helen, I didn't think you would—not really. I thought you were loyal, that you'd fight to the death for those you loved, putting them first. But no, Helen comes first. Helen will always come first.'

A crawling hansom stopped with a clatter of hooves, and he ushered Helen up. Putney being beyond the six mile limit, it took the usual haggling with the driver before he would agree to the journey, while Helen waited impatiently. He must come with her. Reluctantly Jack climbed up beside her, realizing it was too late to allow her to go unaccompanied. The distance between them was only inches, but it was impenetrable.

There was silence between them as the horse clip-clopped its way to Putney. Then Helen said, 'I had another nightmare last night, Jack. Always the same one. Mrs Blades. She was a monster from my childhood. They used to make me get her shopping. She was dying of dropsy and—and sailor's disease. She had a great moon face, red and angry, and whiskers, and she was evil. I used to scream when I was in there sometimes. I was only five. They made me go. She had a doll, a lovely doll in a red dress. But I couldn't touch it because she was always in the way. Whenever I reach out for something in my life, in my dreams, her face looms up. "Don't touch it," screams Mrs Blades. "Don't touch," and her face looms over mine closer and closer till it blots everything else out. I scream and scream but I drown in it. But I swore that I'd get that doll one day, nothing or nobody would stand in my way until it was mine. That I'd never be poor again. It seemed to me if I could reach that doll I'd be safe and she couldn't ever harm me again. And I wanted to prove to Mr Hewson, before I saw him, that I could make it...become famous. I so wanted to make him proud of me. That's why seeing Frederick Glaser was so important.'

Jack had not moved but she sensed he was listening.

'I love you, Jack,' she continued simply, 'and,' her voice breaking, 'I need you.'

He turned towards her, and suddenly the hard look on his face was gone.

'Helen,' was all he could say, huskily. He leaned towards her and her heart singing again she took him in her arms. After a moment he pulled himself away, and looked at her questioningly. She nodded slightly and he leaned out to the driver: 'Cabbie, change of plan. To Chelsea, Tite Street.'

'Overture and beginners, please.'

Helen cast a nervous glance in the mirror in the dressing room she shared with other minor principals, and rubbed out a touch of the carmine; she wished herself luck, and she made her way down the narrow passage towards the stage, the gaslight hissing gently.

The first night, and if she made a success in this production, she might get the lead in the next one. That was her goal. She could go no further. Then she could feel safe to marry Jack. It wouldn't matter that he lacked ambition, for she would have an assured position.

She had a moment's panic as she made her first entrance, but her first joke went down well: 'Oh, Romeo what a whig you are!'

It hadn't seemed very funny at rehearsal but somehow now on stage it did, and the audience laughed, and were immediately well disposed towards her, a disposition that continued to carry her through her first song; mocking Romeo and sung to Figaro's song to Cherubino in the *Marriage of Figaro*. She didn't know who Figaro was, but his tune was difficult. She'd managed it though and found it quite catchy. The days of burlesque were far from dead, whatever Jack said, judging from the bouquets from the auditorium when the last curtain fell. One landed at her feet, and when she picked it up, she saw one of the flowers was made of tiny sapphires. She was so excited by this that she hardly noticed the tiny card tucked in with it, bearing the name Randolph Swithin.

Soon she was changed, and in Jack's arms. 'Rules, I think again,' he said. 'Let's have our anniversary. Only this being 1886, almost a new century, we'll forget about the chaperone this time. If you can trust your honour with me, that is.'

She laughed. It had become a joke between them, ever since that morning when she had to creep out of Jack's apartments and return to face Etty's shocked look. She had met it defiantly, offering no explanation and assuming that none was needed. And anyway it had been worth it, to spend a whole night with Jack.

They had the same table at Rules as they had four years ago. 'Do you remember the lobster?' he teased.

She blushed, annoyed that he should remind her, but then caught his eye and laughed.

'Anyway,' he went on, 'I've ordered the same meal for tonight.'

'You're just a sentimental old thing. Are you going to get me drunk again?'

'No knowing what I'll do, let loose with you without a chaperone.'

'You'll be limited in the middle of Rules, me old cock sparrer.'

'I might manage a daring clasp of your hand.'

'And you might get a daring blow back with me other one. I don't allow no liberties with my hand.'

'Have an oyster.' Jack picked one of the oysters garnishing the lobster for her plate.

'Well, I'll go to Father!' exclaimed Helen, in amazement, looking down, 'they've left the pearl in this one.'

Sitting in the middle of the oyster shell was a gold ring with a heart shaped cluster of tiny pearls.

'I hope you don't mind smelling fishy for the rest of the evening,' he murmured as he slipped it over her finger. She looked at it, her mind in a whirl of differing emotions. Safe for ever with Jack. It was settled then. She'd marry him. Then almost against her will she remembered the curtain calls that evening. She saw the bouquet flying through the air, she remembered the smell of greasepaint all around, the smell of hot but triumphant bodies, the common feeling, the exultation that held them all. And she had not yet done as she had vowed—reached the top.

'I want to be yours, Jack,' she whispered, full of love. 'Your wife. For always. But can you wait till I get the lead? Just to prove I can do it. Before we get married?'

'Is it so important, Helen?'

'Yes.' It caused her anguish to wrench the word out, but it had to be done.

'But you don't have to give up the stage when you're married, darling. You can go on being Mary May. Lots of actresses do. They even have babies and then go back.' It cost him something to say this and she knew it, for he heartily disapproved of actresses having babies and continuing to work.

'No, I must do it first.' She looked at him pleadingly. 'I don't know why it's so important, Jack, but it is. I have to do it on my own, make Mary May a real person, who'll never drop her aitches again. But Glaser has promised me the next leading role. You'll see. It won't be long.'

It was getting on for a year, however, when he announced that the show would close in three weeks' time and that another burlesque would be put on, and to her great joy, with Helen in the leading lady's part. It was goodbye to her tights, but she was too short to play the leading boy at the Gala.

The play had a further significance for her—it was a burlesque on the story of Helen of Troy. When Glaser told her she was taken straight back to Mr Hewson's saying 'Helen of Troy, Miss Jarvis. The most beautiful woman in the world.' Helen's gold. And now she had it in her grasp.

It was the crown of a glittering year for Helen. The world of the Gala was a heady one, a world of silks and satins, of beautiful furs and jewels—once these had been earned by one's hard work on stage. Helen's salary was reasonably generous, but she seemed to save none of it now, much to Etty's disapproval. One had to spend a great deal always to look luxuriously dressed. And indeed

151

she needed to keep in social circles she reasoned, for her career. It was all very well for Jack bumbling along merrily behind the scenes at the Marylebone but she had a public reputation to build and to maintain. Her life was split in two. There was her theatre world and the life she led offstage, and divorced from that her afternoons with Jack when they would love and laugh, before they reluctantly tore away from each other's arms and go to their respective theatres. And then because Jack often had to work much later after the Gala show ended she was left to go home, often to an empty house for Etty was now betrothed to her Paul.

Helen tried hard to be glad about this for Etty's sake. She would have someone to look after her. That was what she needed, and it was time she married. But still that old niggle was there. *She* was the one to look after Etty and she had an unreasoning jealousy of anyone who stood in the way...they might not need her, Helen; she would be shut out from their love. Not that she didn't like Paul. She did. He was quiet, with a sly sense of humour that amused Helen. Nor was he intimidated by her.

It was not long before Jack's long hours began to rankle with Helen. She wouldn't have minded if he'd been working hard, but he was intent on going nowhere in his trade. Well, he wasn't going to take her with him, and in the meantime she would *do* as *she* liked too. Gifts from her admirer had been getting more frequent, much to Jack's annoyance.

'They're to go back. You're not accepting gifts from strange men.'

Helen pouted. 'I can't. I don't know where they come from. Anyway there's no harm in it.'

It was a slight distortion of the truth. They were from Randolph Swithin, the tall young Guards officer who hung about optimistically outside the stage door night after night in the hope of persuading her to dine with him. She hadn't yet, but the idea was tempting.

'You're just jealous,' said Helen pettishily.

'I'm jealous all right. That's my ring on your finger and I mean to protect you as long as you wear it.'

'Phooey,' said Helen defiantly. 'Mr Glaser expects us to entertain the clients.'

'Indeed,' Jack retorted coldly, 'I was under the impression the Gala had a good reputation, not some kind of whorehouse.'

Helen was pink with fury. Up till then she had had no intention of doing so, but she was not going to be dictated to by anyone. She controlled herself, merely replying, 'Very well, Jack.'

Randolph Swithin was respectful, and took no liberties even though she carefully removed her pearl ring. Everyone seemed to know him, best tables were automatically available in restaurants for him, the best seats in the Gala. Helen was impressed. He was strong and forceful, like his uniform, she thought. He didn't seem to have much sense of humour, but that could be an advantage when she considered Jack's mocking eyes. Randolph just thought everything she did was wonderful. He was overwhelmed by the mere fact of her condescension in accompanying him to the restaurant, and she hung admiringly on his every word as he spoke of the regiment.

'I expect to be a captain before I give up,' he mentioned modestly.

'I thought you stayed in the army for ever and ever.'

He looked embarrassed. 'Dash it all, Father's not immortal. I'll have to resign my commission when the old fellow passes on.'

She was still puzzled. 'Damned titles,' he went on. 'Don't choose to be born the way we are. Rather stay in the army. But I'll have to knuckle under.'

She had not known that he was in fact the Honourable Randolph Swithin, son of the Baron Gleven.

'Think you can handle it m'dear?' asked Glaser after the first rehearsal.

'I'm sure I can,' she said confidently.

The first night of *It's All Greek* was one of triumph for Helen. She felt tears come into her eyes as she took her sixth curtain call. She surveyed the white blobs of faces out there beyond the footlights. I've shown them, she thought. I've shown them what someone from Bethnal Green can achieve. A greater pride filled her heart than she had ever known before. If only Mr Hewson could have seen her... She wrenched her thoughts away lest guilt flood back.

She waited impatiently for Jack after she had changed into her new blue taffeta dress with the elegant bustle. He had promised he would come to take her for a celebration even if he couldn't get away to see the performance. But nearly everyone had left and there was no Jack. She stood there by the stage door fighting back the tears of anger and disappointment. It was too bad on this night of all nights. The night when she was going to tell him that now she was established as a leading lady she would marry him. They would be together always. And he couldn't even be bothered to turn up. She was sorry that she had let Etty and her Paul depart.

She felt a light touch on her arm.

'Miss May?' It was Randolph Swithin.

Startled, she heard him say something about 'Do me the honour' and saw awaiting him in the road the Swithin carriage emblazoned with crests.

'Gawlimy,' she muttered under her breath. 'Oh well, why not?' She allowed herself to be handed into the carriage, and surreptitiously slipped her pearl ring into her bag.

Helen had never been to Kettners before, though she had heard much about it, and the warm friendly atmosphere and little tables with their lamps impressed her greatly. But what impressed her even more greatly was to be introduced to the most beautiful young woman she had ever seen, even momentarily eclipsing her memory of 'The Lady', and to be told that she was Lady Brooke, wife to the heir of the Duke of Warwick.

'Me,' she said without thinking to Randolph, 'to meet a nearly duchess!'

He smiled. 'Even greater fish are in the sea, Miss May. The fat gentleman coming in now—no, don't turn round, Miss May, is anxious not to be recognized. But it is our future king. Dining with the fair Mrs Langtry, I see. How very embarrassing.'

And seeing that Helen looked puzzled he went on to explain in a whisper that although Mrs Langtry remained a friend of the Prince of Wales she had been superseded as—er—*very* close friend by Lady Brooke. Thus the situation was a delicate one.

At this Helen simply had to turn round. She saw the Jersey Lily, a tall statuesque swanlike creature with the most lovely profile and skin, quite eclipsing the portly gentleman by her side. Helen nearly burst with pride when she saw Randolph catch the Prince's eye who gave a slight acknowledgement. She sat in a daze. It was too much for one night. First the Gala and now this. It would be one in the eye for Jack. Serve him right. She began to wonder what it would be like to be married to someone like Randolph—always dine at Kettners, lead this exciting life, be addressed as 'my lady', entertain duchesses. She let her mind rove over the idea for a time until a picture of herself and Jack on their hillside floated into her mind, and obstinately stayed, flooding her with desire and guilt.

Jack arrived contrite the next morning. She found him twisting his hat over and over in his hands in the morning room. He came towards her and took her hands.

'Can you forgive me, Helen? I couldn't get away. The show went on and on because of the extra song Marie Lloyd agreed to sing. By the time I arrived you'd gone. I'll never forgive myself that I wasn't there on your big evening.'

Up till then Helen had been longing to feel his arms about her, but at the sight of him being so contrite, self-pity at being forced to dine 'alone' overcame her, and made her act in entirely the opposite manner. She flounced away from him, saying in an artificial voice, 'Oh that's all right, Jack. I went out to dinner with a friend—I'd forgotten you were coming anyway. We were dining with the Prince of Wales.'

Jack looked startled, then angry. 'What friend? Who escorted you? What's all this about the Prince of Wales?'

She ignored the interruption and swept on, 'Mrs Langtry was there too of course. And Lady Brooke.'

'It was a man, I suppose. Did you have a chaperone?'

'I never do with you.'

'That's different, and you know it, Helen.'

'He treats me like a lady,' she flung at him. 'And he'll be a lord when his father dies.'

'And that makes him the most wonderful

person on earth, I suppose,' he replied coldly. 'He's taking advantage of you, Helen, because you're at the Gala.'

'He's always respectful to me,' she shouted.

'So you've seen him before.'

'Yes, and I shall go on doing so while I'm leading lady at the Gala. I must be seen in the best places. I have a position to maintain, now I'm at the top.' She would defy him, she *would*, then he'd appreciate her.

'The top?' Jack laughed in scorn. 'I thought you wanted to be a great actress. And here you are content with being just one of the girls from the Gala.'

Helen cried with fury and pummelled him with her fists.

'What do you mean, *just* from the Gala. It's the best. I can't get any higher than that.'

'Maybe *you* can't, but real actresses can. Do you think Ellen Terry would have been content with playing the Gala? Or Mrs Bancroft? Have you no ambition?'

'*You* talk about ambition,' she said bitterly. 'You don't care a monkey's paw what you do. You just want to waste time knocking bits of wood around, and painting scenery. Don't talk to me about ambition. I've got the top and now I shall go and marry my lord like I always said I

159

would.' Inside she was crying out for him to take her in his arms, trying to force herself to bury her pride and go to him, but she could not.

'Go and marry him then.' Jack spoke with deadly calm. 'If you can. Go and sell yourself body and soul for a coronet. You've cheated all your life, and everyone you come into contact with. But now I really feel sorry for you. Because now you're going to cheat yourself.'

It took Helen another two weeks, during which there was no word from Jack following their bitter row which had ended with her throwing the pearl ring back in his face, to bring Randolph Swithin to the point of proposal. He was rather surprised, because he had not started out with such intentions. But by that time she had bewitched and tantalized him to the stage where he did not know what he was doing, while she always remained just out of reach—physically and emotionally. Helen had not used this technique for some time and then for different motives. But she had not lost the art.

Over dinner one night after the performance she heard the words she had waited for: 'May I call you Mary—Father getting older...anxious for me to marry...find a little woman...not much to offer you and

160

all that…but do you think you might one day be my wife?'

As she looked into his pleading eyes, she saw there the answer to her life's problems. She would be sheltered, her life would be one of ease, the life she had so richly deserved. She listened to his words, as if she were in a dream—a dream in which Jack played no part.

Suddenly once again Jack's face blotted out the handsome one opposite her. And again it wouldn't go away.

Stricken she looked at him, and put her hand out to him slowly. 'Randolph, I can't!' she cried in anguish.

Jack opened the door himself. She thought he was going to shut it in her face, but he didn't, merely motioned her to come inside. She did not stop for ceremony. As soon as he had shut the door of his sitting room behind him she threw her arms around his neck.

'Oh Jack,' she cried, 'I've been such a fool.' She felt his arms creep slowly round her. 'I couldn't. I tried so hard. But when he asked me, I just couldn't. I couldn't marry him.' And she burst into a flood of tears.

He stroked her hair, kissed her neck and muttered endearments into her heaving shoulders. Gradually his embrace grew rougher, the kisses fiercer, as he held her closely to him. Then she was returning them with such passion it might have been the first time they had come together. Then he was removing her clothes and laying her down on the old chesterfield, and they were making love with a passion that shook them both.

Afterwards, when they had dressed, they sat silent for a time, hand in hand, till at last Jack lifted her hand and looked at it. Then he fetched the pearl ring from the overmantel and fitted it onto her finger again.

'Leave it there, this time, Helen,' he said gravely. 'And we'll be married just as soon as we can.'

She leaned against him, and sighed. 'Soon, please, Jack. Oh please make it soon.'

'Just as soon as I can afford to buy a wedding outfit for myself.'

'What do you mean?' she asked lazily.

'It looks as if I'll be dependent on you for pocket money when we're married, unless another job turns up.'

She was startled by his cheerfully spoken words as she took them in. 'Another job? But—'

'I've thrown up my job at the Marylebone. Too much hard work.'

'But what are you going to do? Be a

stage manager somewhere? Where?

'No, too ambitious for me. You know how lazy I am,' he said laconically. 'I'll fill in my time somehow. Take up cooking for when you get home from the theatre.'

'But don't you want to do anything?'

'No, I told you that the first time I met you. Don't you remember I told you I couldn't do anything?'

Helen stared at him, that old panic rising in her. He meant it. He really meant it. He had no willpower. No ambition. He would depend on her money. If she fell sick, if she had a baby, there'd be no money then. What would happen to them? Visions of poorer and poorer lodgings filled her mind already overcharged with emotion. Hoxton, Bethnal Green—the Nichol. That cesspit of humanity. They might end up there. Mrs Blades's face rose up in front of her, taunting her, beckoning her, *'back, back dearie, back where you belong.'* Jarvis's face gloated over her, *'Dahling daughter mine. Dahling daughter...'* Swains' lecherous face... She couldn't go back. No, no no. *'Where you belong, dearie,'* Mrs Blades went on whispering, *'you'll never get away, oh, no, dear...'*

'Mrs Blades, Mrs Blades,' she screamed out loud, bursting into a torrent of tears.

'Helen, what is it? What is it, dearest?' cried Jack, catching hold of her as she rose

163

to her feet in blind panic. But she broke away from him hiccoughing and crying, and fled from the house.

Four days later she married Randolph Swithin.

PART TWO

The Phoenix

Chapter Six

Ten years later, in 1897, at the time of Queen Victoria's Diamond Jubilee, Helen Swithin returned to London...

It was raining. Huddled under her umbrella, Helen cast a baleful eye at the heavens. Would the omnibus ever arrive? Should she spend yet more of her dwindling hoard of money to take a cab? For heaven's sake, why must Etty still live out at Putney? Why couldn't she live in some more fashionable area? They could afford it. Paul was a capable young solicitor, and a partner now.

Rain or shine, in a few days the whole of London would be cheering a little old lady. And she would be sitting in a place of honour to watch her, if only Randolph weren't so spineless now he'd left the army; he couldn't face his old cronies at White's now the parlous state of the estate finances was public knowledge.

His father, Lord Gleven, remained at Monkswater, his snug little estate in Devon, leaving the Kentish farms to be run by Randolph, and ignoring the fact that Randolph couldn't run out of a field with a bull in it. He even joked about it to her, but it was no joke. She had to run the estate herself by working sixteen hours a day trying to make the farms pay, but they had been let go too long. Low rents, bad yields, inefficient managers, had wreaked its toll. Someone had to earn some money from outside, bring it in to run the failing estates, just so that they could go on living in some sort of comfort. And as Randolph could not provide this, it had to be her.

She'd go back to the stage... Once the idea had come to her, she seized on it. She would go back to the Gala. Randolph had objected bitterly at first. They had had the first serious disagreement of their marriage. Normally he gave in after a token resistance. But this time it had taken all of Helen's wheedling, blandishments, and finally threats, before he succumbed.

The little orphan girl, Etty and Paul's general maid, fell back timidly as Helen's wet whirlwind figure brushed by her, flinging off her ulster, scattering water everywhere. Marie cast an anxious look first at Helen's fine French merino skirt which, now caked with mud, would need an hour of brushing at least, and then at the carpet. Madam didn't seem to care about mud and dirty footprints, but she did. She had to clean them up or Mrs Hoskins the housekeeper would be after her.

Helen hurried into the parlour where Etty was having tea with the eight-year-old Paul and six-year-old Constance. They cast one eye at Aunt Helen to see what kind of mood she was in, and vanished. No one could be more fun on a good day but today was not one of them.

'Hell, Hull and Halifax!' Helen relieved her feelings by flinging herself down on the sofa, regardless of Etty's anxious look at the springs.

'Another No thank you?' asked Etty tentatively. Ten years had dealt kindly with Etty. Her face had widened out into a full placidity, suiting her fair complexion. Her hair was drawn straight back, reflecting her calm serenity, and the old fashioned bustle and plain bush rose dress, gave her dignity. Already she looked matronly.

'Another, No thank you Mrs Swithin—perhaps in our next show, Mrs Swithin—what nothing for ten years, Mrs Swithin? May? Mary May? But the days of burlesque are over, Mrs Swithin.'

Etty privately thought that they took one look at the determined face and failed to see it fitting in with the current vogue for musical comedy heroines.

'I'm thirty-two,' Helen declared in despair. *Thirty-two.* And what they're looking for, Frederick Glaser told me, is winsome little blondes who'll simper little songs. But I have to sing right out. You know what my voice is like. Oh Etty, what am I to do? I'm just a burden to you, I can't go on staying here. And I can't go home until I earn some money.'

Etty put her arm round Helen's shoulders. 'You mustn't say that. Look at the way you looked after me all those years ago. And you went through just as bad a time as now? Remember how they turned you away time after time? But you still went on.'

'It's different now,' Helen cried. 'I'm the Honourable Mrs Swithin. I can't go on the music halls again, even if they'd have me, burlesque is finished, and I'm not trained for anything else. And managers, just because I'm an honourable, won't take me for a chorus, or train me. I can see it in their eyes.'

Etty was silent. 'Are you sure the estates...?'

'Paul must have told you what a mess we're in—he's done his best to straighten things out. But, Etty, you can't imagine the tenants, all demanding this, that and the other. And the farms just can't produce enough to pay for it. And, oh the complications, the entail; we can't sell this, can't do anything with that, and please Mrs Swithin, it's little Sid Perkins—can't work no more—you'll look after him, won't you Mrs Swithin? I'd like to, I really would but *how?*'

'And Randolph?'

Helen shrugged. 'He's such a dear, Etty, so kind, so thoughtful, so considerate—and so helpless. You can't imagine. The children adore him. But someone's got to make money so that we can feed them—Randolph can't, so it has to be me. That means I can't be with them all the time too, can I?' It had been hard at first, almost unbearable, to see them running to him not her, but she had had to harden herself.

Etty tried to imagine a life where she lived apart from her own children, a life which didn't begin each day with two children falling breathlessly on top of her, covering her with kisses. She couldn't.

'But don't they miss you? They need you, Helen. Don't they mind your being here?'

'Julia's busy with her puppies all day, and Robert,' Helen's voice softened as she thought of her roly-poly two-year-old toddler, 'is so busy wobbling around after Randolph that I don't think he notices I'm not there.'

'You can stay here as long as you like but—'

'I can't and you know it,' said Helen warmly. 'Look what I'm doing to your

171

household—Marie jumps like a startled rabbit every time I address her, the children treat me like an unexploded bomb, Paul must be getting tired of making bracing remarks of encouragement and you—dear Etty—you can't wait to get back to your peaceful way of life without me raging all over the house like—a caged-in puma.'

Etty had to laugh. They had been to the London Zoological Gardens last Sunday in an effort to break Helen's gloom and there had indeed been something about that restless, pacing, dangerous animal which reminded her of Helen. All that energy. The handsome face, with the large dark eyes staring defiantly at the world, eyes that could at a kind word, a loving gesture, the right man—dissolve into a pool of softness.'

The right man. Involuntarily Etty thought of Jack. What should she do? Should she tell her? Would it make matters worse? She felt it might be like throwing a match into cauldron of seething oil. And yet it was all a long time ago. Helen was married long since, with two lovely children... Ten years. She had never been sure why Jack and Helen had never married, but one thing had been blazingly obvious—they were Barnum and Bailey, Romeo and Juliet, whatever couple you cared to name. Or they were then, no matter what fogs had parted them since.

When Helen married Randolph, so suddenly, so secretly, Etty had been stunned and devastated. She could hardly hold her tears back at the wedding. She could not imagine her beloved Helen with any other but Jack. Her gentle heart grieved for him, and after the marriage she had never seen him again. Their friendship was abruptly broken. He had simply disappeared from her life. She did not mind too much for herself, for by that time there was Paul.

She made up her mind. 'Helen, have you heard of Duke's?'

Helen looked at her in surprise. 'Of course.' Everyone had heard of Duke's Theatre. It had had a chequered career. Built in the 1840s for operatic performances, it had never succeeded, being in an unfashionable part of London so far as theatres were concerned. Occasionally it would have a success, but then it would slip back. Everything had been tried, from variety to cheap melodrama and spectacle to opera, but theatre audiences obstinately refused to include Duke's on their itinerary.

Four years ago quietly, unostentatiously, the theatre began a new policy of straight plays, mostly comedies, with the occasional drama thrown in, by new untried play-wrights. It had a slow start. Audiences wanted famous names to lure them, and the new management could not afford them. But gradually now it was gaining a hold. Comedies of manners in the Pinero style, plays that were excellent vehicles for stylish acting by a good all-round company.

'And did you know that—that Jack is the manager?' asked Etty in a rush of nervousness.

Helen sat very still. An iron band seemed to be constricting her chest; her face felt cold. If I try, she told herself, I can keep this horror outside. She couldn't re-open that wound by her own hand, the wound she'd so consciously plugged so many years ago. It had seemed easy, so easy. She'd married Randolph. She had cut off part of her life, left London, left love, far behind her—and started her new life. She hadn't seen or heard of him for ten years. And if in those ten years, in moments alone, or in the great double bed at Swithins, the thought came to her of what life might have been like, laughing with him, walking along gaslit London streets, that smoky smell in their nostrils and love in their hearts, of being in Jack's arms—she had promptly banished it as part of another life, a life that was Helen Jarvis and nothing to do with Helen Swithin.

Taken by surprise, pain swirled over her as ten years whistled down the wind, as the well was unplugged.

'No,' she managed to whisper, 'I didn't know.'

Already regretting what she had done, Etty went on to tell her as much as she knew, which wasn't much. Helen tried to concentrate on what she was saying, but all she could think of was that one name—Jack.

'His father, I suppose?' Helen pulled her thoughts together.

'No,' said Etty. 'He's still running the Marylebone. This is Jack's theatre. He was in partnership for a few years at the Duke of Cambridge Theatre and took over Duke's a few years ago. He's beginning to do well too. I'm glad, for you know how ambitious he always was.'

Helen stared at her, suddenly tired. Ambitious? She fought to keep tears back but failed.

Helen walked up and down outside the theatre for half an hour, then rapidly away through the Square to St James's Street. There she stared blindly at the crowds and the ornate decorations adorning the specially erected pillars. A Jubilee. She wondered how many others in this milling throng were so torn, so unhappy as she.

She walked slowly back to Duke Street. Randolph and the children...she had to get work for their sakes. Just a friendly greeting to Jack, ask him to put in a word somewhere, a pleasant chat about old times; it was ten years ago after all. What harm could it do? He was probably married with a brood of squalling children. He might not even remember her. This thought gave her little consolation, however. But then what if...? No, she should go home now, and try again to make a success of running the estate. Perhaps she should grow a different type of apple with a better yield. Perhaps Paul hadn't got his figures right? Yes, go home now, Helen, and forget about Jack...Jack...

She was here. Outside Jack's theatre. In a few minutes she could see him. All other thoughts faded from her mind. There had never been a choice.

'Mrs Henrietta—er—Jarvis,' she told the doorman firmly. He might not know Etty's married name and she could not risk his refusing to see Helen Swithin.

A chirpy youngster disappeared at a snap of the doorman's fingers and Helen endeavoured to calm her beating heart by paying attention to the photographs and playbills adorning the green painted walls. There were photographs of a recent production, a print of one of the early musical turns, and a drawing of the theatre before it had been renovated twenty years before. She became aware of what had unconsciously been troubling her. This cool, elegant decor like an eighteenth-century drawing room—was this of the Jack she remembered? The feckless, carefree, no-thought-for-the-morrow Jack? She recalled Etty's words: *'You know how ambitious he always was.'* Fear plucked at her again.

The youngster reappeared and invited her through the pass door. Jack's office was on the first floor tucked at the far end of a passage with several open doors; through them she saw scenes of activity: piles of costumes being sorted; a spare props room with stage hands hard at work, and from one a smell of greasepaint and stale make-up so overpowering that Helen was overcome with nostalgia. She'd forgotten the smells of theatre, the warm, fetid close embrace it laid on its servants. Now she wondered how she could ever have left it.

He was standing by the window. He turned as she came in with the words of welcome on his lips.

'Etty, my—'

His whole face changed as he saw her standing there. A shutter seemed to come down over his face, as the smile went from his lips and from his eyes. He seemed hardly to have changed in ten years. Then she saw the lines etched on his face, the dimple more sharply defined, giving maturity to a face that had seemed to lack purpose. Yet that too had been an illusion, she now realized. For Jack's face had never lacked purpose, if you had the wit to see it. Your attention had been caught by the laughing eyes, eyes that were stony and hard now as they looked at her.

'Mrs Swithin. A pleasure indeed.' He did not ask her to sit down. Did not move. Her composure returned. The worst was over.

'Don't be stuffy, Jack. I'm here on business.' An eyebrow lifted. She hesitated but ploughed on. 'I want a job.'

It cost her a lot to humiliate herself so, though he could not have guessed it from her tone. It remained brittle and arrogant.

'Sit down,' he said abruptly. She took the comfortable shabby Queen Anne armchair. 'There,' he added drily, indicating the chair positioned by his desk. 'This is the chair for business.' He sat in the chair on the far side of the desk and waited for her to speak.

'You're not making it easy for me, Jack.'

His laugh did not reach his eyes, but it somewhat reassured Helen. She must not give an inch in front of him. Her recital was brief, for it left out many humiliating facts. How could she tell him that the Swithins' estate was all but bankrupt, that the wealth and power she had been determined to marry had disappeared like leprechaun's gold under her fingers. Instead there was talk of the need to return to the theatre now that the estate was on its feet again, that Randolph was urging her to return, that she had come first to him since he might know of something suitable.

Jack said nothing when she finished. He seemed to be giving his whole attention to a brass letter opener which he turned over and over in his hands until Helen thought she would scream. At last he looked up.

'You always were a liar, Helen,' he said pleasantly.

She gasped, indignant and furious. The colour rushed into her face, whether from shame or guilt she did not know. She gathered the skirts of the smart midnight blue walking dress that she had donned to impress him, and rose to her feet. How dare he insult her? After all they had been to each other. Then she recollected that she could not leave. This was her last chance. With a great effort of will, she sat down again and smiled sweetly at him. 'Jack, don't blame me too much. It is *partly* true. But I wanted to see you again. I had to.'

The shutter came down again. 'I'm honoured, Mrs Swithin,' he said formally. 'Now having achieved your object, you won't be too disappointed when I tell you that I would not recommend you to my fellow managers even if I knew of a part on offer. You've been ten years out of the profession, you had precious little experience then, your only attributes exuberance of youth and a foghorn voice; moreover that your arrogance and self-centredness more than outweigh your talents.'

This couldn't be Jack, this alien cold man. Her numbness went and she blazed at him: 'I don't need your help, Mr Waters. I've always managed on my own. I don't need a job with you or anyone else.' Even as she said it, she felt tears welling up inside her.

'You're lying.' His voice rose slightly and his eyes at least seemed to betray some emotion. 'You're on your beam-ends. Swithins' is on its last gasp, and club gossip has it that the Honourable Randolph Swithin is content to sit back and let his wife work at the farm, work in the fields, hold the purse-strings, be the total bread-earner. Oh Helen...' he shook his head mockingly, 'where be your dreams now?'

She gave a choking cough and rushed to the door. She clutched at the handle to steady herself. She heard him say with a quick intake of breath, 'Helen.'

She could not see him now for her eyes overflowed with the threatened tears, but she heard his quick footsteps as he crossed the room, then felt his arms go round her. Her head was on his shoulder and there seemed to be more tears than of her making.

'Helen, Helen. Why couldn't you have waited? Why, oh why?'

She cried out in anguish. 'Don't, darling, don't.' It was no good. That careful dam of her emotions built up over ten years was swept away by a single breach. What a fool she'd been to come. Yet how could she have borne not to?

'I had to,' she whispered. 'I had to. I couldn't ever be poor again. You'd thrown up your job. You had no purpose. You cared for nothing, a wanderer; you didn't want to achieve anything. Money meant nothing to you. But I had to go on. I couldn't have married a man I had to support, going nowhere, except down...' She broke off. There was no need for either of them to say that that was exactly what was happening to her now. 'We'd have grown to hate each other. I couldn't have borne that... I couldn't have known... You didn't explain.'

He looked at her in despair. 'You only see what you want to see in people, Helen, hear what you want to hear. Never more. I was as ambitious as you. I'm of the theatre. I always have been. I never intended to be a lawyer. But I had to learn stage crafts first. Everyone has to learn, but I always intended to have my own theatre in the end. That's why I left my father. It was time then. I was already talking to people about a partnership.'

She gazed at him in stunned horror and cried, 'But why didn't you tell me, Jack?'

'Why didn't you trust me, Helen?'

Etty's feelings were mixed. One part of her rejoiced that Helen had found a job and that Jack had received her warmly (Helen said) and was therefore likely to become a friend again; the other part of Etty, the part that knew Helen of old, suspected that it wouldn't be quite as simple as that. Yet she had been the one to suggest that Helen went to Duke's, and now everything appeared to be all right, for Helen had been given a small part in the new production going into rehearsal. A very small part, Helen had admitted honestly, for once. She was mindful of the stringent conditions Jack had laid down for her return.

'You are *not* the Honourable Mrs Swithin. You are *not* the Queen of the Gala; you are an untried minor actress competing against hundreds of younger actresses...' and much more in a similar vein.

'I shall get some lodgings,' Helen said excitedly to Etty. 'Or even rent a small house.' Her mind raced ahead.

'But what about Randolph and the children?' Etty was bewildered at the pace of events.

'I shall see them on Sundays,' said Helen. 'And then when I'm not in a show'—though she could not envisage this as likely—'I can keep an eye on the estate.'

'But the children—' Etty started to say again, but then thought better of it. It wasn't her place to suggest that growing children needed a mother, to remind Helen of their own childhood. So she switched her focal point of worry.

'Who's going to run the farms, while you're up here?'

'We'll get a manager.'

'It doesn't seem to me that there will be much money to send to Swithins' if you are going to live independently in London.' Etty was doubtful. 'And how can you live alone? Apart from your husband? What will people *think?*'

'What will Mrs Grundy say?' quoth Helen blithely. 'Mrs Grundy can say what she likes. I won't be listening.' Then seeing Etty's shocked expression she said mollifyingly, 'I'll have a housekeeper. And you'll see, once I'm the leading lady, people won't care if I live apart from Randolph or not. It's me they'll want to meet.'

Despite Jack's strictures she had little doubt of her destiny. Her heart was singing, although he had quickly returned to formality when he'd released her from that quick hard embrace. He still loved her. He must do, for he hadn't married. Everything would be as before, she had no doubt of it. She had listened docilely while he told her in a clipped cool unJackish voice that he would give her a part, a very small part, in his new play, which wasn't a burlesque.

'Do you realize what that means, Helen?'

'Yes, Jack,' she said meekly. 'I'm not to overact.' She laughed at him.

'I'm taking a chance, Helen. I don't even know if you *can* act. You can stride stage front and put over lines direct to an audience. But can you play a part for itself, for its own sake, regardless of audience, play with other people, think of their lines, their feelings, who they're playing—?'

'Of course,' said Helen indignantly. She did not need him to tell her that if she was to succeed in building a career she had to become a straight actress, and start again. And if that meant playing second, or even fifth fiddle to inferior actresses for a time while she learned the trade then she would. She could not afford to offend people this time. The last traces of Helen Jarvis would be buried forever, and in their place, phoenix-like, would rise—

'We'll have to think of a name for you. It would be unwise to go back to Mary May—and you wouldn't want to use Helen Swithin, would you?' Jack cocked an eye at her.

'No.' If she was going to be an actress she was not going to get there by using her husband's name, especially in Jack's theatre. 'I know,' she said triumphantly, 'Helen Hill.'

He tried it. 'Yes,' he said. 'That's all right. If you like it.' Then he realized why she had made her choice. Caught off guard he flushed. The hill. Their hill.

Helen had another reason for choosing that name too: 'drop your friends before you drop your aitches'—the last trace of 'Elen Jarvis should be dispelled for ever. Helen Hill. She had mastered her aitches now.

Working at Duke's had none of the chaos and good-humoured rowdiness she remembered from her days in burlesque. At first she found this surprising, then she recalled the same orderliness and quiet organization had characterized the backstage work at the Theatre Royal when Jack Waters was in charge. He seemed to have the knack of allowing everything to fall automatically into place without his appearing to make the least effort for it to do so. His supervision of rehearsals was minimal, and yet somehow one was aware all the time of an overall control and pattern to the production. She found this strange at first, but gradually began to relax in the friendliness and professionalism of the theatre that prevailed in everyone from the leading players to the boy who took the patrons' hats.

The play, *Lady Castleton's Dilemma*, was a frothy unpretentious comedy based on the usual misunderstandings of marital infidelity, and she had the small role of Mrs Tankerton, a society friend in whom the heroine mistakenly confides her famous dilemma.

All went well, Helen congratulated

herself, until one day the leading lady, Margaret Cunningham said gently, 'You're not playing with me, Miss Hill.'

Helen was puzzled. What could she mean? She was saying the lines properly, wasn't she?

'Try placing your feet towards me when you speak, Miss Hill—you're facing the audience and if your feet face the audience you'll play to the audience.'

Helen was about to make a crushing retort, when she remembered Jack's orders. She mustn't upset his beloved leading lady. Even if she wouldn't be his leading lady for long once Helen had found her feet—whichever way they faced! So she tried it, and found to her surprise it was much easier to say the lines direct to Lady Castleton. She began, moreover, to listen to the replies.

Miss Cunningham had won that time, but she wasn't so successful on the next occasion when she gently tried to tell Helen, offstage, not to move around and upstage her in their scene together. This was more than Helen could take and in high dudgeon told Jack of her wrath.

'I think she must be jealous of you and me.'

Jack stiffened. 'What do you mean, Helen?'

She was surprised. 'Our feelings for each

other—she's seen how we feel about each other.'

'There is no you and me, Helen. Don't you realize that?'

'But, Jack—' What was he saying?

'There is no but, Helen. Have I ever said that these ten years could whistle down the wind? Have I ever made one move towards you after the shock of seeing you again?'

No, he hadn't, she admitted unwillingly to herself. But that was because they'd been busy with the new play.

'But when I move into my new lodgings—' she burst out.

'Our romance ended ten years ago, when you married another man. You needed a job and for—well, because of old times' sake—I couldn't see you starve.'

'But you still love me, I know you do.'

'Love? Helen, ten years ago you left me and married someone else. You're still married to him. And you've two children. And if you can forget all that, I can't.'

'But we love each other.' She was stricken by the harshness in his voice. 'It wouldn't matter to Randolph—he and I—well, we—' She stopped. Pride would not let her tell him that sexual relations between Randolph and herself had dwindled to a polite minimum; that she guessed he found more loving arms in the Swithins' nanny, a 21-year-old English rose by the name of Jane Wickham. She could not bring herself to admit to Jack that Randolph's adoration had vanished as surely as had his liquidity.

'It's not just for Swithin's sake, but mine,' Jack said, coolly. 'Even if I did still love you—' she shivered—'I wouldn't go back, not after all the misery you put me through then.'

'Was it all misery?' she asked, beaten.

He stared at her across the years. 'No,' he replied at last. It had been a kaleidoscope of joy and pain, ecstasy and anguish. The greater the happiness the sharper the wound. 'But one can take suffering like that at twenty-three. Not at thirty-three though. One grows wiser. It's over, Helen, over.' He slammed the door irrevocably behind him.

Helen continued her rehearsals, overcoming her first inclination to creep away like a wounded animal. She threw herself into the work to overcome the numbness in her heart. To be so near to Jack, not be able to touch him. He no longer loved her. Would never hold her in his arms again. Very well, then, she would become the very best of actresses. She could at least justify his gamble for him. Show that she could play in a company as well as any of them. She took the bull by the horns by apologizing to Miss Cunningham. The actress hesitated for a second startled at this uncharacteristic gesture, then seeing Helen was sincere, from that moment on was her staunch ally. During the weeks that followed she taught Helen to listen as well as to speak on stage, to catch a cue, to time a pause, to yield laughs to her fellow actors, when to cut audience laughter, and when to portray emotion.

'You're still playing Columbine,' Margaret said critically one day. 'You strike an attitude, and like her you've only got four of them.' She parodied them, laughing. 'Hand to head, despair, hand to heart, sincerity, hand clasped in hand, joy, and—'

'Show me how to do it then,' said Helen resignedly.

'I can't. Just listen to the words, remember there's an audience out there and the emotion will come naturally.'

Often Helen was on the point of giving up, but Etty would urge her on giving comfort and support: 'Go on, Helen, go on. Remember how you told me after that penny gaff that you were going to be the world's best actress. You must go on. You can't give up now.'

Jack watched her work with a dispassionate eye. He took no part in her training, but waited to see whether she would sink or swim. They had not spoken and scarcely seen each other since their encounter. But Helen was constantly aware of his presence. The whole theatre seemed imbued with it. She simply could not believe that love such as theirs could die. The hill must mean something to him. He couldn't pretend it hadn't happened... She forced herself back to the present to concentrate on the play, forced herself constantly to stand in the wings observing the other members of the cast, absorbing nuances of technique, picking up their stagecraft, at first for something to fill in the long stretches of time when she was not on stage, then from genuine interest. By the time the first night arrived she was confident that it lay within her powers to be an actress, and the knowledge filled her with calm assurance.

As the curtain rose, however, she was more nervous than ever before, aware that on this one night hung the whole of her future dreams and ambitions. She saw Margaret's encouraging face, and then she was on stage. Immediately she found that the experience was opposite to her previous performances. Gone was the necessity for febrile excitement; instead her brain needed to be ice-cold, telling her, analysing what to do, how the audience was reacting; something ticked away like a metronome inside her regulating and disciplining her performance.

Her part was over, in a flash. How had she done? She could not tell. Then Jack was by her side, touching her shoulder briefly, impersonally.

'Well done.'

So it was all right. It was a beginning. She had a future. Slowly, steadily her spirits began to rise. Anything was possible now.

Jack's house in Montpelier Walk was not large but furnished in a style that Helen remembered intimately. Everything spelled out his personality. With a pang of grief she recognized the sketch of Peg Woffington on the wall that had adorned his home in Tite Street. As the first night celebration was being held in his house he could not exclude her; she was part of the cast, but she sensed his antagonism as she entered the door on Randolph's arm. He greeted her and shook Randolph's hand, as though forcing himself to withstand an enemy intrusion into his territory. She was confident enough, however, to brush close to him so that he could smell the Floris rose scent in her hair, be aware of the low-cut, dark green, rustling dress that suited her dark eyes and hair so well.

Jack took little notice of them during

the evening. He laughed, he flirted with Margaret, Helen jealously noticed. He was the perfect relaxed host chatting to all in turn—all save Helen. But nothing could shake Helen tonight. As the cast, growing weary, slipped away one by one, the guests were reduced to three. Margaret, Helen and a yawning Randolph. With perfect good manners Helen thanked Jack for his hospitality and departed with Randolph in the cab waiting outside; as the horse ambled away she turned to see Jack walking towards the cab stand to hail another to escort Margaret home. A small smile crossed her lips.

Half an hour later Jack wearily opened his front door. It had been a long day, his reserves of nervous energy used up. He needed a brandy and soda. He entered his drawing room to find a small figure curled up on the sofa.

'Hello, Jack,' said Helen softly.

He did not speak.

'You couldn't have expected me just to go quietly away.'

'No,' he agreed wearily, 'I couldn't have expected that.' He passed a hand over his brow. 'What have you done with the heir to England's heritage?'

'I told him he had to sleep at the club.'

In silence he poured a large drink for

himself and one for her.

'I'm not going to argue with you, Helen,' he said, as he handed it to her. 'I'm too tired to take you home and I can't send you home alone. There's a perfectly good sofa there; you can sleep there till morning and to hell with your reputation when old Groves sees you.'

She plumped herself on the cushions and smiled at him.

'Very well, Jack, but do sit down and finish your brandy first.'

He sat down reluctantly at the far end of the chesterfield.

'The last time we were on a sofa—' she began meditatively.

'You ran away from me ten minutes later,' he interrupted bitterly.

'So you do remember, darling, you still care,' she whispered triumphantly. Then her arms were round him, the smell of her hair in his nostrils.

'Helen, leave me alone. Leave me alone for both our sakes. Don't ruin our lives again...'

But it was already too late. His hand was on her breast, his body responding.

'Sofas,' he whispered, *'Goddam* all sofas. Helen. Helen...'

'Jack?'

'My lady?'

'Are you very cross with me?'

'You're like William Grace, Helen. You'd make a good cricketer. No half measures. Just hit them for six.'

'You don't mind?'

'From the moment you walked through my office door, Helen, I had no choice. I tried. I still clung on to that dream of a fireside with two kids. But it was hopeless. It was always your face, Helen. Somehow in my dream the slippers never fitted—I could never get them on and the pipe smelled rancid.'

'You do still love me. You won't leave me again, Jack?'

'Leave you? Helen, I'm Lochinvar, Casanova and Lord Byron rolled into one.' He was light-hearted, seizing Helen and rolling her off the chesterfield onto the carpet in a tangled heap of arms and legs. 'Remember the barrow? Oh no, I won't leave you. I'll plaster you to me with carpenter's glue this time, fix a counterweight to you to toss you back to me when you stray. We're on the same travelling iron, Helen, strapped together, we'll shoot up through the star trap together, Pantomime Queen and Demon King. For you are April's lady and I am lord in May, up, right up.'

'Up where?' Helen laughed. 'Up through old Rodgers' beloved paper trees?'

'To the top of the theatre tree.' Jack was serious again, kissing her eyes, her lips, her chin. First its queen, then its dame then its grande dame. A lifetime of service to the theatre, Helen, and the top of that tree. And I'm going to put you there.'

Chapter Seven

'Have an éclair, my dear.'

The rich plummy tones of Maude James's voice rolled round the words as though intoning Lady Macbeth's soliloquy. Helen sighed. Not another one. It was the good conduct prize, the one sign of approval that Maude would give.

'They're French éclairs, you know. The real chocolate *crème.*' Maude licked her lips appreciatively in anticipation of the treat to come. 'Jean-Pierre Colombe makes them specially for me. I remember when he started.' A reminiscent gleam lit the old lady's eyes. 'I was able to bring—ah—a certain gentleman to his establishment. Monsieur Colombe never forgets a friend. Does he, my pet?' This last was addressed not to Helen, but to the snappy little white-haired poodle who grew fat and indolent in her rooms. A French poodle naturally. French, like all things in Maude James's life (Maude, spelled the French way, she would point out). It was strange in one who remained so unmistakably English to look at.

Maude was eighty now. She had been

on the stage even before Ellen Terry, back when actresses were little better regarded than prostitutes. In her time she had seen the stage gradually become a respectable calling even for women. She was so fat now she could move from her chair only with difficulty, yet each gesture or movement she made illuminated the words, a mere difference of intonation would give point to a whole speech. She had first learned her stage business over sixty years ago from the old stock actors, who in turn had learned exactly the same business from their mentors; Shylock shall look so, Othello shall move here and not there. She had worked with people who had worked with Kean or Kemble, she had acted with Ellen Terry, with Mrs Bancroft, met those that had been taught their business long ago by Garrick.

'I'll send you to Maude James,' Jack had said reflectively. Helen had instantly rebelled.

'I don't need to *learn* to act. I'm learning by experience. I did well enough in—'

'Well enough is not good enough,' Jack cut in firmly. 'Trust me, Helen.' He paused as her eyes fell away, then: 'I'm going to create a theatre to be remembered, Helen. I'm going to be a manager people will remember, of a theatre with a style of its own, a tradition of its own. And, to crown it, I'm going to create you, Helen. So you're going to see Maude James.'

Day after day, éclair after éclair, apparently pointless exercises were shot at her. However, to her interest she began to notice a difference in her performance in the evenings, gradual though it was. A certain grace began to characterize her movements, a flair and expertise. Much less rewarding, for they seemed to bring such slow dividends, were the elocution lessons.

She learned to speak softly, yet still be heard, a revelation to Helen. 'Like sweet bells jangled, we are today, aren't we dear? Suppose we try it a bit lower, sweeter, dear, not harsh and out of tune.' It was a surprise to Helen, trying it in performance that evening, that speaking softly still enabled her to make the audience listen.

In that tiny crowded room close to Covent Garden, stuffy, overloaded with aspidistras, playbills and photographs, an atmosphere of professional stage seemed to be created, so that when Maude bellowed, 'Don't pause when you come on the stage, dear Miss Hill. I know dear Sir Henry still stamps when he enters, but those days are over, dear. We can see you perfectly well with all this newfangled electrical lighting. Have an éclair, my dear, that's right. Real chocolate *crème* you know. None of this nasty English stuff. Now, dear, how about a bit from naughty Oscar's play? I know we don't mention him, dear, but he did write nice plays. How about a piece from *Lady Windermere's Fan?* Lovely lady falls to sin. Well we can all fall to sin, can't we?'

Helen looked at her sharply, but the old lady's face seemed innocent.

'Let's try this big speech here. I'll be Lady Windermere dearie, you be Mrs Erlynne—lovely lady stoops to folly.' She heaved her bulk out of the chair.

'Now pause, dear—think about where you'll go for luncheon tomorrow, that usually takes about ten seconds, dear, no, not that tone of voice, that's not a fallen woman, dear, that's a lady been told she can't buy a new dress.'

'You don't know what it is to fall into the pit,' Helen obediently declaimed, 'to be despised, mocked, abandoned, sneered at—to be an outcast.'

'I thought I heard some light comedy going on in here.' Jack popped his head round the door. 'Any *petits-choux,* Maudie?'

She chuckled. 'Always one for you, me duck.'

'Jolly good these things, aren't they, Helen?' Jack munched his way through a concoction sticky with heat.

Helen marvelled. This was the man who

couldn't bear sweet cakes. And here he was eating one just for an old woman of eighty. What was her attraction? Jack wandered over to the piano, almost entirely hidden under its weight of photographs and memorabilia.

'Play me a tune, my dear,' gulped Maude, sinking back into the armchair.

He began to play 'Love's Old Sweet Song', and Maude began to sing in a cracked wandering voice, but Helen's voice soared over it. It was a soft and sentimental tune, and Helen had toned her voice down suitably. When the song was over, Jack played absently on. Suddenly he stopped and spun round on the stool.

'Helen, do you play?'

Helen grimaced. 'Yes. Randolph made me learn. It fitted his ideal of the country lady, tinkling away at the Steinway. You should have seen those country aristocratic dummies down there clapping politely, and secretly hating me. I wanted to shout out Nelly's Song. I did once too,' she giggled, 'but Randolph was so upset, I gave in and went back to "I Dreamt that I Dwelt in Marble Halls"—'

'Sing it now,' he interrupted, 'and play it.'

She shrugged, a patently insincere smile appeared on her face, and in soft tinkling tones she parodied it, much as she used to caricature her escorts on the hill years before.

'Now, Helen,' he cried urgently, *'sing it as Helen Hill.'*

Over the top of Helen's head, a suddenly comprehending Maude nodded to Jack appreciatively and popped a chocolate almond in her mouth.

Helen began again uncertainly, and much as she had before. Then she stopped and concentrated. She began to play again. This time a warm richness filled out the empty tinkle, emotion culled from years of responding to an audience, coming straight from the heart, was refined to pure gold, disciplined into maturity.

'Yes,' said Jack quietly. 'Oh yes, Helen.' He took her in his arms and kissed her. Maude patted her poodle meditatively.

'I have an idea,' he said, 'that will make Duke's productions different. Something to stamp each show with a mark of its own, a Jack Waters' presentation, a Helen Hill performance. Dramas, Comedies, polished plays, true theatre, but—'

'But what?' asked Helen, agog.

'A song sung by you playing at the piano. At some point in each play, you will wander over to the piano and play and sing one song. Just one. It's not going to be a musical comedy, just a moment the audience will come to expect.'

Maude looked interested. 'Jack you've got a brain. Wish I'd known you when I was making my way.' She sighed. 'But you didn't have time for such things then, two or three different plays a week, a day of rehearsal and you were on.'

'Well, Helen?'

'Yes.' Her eyes were shining.

'No throw-back to Mary May, remember.'

'No.'

'Then there's only one thing left to know. Maudie?'

'Yes, dearie?'

'Is Helen going to make an actress? Can she do it?'

Helen reddened. How could he doubt her?

Maude met Jack's eyes.

'Oh, yes, we think so, don't we pet?' She bent down to pat the poodle. 'Have an éclair, dear. Real *crème*.'

Over three years of steady patient work at Duke's Theatre followed, building up a faithful audience for a Helen Hill play. It was difficult at first to introduce the novelty of a piano and a song into a straight play or comedy, and playwrights objected to their dramatic tension being broken by what they saw as extraneous business. Three years of soothing people, making them see how it could fit into a pattern, wooing audiences so that other plays put on in between Helen Hill productions no matter how good, were mere interludes while people waited for the next Helen Hill appearance.

Jack's main worry was Margaret Cunningham, of whom he was fond and in addition owed an obligation to for her years of hard work to build up Duke's. Fortunately this problem solved itself. She married and while not leaving the stage was available only for a few productions, a time when Helen could reluctantly make her visits to Swithins.

'In five years we shall have conquered London,' Jack had prophesied at the beginning.

'I shall be nearly forty by then.'

'You my love,' said Jack, flicking a black curl with his finger, 'will age gracefully. That firm little chin will soften down a little with increased weight by then, the dash of grey in the hair will add distinction; at forty you will be known as the distinguished handsome Helen Hill. By sixty, you will be gracious. By seventy you will be an institution.'

'Or in one,' grunted Helen, secretly delighted.

Jack was right, for it was beginning to work, and moreover these three years had seen the fulfilment of their love. It hadn't been easy at the beginning.

'I can't stay here any longer, Etty darling. I've rented a small house.' Helen did not labour the point that the house was conveniently close to Montpelier Walk.

'But Helen, what does Randolph—?'

'Bother Randolph.'

'But Julia and Robert,' wailed Etty. She had never believed it would happen.

'It doesn't affect them either.' Helen believed this. When she paid visits to Swithins now, she forced herself not to mind when they ran to Randolph or Jane with their childish worries and joys, reminding herself that it was inevitable. She stifled anguish for what she could not take with her from the past by dedicating herself wholeheartedly to the future.

'Yes Helen,' Randolph had agreed readily, when she told him crisply what arrangements she proposed to make. If he had had any qualms about what his wife might be doing in London when off the stage he did not display any anxiety, and Helen shut her mind to the problem. After all, he hardly ever came up to London, and his club was no hotbed of theatre gossip. When she married Randolph she had shut Jack from her mind—or tried to. She had not talked of him to Randolph, and if others had, he did not speak of it to her. No, all would be well. She knew

Randolph. If gossip reached him, he would simply turn it aside, disbelieve it or ignore it—anything rather than have an emotional crisis in his life. The Swithin family *never* had emotional crises.

Her salary, she informed Randolph, was not going to contribute very much at the moment but it would increase. It would pay the servants' wages and those of a manager. He would ensure the estate did at least pay for itself. Thus she chose a manager she could trust, not a man from the ranks of their country friends but someone from an East End background—she could tell it a mile off for all he tried to conceal it—who knew the value of money as well as she did. She did not like him but she understood him, how to deal with him.

'Look here, me old cock sparrer,' she informed him. 'I know the books, see, and I'll be down every month to look at 'em, so no use thinking you can pull the wool over our eyes and have your hands on the fiddle. See this estate makes a profit, and you'll get a share. If it doesn't, you're out. Fair and square?'

Jennings looked shocked at this full frontal assault on his integrity. He had indeed been thinking along those lines, having quickly sized up Sir Randolph's business capabilities, but quickly changed his mind. There was more to be had by going along with her ladyship.

'Your hand on it, Jennings.' Once a coster had shaken hands, the deal was fixed. He hesitated an instant, then shook it. Helen was satisfied. Randolph proved almost as easy.

'I intend to have my own house, Randolph. There'll be just enough money left for it.'

'Alone? My wife?' Randolph was shocked —to her surprise.

'As Helen Hill. I'm only Mrs Swithin down here.'

He looked at her suspiciously. It was true that physical relations between them had all but ground to a halt, after he had given up the struggle of keeping up with her. Centuries of Gleven blood recoiled from the idea, and surrendered—there was no gainsaying that Miss Wickham's arms were a great deal more restful than Helen's.

'No, Helen, no.'

Jack was gentle, but adamant. He would not move in with her to her new house in the Square. Nor would he allow her to come to live with him in the Walk.

'You don't love me,' said Helen threateningly.

'You don't persuade me that way, Helen. It's beneath you. You know very well why I can't move in with you. Because you've got a husband and two children, and a reputation to maintain.'

'Randolph doesn't care. And he's got his little nursery governess.'

'Irrespective of your husband and his feelings, there's my own and my leading lady's reputation—not to mention the theatre's.'

'What does that have to do with our private lives?'

'Everything. Think of the theatre gossip. Think of the audience we're trying to attract. From the very people that would cold shoulder us. If you don't care what society thinks, then I do. You'd be ostracized. We both should.'

'And do you mind?'

'Yes, I do. We made a bargain, remember. The top of the tree. We won't get there this way.'

'Does this mean that we won't—' asked Helen bravely. Not again, she couldn't lose Jack again.

'No, it doesn't, Helen,' Jack sighed. 'You know I can't give you up. You're in my blood. I love you, and heaven knows I need you.'

She was in his arms. 'And what about your slippers? I won't be there to warm them for you.'

His arms tightened around her. 'I want you more. More than all that. Much more—Helen,' he said fiercely, 'I want to marry you. Don't you think I want to live with you, every day, sleep with at night instead of snatching odd hours? I want us to be married. I suppose Randolph wouldn't let you divorce him, would he? Or even, if we gave him evidence, divorce you?' Even as he spoke he felt her instinctive reaction.

Helen went rigid with shock. Divorce? *No one* got a divorce. That really would be a social disaster. However could Jack think of it? Randolph would never divorce her, or let her divorce him. Besides, once she was in London, she felt she was Jack's wife already. Randolph never entered her head. She was already as good as married to Jack, so why should they not live together? There was no need for it to become a society scandal. But divorce! She shuddered at the thought. Besides, the old earl was failing now, it couldn't be long before Randolph came into the title, and would need her at least for appearances' sake. Once that had happened, she could relax. The terrible past would be over, and *then* she and Jack could decide their future.

'Jack,' she said, 'you know how much I want to marry you, you must do, to be together always. But we are now. There's no one but you and I for ever. If I were divorced, think of the scandal. You would be named—dearest, what would that do for Duke's and our plans? No, much better to remain as we are—all in all one to another. I love you, Jack, you know that, don't you?'

He was silent, then said, 'Take care, Helen, take care.'

It had not been easy in the theatre either. Secure in Jack's love, Helen tended to slip back to her former queenly ways of disregarding anybody other than those she needed. As a result early rehearsals were a fiasco with no sense of company unity and Helen blithely forgetting all the lessons on stagecraft she had learned from Maude James.

Flummoxed by the lack of support she got on stage, and not appreciating the reasons for it, Helen floundered and stumbled through rehearsals, found it difficult to learn her words, and a general apathy pervaded the company. Jack watched grimly. Extreme measures might be necessary.

On stage Helen fluffed. It was entirely her own fault, but when a small part player failed to come in with his speech, she turned on him in fury, not mincing her words.

'But, Miss Hill you forgot my cue,' he ventured defensively.

Helen went purple with rage. How dared he answer back? Torn with vexation at her own ineptitude and rage that it was commented on by such insignificant fry, she slapped his face.

An arctic voice from the stalls cried, 'Break for ten minutes. Now! But not you, Miss Hill, come here.'

She sped down the steps to the auditorium eager to justify herself to Jack. But Jack wasn't there. Instead a huge reproachful figure, in mauve velvet and matching hat with long dangling plumes, wagged a finger at her.

'Naughty, naughty girl.'

She gasped. 'Miss James. What are you doing here?'

'Mr Jack called me in. Said I was needed. I knew it must be important to get me out of my nice warm chair. He sent a cab for me too. Now, dear, you've disappointed me. You think you're the most important person on the stage.'

'I *am* the leading lady. Who's more important than me?'

'The person that's speaking the author's lines, dear, whether it's the butler with his one line, or you with your two hundred. And it's your job as leading lady to make them the most important.'

Helen flushed. 'I didn't realize—'

'No, but they do, dear. Now I'll tell you

211

something. I didn't like you one bit, not one little bit, when Mr Jack sent you to me. Lady Nose in the Air. I went on not liking you even when I saw you were going to be quite a good little actress, dear, and I can always tell. But then,' she paused, 'one day you suddenly looked at me and smiled. Straight at me, instead of through me as though I was a mirror for yourself. And I thought she likes me, that little girl, and I felt all warm inside, although I've been on the stage sixty years or more. Now I don't know whether you like me or not, dear, but you convinced me you did and that's what made me go on. I'd been going to give you up.'

Helen thought back. She remembered the moment—she'd been in the middle of a long speech from *Olivia* and doing it very well, she thought, when she'd suddenly looked up to find Maude's eyes not on her but straying to a photograph by her side. As she stopped Maude had said, 'Sorry dear, I was thinking of when I played it—just after dear Ellen.' It was a photograph of Ellen Terry in her most famous role. ''Course I wasn't so good—like a feather she was, dainty, still is, bless her'—and Helen, seeing the loving look in her eyes, the wistfulness for days and beauty now gone by, had smiled in sympathy.

'Make them think you like them, dear.

And apologize to that poor little man.'

She apologized and she tried. It hadn't been easy, but little by little she managed it. And little by little the company responded. And what was it Maude had said? 'Listen, dear, as well as speak on the stage. Listen to them.'

Instead of concentrating on her own lines she listened, and was surprised to find that her own words then came quite naturally, that the pauses were simpler to judge and a natural rhythm took over.

Jack's worries began to recede. His visits to her in the afternoons became more relaxed, for they were able to talk of the play now without having to avoid the subject.

The play was a mild success; a few critics disarmingly pointed out that here was a possible star in the making. The next play confirmed their hopes. The next one dashed them. They had become too confident too quickly, Jack as guilty as she. They ignored Maude's warnings that society didn't yet want to laugh at itself, that plays with the mingling of class couldn't yet be accepted. The old queen and the old order ruled. It was a setback. Let's brazen it out, was Helen's view. Put on another one just the same.

'No,' said Jack. 'The audience is the

arbiter. Never fly in their face.'

So they put on *Lady Castleton's Dilemma* again, this time with Helen as Lady Castleton as Margaret Cunningham was expecting her first baby. Mollified the audience returned. After that, they tested out each idea cautiously, discussing and constantly amending scripts. But in each play there was built in one song for Helen to sing.

As the bells rang out for 1901, Duke's celebrated the twentieth century with Helen Hill in *A New-Fashioned Duchess*. Her song became known everywhere; delivery boys. road-sweepers, milk roundsmen whistled cheerily, 'A Century of Love'. Helen Hill was on her road to fame—but every song that Helen sang, she sang for Jack. During the week they had to be satisfied with afternoon visits, at the weekend they would go out perhaps to Richmond, far from everyone. Helen would then forget that she was a matron in her mid-thirties and Jack that he was a respectable theatre manager with a thriving business. They would dress simply, and few would recognize in the flannelled, blazered curly-headed man, and cotton-frocked woman a pair becoming famous all over London.

'Jack,' remarked Helen, carried away by

the warmth of the spring sun. 'We're on a hillside here...'

'No,' said Jack swiftly. 'No, we can't, Helen.'

'Are you sure?' She leaned over him, and it seemed to him that she was the same young girl he'd taken into his arms on that northern hillside all those years ago.

'Quite sure,' said Jack forcefully. 'We're far too old and far too respectable to roll around on a hillside.'

'Are you very, very sure about that?' whispered Helen tickling his nose with a piece of grass.

'Almost sure.' His arms folded around her.

'Very secluded indeed,' she murmured in his ear.

'Helen—don't—no we can't—get away from me—'

'I don't think we're too old at all.'

Early in the year, the old queen had died, and Duke's, when the theatres had reopened from national mourning, celebrated the arrival of a king who loved the theatre and patronized it so extensively. Jack put on a light farce, to follow the *Duchess;* a new challenge for Helen, for there was little drama or pure comedy in it, at which she excelled. This was all sparkle, all pace, demanding new

215

timings, new techniques. It was exhausting. Far harder work than straight drama. Visits were paid anew to Maude, now eighty-four, and bulkier than ever. She seldom moved out of her chair now, and her beloved poodle had died the year before. Even the supply of éclairs had dried up as Jean-Pierre himself had passed on to the Great Kitchen in the Sky. Her eyes gleamed appreciatively, therefore, when Helen wafted through the door bearing a large box tied up with pink ribbon.

'Not yet,' said Helen warningly. 'You've got to teach me my lesson first.'

'Rather like naughty Oscar's play *The Importance of Being Ernest*,' said Maude. 'Without the wit,' she added caustically—looking down the script. 'Yes I see just how to play it dear, but I'll have to play it from here. No dancing round the room now.' Such was her craftsmanship that she managed to sound like an eighteen-year-old girl as she instructed Helen.

It was hard work, that play, but Helen succeeded. This was in no small part due to her leading man, Michael Selling, imported by Jack for the occasion. His love for Helen did not blind him to objectivity on her abilities. Farce was an unknown field for her yet, so find her a leading man who could play it and Helen would respond. If she were willing to be led

216

on stage, that is. He would be interested to see whether she would, and whether her instinctive feel for theatre was strong enough to overcome her personality.

It was the first time she'd shared the billing but she'd enjoyed it, although she'd been doubtful. 'It won't do you any harm,' Jack had said casually. She trusted him now, and it marked another beginning. She learned that she could share but still shine, that her own performance gained, not lost, from having a good partner. Michael Selling was also a very good-looking young man. Excitement and relief that the first night was over and successfully so led her to flirt outrageously with him.

'Jack,' she cried in mock horror, 'however can you sabotage your reputation by insisting on coming home with me tonight?'

He did not answer her, but sat silent next to her in the cab.

'Very well,' she shrugged, 'if you must be moody...'

He paid off the cab, and they went indoors. It was two o'clock and Helen was tired. But Jack was in no mood to go to bed. He flung himself down on her sofa, having helped himself to a large whisky.

'Very well,' she yawned, 'if you're not going to bed, then I am. I feel like a ship's figurehead trussed up in these S-bed corsets.'

He caught her by the arm as she went out of the room and twisted her round to look at him.

'I can't go on, Helen. I've had enough.'

She stiffened and tried to free herself but he held her in a vicelike grip.

'I won't go through another evening like tonight, having to watch you with another man, not being able to march forward to claim you for my own. You've got to marry me, Helen, it's the only way.'

'We've been through all this.' Panic swept through her. 'You know it's impossible.'

'I know no such thing. If Randolph divorces you, quietly, it will be a nine days' wonder. We'll keep out of the public eye for a bit, go on tour abroad perhaps and get married there. We must, Helen. Either that, or we must part.'

'Part?' Helen was terrified.

'Yes. I can't go on loving you as much as this and continue as we are. We must stop being lovers, and if we then cannot bear to be near each other, we must part professionally as well.'

'But we can't.' She was aghast. 'What about the pact we made? The top of the tree—you promised.'

'Some things come before that,' Jack said quietly. 'Ambition is all very well, but not at the cost to one's reason.'

Helen was thinking and thinking quickly, fighting down her trembling fear. She could not lose Jack again. Nor could she lose him professionally either. Yet he meant what he said. Not a shadow of doubt. Would divorce be very terrible? What was a coronet besides love? She'd made one great mistake in her life, she couldn't make another. She was at a crossroads. She hadn't seen them coming but here they were. This time she knew which road to take, because there seemed no alternative.

'Very well, Jack. I'll ask Randolph for a divorce.'

The lodge gates flew open and old Jacobs stood beside them. It was a long time since she'd been to Swithins', and she was surprised how much pleasure she had in seeing the old man again, cross and crotchety though he usually was.

'Afternoon, Mrs Swithin.'

The carriage proceeded up the drive. No expensive new motorcar yet, for Swithins'. The estate was doing reasonable well, now that Jennings' control was beginning to tell, but profits did not run to luxuries. Swithins' red brick façade looked mellow and welcoming in the afternoon sun. Down the front steps ran nine-year-old Julia and her six-year-old brother. A surprise visit from Mother meant presents. She jumped down from the carriage not waiting for the groom to hand her down and scooped Robert up. He'd grown even chubbier in the two months since she had last seen him. His blue eyes beamed back at her; Randolph's eyes. By his side Julia waited more decorously to be greeted. Dark-haired and tempestuous she took after Helen, yet she was reserved and wary. Had Helen been more perceptive she would have seen in her a picture of herself at the same age. Helen planted a kiss on her cheek, but she was never sure how Julia felt about her. She was her father's girl, maintaining a formal politeness towards her mother. Randolph was in his check trousers and Norfolk jacket, every inch the country landowner. He took Helen's hand and kissed it, his blue eyes lighting up with genuine pleasure at seeing her. Nervous of her he might be, but she still exercised an attraction for him. Life always seemed to be more lively when Helen was around; too lively sometimes. She'd sweep into the drawing room, fling back the piano lid and start singing. Normally it was the husky lilting songs for which she was now famous, but after the guests had gone she would revert to the music hall songs from her past. The children loved this, though Randolph blinked a little. Julia would glow with pleasure and Robert would clap his hands and jump up and down saying 'More, more,' and strut around singing the choruses with her. She omitted the innuendoes on these occasions.

'You heard Father's ill?' said Randolph after dinner.

'No.' Helen was sorry for she always got on with the cantankerous old man.

'He's thinking of living at home for good, giving up Cannes.' He paused. 'He thinks this may be it. He's seventy-five you know. Matter of fact, doctors say it will be only a year at the most,' he added awkwardly.

Helen sat still at the huge dining table, her fingers round the stem of her crystal wine glass, looking at her reflection in the polished oak. The Swithins' silver, adorned with the family crest, gleamed in front of her. Only the Stilton and port adorned the table. Around her the Swithins' forebears looked down at her severely from the walls, youthful portraits, by second-ranking artists. When they came into the title, the Van Dyckes and the Gainsboroughs were commissioned to paint them, and these memorials hung in state at Monkswater, but those at Swithins' were awe-inspiring enough to Helen. How did they see her, she wondered? As an upstart or an asset? She'd saved their precious Swithins for them after all, even if they did think of her as a cuckoo in their midst. It was a long, long way from Spitalfields. She had earned the right to sit here, and now she belonged here. When Randolph's father died her portrait would hang at Monkswater too. Wife of the twentieth-century baron. Who'd paint it? Perhaps Sargent would paint her portrait in her peeress's robes. Or on the stage might be better perhaps, but the stage seemed a long way away. Just to be a peeress, even for a short time before she broke the news to Randolph... A *very* short time.

She went back the following day in time for the evening performance. The children and Randolph stood on the front steps, and she turned and waved to Swithins: the house, her family on the steps, the staff. She hadn't mentioned the divorce once. There was no immediate hurry after all. They were happy as they were, she and Jack.

'He won't Jack. He just refused to listen to me,' Helen wept in his arms. 'He just said I was his wife, there'd never been divorce in the Swithin family, and there never would be.'

He held her close, his face a conflict of emotions. 'And can't you divorce him? The nanny?'

She shook her head miserably. 'No, adultery isn't enough as you know. And I've no evidence for that. Nor could I prove he's insane or cruel. What are we going to do?'

Jack banged his fist on the mantelshelf. His face became red with anger. 'Very well. We'll do as you wanted all along. No matter what you do, eh? We'll give him grounds to regret that statement. You'll come to live with me, openly. And to hell with what the Mrs Grundies say.'

His mood suddenly changed from anger to joy as he swung her high in the air, crying aloud with happiness.

'Mind, I shall want my whisky and soda at exactly 6 p.m. and my slippers—and you mustn't interrupt my reading of *The Times* at breakfast.'

They rented a country house in Hampstead where the news took a little time to spread. Theatre gossip moved more quickly, but Helen was respected and liked now, and Jack loved, so in theatrical circles the storm quickly died down. When the gossip filtered to the outside world, they had been living together for two months, and in their happiness buttressed themselves against it. That the news might reach Randolph, Helen did not doubt, but the thought caused her no anguish.

Kent was another world. She counted on the fact that not even Nelson had a blinder eye than Randolph when it came to unwelcome news.

She and Jack were remorselessly and unsurprisingly dropped from all circles that knew the Swithins and Glevens, but gained a wider fascination for a different circle. After all, society argued, Hampstead was a long way from London, and a theatre manager and a leading lady were far too good company at a luncheon table to be ignored. What little time that Helen and Jack had for social functions was easily filled. They were still invited to most of the houses, but never together. This was society's solution to its problem, and caused them much amusement.

'Trout for luncheon,' Helen would announce.

'I did better than you,' Jack would proclaim, lunching at the same house a week later. 'Lobster. New chef.' They ran a scoreboard keeping their totals with satisfaction. To one person, however, it did cause great distress. Etty.

Through the years of Helen's and Jack's partnership Etty had remained devotedly in the background, raising her children to admire and love their aunt, making visits to Swithins' when Helen went so that the cousins could get to know one another.

Their news, when Helen broke it to her, hit her very hard. Etty had turned red, then white. Then red again.

'But Helen—Randolph—the children—'

'You're like a gramophone recording,' said Helen gently. 'You must leave them to me to worry about. You know that Jack and I have loved each other for a long time. Since Halifax.'

'I didn't realize. I must be very stupid. I did think so at first—but then you married Randolph.'

Helen winced. 'It's a long story, Etty. I can't explain; it was to do with Father, with Bethnal Green, with poverty that made me marry Randolph. Do you understand?'

'No,' said Etty simply. 'Not if you loved Jack.'

Helen stared at her. She suddenly felt utterly remote from Etty, as though she was the younger sister and Helen the older, wiser of the two. And a little angry too. What right had Etty to judge her? Etty had been looked after all her life by someone or other. The fact that she had been equally eager to look after Etty did not occur to her. She felt that Etty was slipping out of her embrace, her control. She did not understand her any more, yet she'd always been so sure of her.

'You won't desert me, Etty? You'll come to see us?'

Etty hesitated. 'I—I don't know.'

'Don't know?' Helen felt panic rising, and a constriction in her throat. Tears began to form. 'Etty you must, oh you must. What would I do without you? You're my sister, you can't desert me.'

Tears began to roll down Etty's cheeks. 'Yes, Helen darling. I will. Yes, I'll come.'

But when she came, two days later, it was not for Helen's sake.

A year earlier London had stood and cheered to the announcement that Mafeking had been relieved. Two months ago Paul had been sent out to South Africa as a civilian solicitor to sort out a legal wrangle on the ownership of a diamond mine. But the war was far from over. Caught in a Boer ambush, he was killed outright.

They heard the opening and closing of the front door, and the murmur of voices in the hall. Still at breakfast Helen and Jack heard Etty's voice, and rushed to the doorway in alarm. A grey-faced Etty thrust the dreaded yellow paper into Helen's hands. Helen gave a short moan, and folded her into her arms. Mixed with her grief for Etty, was a small happiness at the back of her mind. Everything was all right. Etty needed her. She was home again.

Chapter Eight

'Trust me, Helen. I tell you this is the most exciting play that has ever been through my hands. And we've got the opportunity to buy it.'

'"My little sister Catherine." What a stupid exit line.' She dropped the script. 'The author isn't even famous.'

'Nor was anyone when they started. Not even Helen Hill,' Jack told her forthrightly.

She subsided; pride would never let her admit that anyone had helped her in her career, not even Jack. She had achieved it all by herself—at the most it was a partnership. Her first thought was to push his nonsense aside; she couldn't waste time on a script that couldn't make up its mind whether it was comedy or tragedy. It was not what the Helen Hill public wanted. Her sense of self-preservation, however, made her think twice. Nevertheless the author was a no one—a tin pot schoolmaster from some obscure part of the country she'd never heard of. She had been nice to him, though, overlooking his perspiring face, and the nervous tic and the pince-nez wobbling on his nose.

'Helen, I tell you that this could be your *Second Mrs Tanqueray.*'

That caught her attention. She saw herself as another Mrs Patrick Campbell, dominating the stage, the audience, sweeping tragically to her doom, the pressures of society at last outweighing the pure gold of her character. She picked up the script again, and turned immediately to the last pages, riffling through for suicides, shootings, heroics—and, most of all, long speeches.

'You see,' Jack watched her carefully, 'social comedy to tragedy. Look at your big scene when you plead with your sister to tell the truth, only to have her turn round and say that you owe her a favour since your husband wanted to marry her first anyway. And so—*bang*. Change from comedy into tragedy. And it's at *that* point you say "My sister—my little sister Catherine" as you see her as she really is for the first time.'

In her mind's eye Helen was already on the stage, playing first this as Jack described it, then the last scene of all which she had just looked at.

A short but powerful ending with her playing her husband's favourite song at the piano and then walking slowly offstage. A shot rings out. Perhaps Jack was right. After all, she'd never played tragedy, and here she could play both tragedy and comedy in the same play. Her spirits began to rise.

'Perhaps we should see Mr Pince-nez again.'

She had made the right choice, for *The Sisters* was to be the play that lifted her out of the ranks of the drawing-room comedy actresses and placed her irrevocably in the annals of British theatre history.

Of her real life sister, Helen saw a great deal, making the tedious journey to Putney two or three times a week. Paul had been dead nearly six months now, and Etty was still in deep mourning, her pale face looking so woebegone in the black that Helen's heart cried out for her. Of money problems she had none, for always frugal by nature she had conserved the income on her capital and with the little that Paul had left managed well enough, and refused Helen's constant offers of financial assistance. But her loneliness, despite her children, was a different matter. It had been Helen's impulsive wish and one she still nurtured secretly that she, Jack, Etty and her children should all live together. She and Jack could afford a large house, and if Etty was stuffy about the conventions she could always live in a separate part of the house. Yet

Jack had obstinately refused to entertain the idea. No matter how she stormed, pleaded, wept, he just shook his head.

'But it's my family,' she wailed. 'I can't be near my own children,'—she saw him wince—'so I want Etty here. I need someone to look after. Lots of people.'

'If, my love, you want a family round you,' Jack put his arm round her waist, 'why don't we have a child of our own—be blowed to the conventions—go abroad...'

Instinctively she pulled herself away. 'Have a child?'

'We could go abroad. Go to New Zealand—or America. They have excellent theatres there. It would be fun. That's if—' he hesitated—'you would like my child?'

To hold Jack's baby in her arms? Stand with him over the cradle with love in their eyes? Teach it to read? Play with it, run on the hillside, fly kites, a Jack parading round the room with a laughing child on his back, at the circus, at the fair, at the zoo... How different it would be from that starchy nursery at Swithins, an awkward Randolph, so proud, so like a child himself, and herself so stiff, so divorced from any feelings that this was their joint achievement.

It had not begun like that, but she had found herself banished from the nursery, her children handed over to the fierce old dragon of a nanny who had looked after Swithins children for two generations and was not going to be dispossessed now, and before her black formidableness even Helen had quailed. Her contact with her children had been the bare minimum each day—a formal hour in the drawing-room—and, if she were lucky, a good-night kiss. Her children had come to regard her as a beautiful remote figure before whom they had to be good. And then Jane Wickham had come...

How different it would be with Jack's child... Her eyes filled with tears. Soon yes, *yes*, oh yes. There was still time. But abroad, and *now?* How could she? Not abroad—there was her career to be crowned first, and not *now*—what about Randolph, her father, and the social disgrace. People might tolerate an illicit union, but never a baby. She would have to retire, before reaching the top which would mark the point where Helen Hill would flower with all the love she had to offer.

'I can't—oh darling, I want to so much, but they told me after Robert that I shouldn't have any more children. Besides, I am in my thirties, and it might not be safe...'

She couldn't bear to look at him. The disappointment showed so clearly on his face. She burst into tears—genuine tears.

'Oh Jack, I do want to. I really do.'

'Hush, darling, hush. There are other things in the world. We have each other.'

She threw her arms around him and hugged him passionately. 'Never let me go. Promise me. Again. Like you did once before. On our hill. Never, never, let me go. No matter what happens.'

He stroked her hair, and waited till her heaving body was calmer. Then he took her face between his hands, and said to her gravely: 'Always, Helen, always yours. Till death us do part.'

Mr Pince-nez, or to give him his proper name Owen Orford, became a familiar sight at rehearsals. Not that he was obtrusive or shouted helpful comments. Indeed he seemed too nervous to speak at all and soon everyone became accustomed to his figure slinking apologetically round the corridors, and sitting way back in the stalls in the theatre in the gloom. Helen was gracious to him, which he rewarded one day by seizing her hand in the wings, covering it with kisses and as far as she could make out, offering her his devotion for life. By now she wanted more from him than abstract loyalty. She wanted his playwriting skills. For the moment she began to rehearse she realized how skilfully the play was constructed and marvelled that such lines reaching into the depths of feeling could emerge from this young village schoolmaster.

Then he announced to Jack that he had decided his mission was to write plays, not to teach Aristotle, delighting him, for as Jack watched *The Sisters* develop, he grew more and more certain of its chances. Much would depend on performance of course. He still worried about Helen herself. The actress that is. For he had long since ceased to question the private Helen at all; he took her for what she was, an intoxicating presence, without whom life had no point, with whom he was so caught up that he could not imagine life without her bewitching magic. He suppressed all thoughts of Randolph; only the children caused him a qualm. Randolph could jump into his own ornamental lake; he had had the perfect opportunity time and time again to divorce Helen and if he chose not to he could take the consequences.

Jack's doubts centred on her career and whether she could make the abrupt change from comedy to tragedy at the end of the second act. It would only take one titter to ruin the whole play. He could not voice his qualms to Helen for fear he would make her self-conscious and ruin the chance of its coming right naturally. It was so nearly there. In the end he had an unwitting ally in Owen Orford.

'Miss Hill,' he stuttered one day, buttonholing her on the way out of the theatre. He nervously removed his pince-nez and began to polish them furiously on the red silk handkerchief he kept for ornamental purposes in his coat, to mark the red rose he always wore. 'I want to express my admiration, my very deepest admiration.'

Helen smiled. 'It's a very good play.'

'Miss Hill, I see you as a flower—'

'A flower?' She was somewhat taken aback. Was this a declaration of love, the silly boy.

'Gertrude. Lady Montjoy. Your part. As a flower. In full bloom, reaching for the sun. Then the sun goes in, and the flower closes it petals over itself, against the harsh winds. Against the cold.' He stopped, overcome by this long speech.

'Do go on, Mr Orford,' Helen said politely. 'A flower, you were saying.'

'The flower wilts, brown at the edges— it's dead. Hour of glory over.'

'Do you think I'm brown at the edges?' asked Helen smiling.

'Oh no, no, not at all, I didn't mean,' he mopped his brow. 'Not a bit. Oh dash it.' He grew purple in the face and rushed away. Helen stifled her laughter.

'Like a flower,' she mocked him later that night to Jack, 'brown at the edges. What *did* he mean, poor boy?'

At the rehearsal, however, as Catherine laughingly refused to agree to put matters right with Gertrude's husband, Helen suddenly remembered, 'closing its petals over itself'. Her body grew still, she looked in chill horror at the little sister she loved and thought she knew so well. The sun had gone in. In her mind she hugged her petals to her. So when the final time came she spoke not with the defiance of melodrama, but with a quiet disbelieving change of mood:

'My sister, my little sister Catherine.'

On the first night, the curtain was going up for the last act. This was the testing time. The audience had been interested and amused up till now, expecting the play to run according to rule. There had been, however, a murmur of surprise after the curtain line of Act II at the sudden note of seriousness entering into what had seemed a perfectly ordinary drawing-room comedy. The plot seemed to have gone too far for the sister suddenly to turn back into a good sort after all, but if she were not, what then? What sort of play would this be?

Jack sat tensely in his box, willing Helen

to succeed, gradually relaxing as from the moment she entered, listlessly arranging flowers in a crystal vase, she held their attention. When finally her husband left her, still intent on divorce, she was sitting at the Steinway, quietly playing and singing to herself the love song of the First Act, 'For my heart is yours...' Then with sudden resolution, she slammed the piano lid, and walked offstage. A shot followed, and the stage darkened. As the curtains swept down, the husband rushed back on to the stage with sister Catherine. Slowly he fell to his knees and wept with his head on the piano stool. After a stunned silence the audience was on its feet, to welcome Helen Hill, as an actress of the first order, and to praise the playwright, blinking at them behind the footlights, his arm firmly in Helen's own.

In his box, the man responsible for their success slumped back proudly in his red plush seat.

'Well done, my darling.' Jack bent and kissed the nape of her neck. She turned and regardless of the cleansing cream on her face she kissed him wholeheartedly.

'Wasn't it marvellous? Oh Jack, Jack, I'm so happy. Are you?'

'Frabjously.'

'There's no such word.'

'There is today.'

They stood smiling at each other, well content. He took her hands. 'Well, now, we've arrived, at the top of the tree, where shall we go next?'

She considered. 'Yunnan-Fou.'

'Never heard of it. Doesn't exist.'

'It does.'

'Then how do we get there?'

'By donkey.'

He grabbed her round the waist, her petticoats a-flying, galloping her round the room.

'Where next, my lady?'

'Katmandu.'

'There's a little yellow idol to the north of Katmandu,' they chanted.

'And how do we get there?'

'By chu-chu.'

They were still chugging round the room to Katmandu, as the door opened. It was Randolph.

Only a slight change of expression betrayed any emotion as he registerd Jack's presence.

'Randolph, may I introduce—'

'I know who it is, thank you, Helen,' he replied evenly.

Jack withdrew his outstretched hand, and walked out of the room.

Helen rounded on Randolph. 'You might at least be polite.'

'If you don't observe the social conventions, I fail to see why I should,' Randolph remarked coolly. 'But I haven't come here to quarrel, Helen. I'm sorry to have intruded on you, but the Green Room doesn't exactly seem the place to greet one's wife. Especially in our circumstances.'

'It was good of you to come to the play.' Helen meant it. She had not thought him to be at all interested, except in the money she was able to send back to Swithins.

'I had a reason.'

Her spirits sank. However low relations between them sank she would have liked to think he would support her at important moments, and even bring the children perhaps. Julia was almost old enough now.

'The old man's really ill, this time,' Randolph continued. 'I came to tell you. They give him six months.' He paused. 'Thought I'd warn you. We'll have to talk sometime. I'm off down to Devon now. I'll need a wife then, Helen. Help me you know.' He stepped forward and kissed her unresponsive cheek. 'Thought you were the tops tonight,' he added awkwardly. 'Funny really, when I think of you as I first met you—kicking your legs around, and shouting. And here you are, another Sarah Siddons. Jolly good.'

Helen forced herself to kiss him lightly.

'I'll come down and see—Father.' She always found it difficult to say that word, with all its connotations of that other Father, blotted out of her life for ever.

What would happen when Randolph's father died? She'd be the Baroness Gleven of course. She put the thought aside. That was another world and tonight was her night of glory. Hers and Jack's. She put her arm through his and looked at him anxiously. She squeezed it slightly and was relieved when he squeezed hers back. So it was all right. He hadn't been perturbed by the scene with Randolph. He was not blaming her. Time enough for worrying about Randolph when his father did die. Meanwhile, she was Helen Hill and her public was waiting for her.

Here in the Green Room was Etty, bless her. Dear, dear Etty, still in mourning of course, but dressed in view of the occasion in deep purple velvet. And it seemed a thousand other people were crowded into that one room. True the cream of London's society was not there, but the people who mattered were, and in particular the critics.

She looked to see if Ambrose Pearl was there. Pompous, precocious and irritating beyond measure, the critic of the *London Witness* had gained an importance for the

239

theatre out of all proportion to the prestige of the paper. He was a short, round, almost ugly man in his late forties who used his wit to charm or to wound, both with deadly effectiveness. His devastating criticism of those who displeased him—by no means difficult to do—expressed with his mordant wit could damn with a phrase. So far he had been ambivalent about Helen Hill. Sometimes indeed he had not bothered to review plays at Duke's at all, passing them off with 'another game of croquet at the Ducal palace' or of a comedy of manners named *The Storm* simply 'In a teacup'. Liked or disliked, he had influence. She looked at him speculatively as she handed him another glass of champagne.

He put down the glass and picked up her hand. 'Dear lady,' he said meditatively. Helen waited, remembering the leading lady who had been rash enough to ask coyly whether he would be mentioning her in his criticism the following day, only to read five hundred words devoted to a description of the set and one sentence 'Mrs—looked divine in a large pink hat.' He knew his own reputation, and savoured it.

'Dear lady, on whom the gods bestowed every gift at birth, it seems. They gave you beauty, they gave you charm, they gave you gaiety, they gave you grace and intelligence.' Helen glowed, as he bestowed a kiss on her hand; then he straightened up, and with a malicious gleam in his eye he murmured. 'The Sleeping Beauty. But they forgot one gift, dear princess. They forgot the gift of tears.'

When his review appeared, however, it made no mention of this. It was full of almost unprecedented praise for an actress, particularly one of whom he had previously entertained—and expressed —doubts. Helen sank back into her pillows with a sigh of relief. It was all right. Pearl had given his approval. She ceased to consider the gift of tears. Jack remembered it, though, after Helen in some puzzlement had related the statement to him. He could see what Pearl meant. Helen's was a crystal-clear performance, ice-cold, objective, the perfect stone without a flaw. In her comedy, her timing was now impeccable, and she had proved that in tragedy her emotions could carry the audience with her. They would pity this proud woman, agonize with her dilemma, and as she went to her death they would remember her, respect her, admire her. But they might not weep for her.

The Sisters opened in January 1902. It played to full houses, and established

Duke's once and for all as a leading London theatre. No more murmurs that it was off the beaten track. For Helen it established her position, not only on the stage but in society. Many doors that had been closed to Helen and Jack reopened as hostesses found themselves eclipsed. For where Ambrose Pearl trod, no hostess could afford to be left behind. After all, they agreed, the couple did live in the country; it was not as though they insisted on flaunting themselves in Mayfair. Up in Hampstead who knows? They might even have separate houses. Society would not know. It was a long way away. Couturiers who once looked slightly askance at the impoverished Mrs Randolph Swithin, flung their doors wide open with the prospect of the fashionable Helen Hill patronizing and publicizing their creations. Thousands of postcard photographs winged their way through the halfpenny post, showing her on stage at the piano, defying her husband, pleading with her sister.

Helen remained in Hampstead, making one excuse after another to delay the journey to Devon. Receiving news from Randolph that his father's condition was unchanged, she almost lulled herself into dismissing it as a false alarm. But one afternoon the telegram arrived: *'Come immediately. Randolph.'* Wasn't that just like Randolph, she thought idly. He spent money as though it was water, and yet when it was really important he couldn't spend money on a few extra words and tell her what was really wrong. She must go, but she would go tomorrow. She couldn't leave tonight's performance at such short notice. It would only be a false alarm.

This time it wasn't. For next morning another telegram arrived: *'Father died last night. Expect you here, love Randolph.'*

'I have to go,' said Helen dejectedly. 'And I have to stay. Goodness knows how long.' An endless vista stretched out in front of her. Nothing but estate affairs, lawyers, servants, managers; yet another estate to sort out. For Randolph would not be up to understanding the complexities of the Gleven estate any more than he could cope at Swithins.

'We'll have to close,' said Jack despondently. 'No help for it.'

Helen immediately cheered up, though she tried not to show it. She could not bear the thought of anyone else, even Margaret, in her part. 'You could do a revival of *Lady Castleton.'*

'How long do you think you'll be? It's May now—a month, say?

Helen shook her head. 'I just don't know. There's the estate to be sorted out.

243

And the will proved. And the house to arrange. And the tutors and governesses, and local duties—'

'Local duties?'

'I shall be the lady of Monkswater now. There hasn't been one for some time. I shall have a lot to do. I shall be Lady Gleven. Baroness Gleven.' Then she saw his face and cried: 'Jack, don't look like that. I'll be back, just as soon as I can. And I'll be thinking of you every minute, every day, every night—'

'I'll write—'

'No, don't do that,' she said unthinkingly. 'Randolph wouldn't like it.'

'Randolph wouldn't like it,' he repeated bitterly.

There was a short pause. He broke it at last with a despairing: 'You must ask him again, Helen. He must divorce you. Perhaps now he's come into the title, he really will object to his wife actually living with somebody else so will agree to divorce you quietly. Or else—' He could not go on, for the alternative that Randolph might try to persuade Helen to remain was so terrifying that he could not voice it.

'Yes, darling, yes of course,' murmured Helen placatingly, but irrational panic was surging up.

'I mean it, Helen. I can't go on like this, knowing someone else has first call on your time—on your body.'

She cried out in shock. 'You can't think—that's all over long ago. I told you. Don't you believe me?'

'I don't know,' he said wearily. 'I only know you're going away and there's nothing in the world I can do to stop it.'

Jack settled her into a first class carriage, tipped the porter, and unnecessarily plumped the cushions. There was nothing to say. He had said it all. She was wearing dark mauve, a compromise for the black she must shortly don. Black had never suited Helen. As the cream and brown train drew out of Paddington GWR Station, he could see her figure at the window through the billowing grey smoke.

'Ch-ch-ch-chu, ch-ch-ch-chu,' he whispered to himself. 'Where are you going to, Helen? Where are you leaving me?'

Helen sank back on the cushions, tears prickling at her eyes. She blew her nose defiantly on her monogrammed handkerchief. After all, what was she crying for? Even if she had to stay down for the rest of the summer she could go back for short periods, take a cab to the Hampstead house and cry out, 'Where are you, Jack? I'm back. Here I am!' and he'd rush out and sweep her up into his arms.

Why it would be like the first days of their romance all over again. No, she was silly to cry. Nothing could divide them now.

The bell boy was already passing through, with his cry of, 'Luncheon please. Announcing luncheon. Dining car this way.' But she had no appetite. Perhaps she would go later. It was a pity to be leaving London now, just when the most exciting season for years was about to commence. The season of the coronation and with a fun-loving king on the throne, there would be celebrations such as London had never seen the like.

Then the significance began to dawn. A coronation... Under two months away, at the end of June. And Randolph was a peer now. He would have to attend. And she was Baroness Gleven, wife of the 20th Baron Gleven. A lady at last. Why did the thought give her no pleasure? She felt robbed, cheated. All she had waited for, and now it had come about in the worst possible way. There must be some robes somewhere. Packed away, probably since the old baron's wife died. All smelly, no doubt, from leather or turpentine, whatever preservatives they used. Still—she'd have to be there, at the coronation, dressed in those heavy robes, all the family jewellery on, the coronet... What a role! And yet excitement failed to come.

The Gleven carriage took her through the lodge gates, unfamiliar lodgekeepers sweeping their hats off, peering in to see their new mistress; then it took her up the wide circular drive surrounding the formal gardens to the front steps of the grey-stone mansion. Monkswater looked forbiddingly cold compared with the warm red brick of Swithins. Randolph and the children were waiting to greet her on the steps. I've done all this before she remembered. This time, however, it was different. From Monkswater there would be no return to London the following day, no return to Hampstead, no speedy return to Jack's arms.

She gave herself a mental spur of courage; up she went, up the steps to where her new staff were waiting to greet her, agog with curiosity for Helen Hill's fame had spread even to this far western county. Jones, the butler, Mrs Palmer, the housekeeper and a whole range of lesser servants stretching as far as the eye could see. Robert was bobbing up and down by her side now, tugging at her, regardless of the solemnity of the occasion.

'I saw an otter,' he told her, with the confidence of the seven-year-old, eyes shining.

'An otter,' she echoed dutifully in her best motherly tones.

She put an arm round her daughter who received it stolidly, but without drawing closer to her mother. Helen dropped it again.

Four days later Helen watched from the window as the long cortège left the grounds, the coffin borne on the shoulders of three stalwart manservants and Randolph, the only son. Thank goodness it was a men only funeral. She had had enough of the village folk staring at her when she'd dutifully accompanied Randolph and the children to church on Sunday. Used as she was to staring eyes, this was somewhat different, for she felt they expected something of her, something she was not sure she could—or wanted to—give. Already she felt like a prisoner, the vast gates of Monkswater closing gently but inexorably behind her. She looked round the vast ornate bedroom with its interconnecting door to Randolph's—firmly bolted, not that it was tested. Flushed with brandy on the Saturday night, he had tried a tentative overture but seemed almost relieved when it was declined. The problem of Miss Wickham Helen solved in her usual fashion by ignoring it.

The affairs of Monkswater were vastly more complicated that she had imagined. For years the old earl, though not business-like, had run it more or less efficiently through the goodwill of his retainers, who had been on the estate for generations, and the feudal loyalty of the village folk. The goodwill would not automatically be obtained for Randolph and certainly would not be for her. It would have to be earned. And that might be hard. For Helen guessed that despite all their curiosity about the famous Helen Hill, it would be difficult for a 'foreigner' to win their affections and earn their loyalties. Mistrust was writ large on their faces. Her usual perversity made her all the more determined to win it.

How she missed Jack. For all the comfortable Victorian luxury of Monkswater and the picturesque village of Monkswell and the estate itself, she longed to be far from these brooks and streams, these quaint thatched cottages, and the strange accents and be back safe in Hampstead, at Duke's with him. It was impossible for the moment. There was hard work to be done, and it could not be done overnight. Yesterday she had interviewed a succession of tenant farmers, lawyers and creditors, determined with all the force of her personality to impress them all that Monkswater was going to continue as a profitable estate. There were rents to examine, takings from sheep, and milk to see, to compare the year's prices with last, to see how it was being managed and if necessary to find her own manager.

It all took time. Mercilessly she delegated tasks to all who were incautious enough to come within shouting distance. Miss Wickham, charmed into a moment's involuntary liking for this imperious hand-some woman, found herself supervisor of all the funeral arrangements; Randolph was despatched to cataloguing the cellars—he would not fail there—the children into jobs around the farms and estate. Children's eyes could tell her much. With the help of their reports, innocently observing men in their work, she began to watch one, Dan Polryn, carefully. He was a quiet Cornishman of thirty-two, not long in the district, a mere ten years. He was still young enough to mould his life to Monkswater, and old enough not to let it go to his head; he was not one of the village, but he understood their ways. She'd keep her eye on him—he was a likely-un.

The days flew and turned into weeks. Weeks that in London were filled with a far different activity. Once June was in, London began to fill up with crowds, foreign dignitaries arrived according to their importance, troops from overseas with strange uniforms and coloured skins—all waiting for June 26th.

At Monkswater robes were unpacked with loving reverence by Roberts, the old valet, with the children's help, watched jealously by the rest of the staff. Out came the large holland storage bags, and a moment's breathless suspense when it was determined which had won the fight of over sixty years—the moths or the borax and camphor powder. Save for one sleeve of Randolph's robes, the moths had had a lean time, and once they had been shaken, the ermine gently brushed with a hat brush, and the velvet sponged with liquid ammonia and water, they were ready to greet another sovereign.

Helen, cross that Randolph's introduction into the House of Lords did not require her presence, consoled herself with the thought that the coronation was only two weeks away. She would be there—and she would ensure that their brief stay included time for Hampstead. To see Jack again... Happiness swept over her at the thought. What a time it would be—a reunion and a coronation. Few people in England could now remember the old queen's coronation. It was another century, another age. There was only one note of disquiet. The king had a cold. He had not been seen out for some time now. Would he recover in time? Before many days had passed the situation had worsened dramatically. It proved to be no cold, but the dreaded appendicitis. Instead of a coronation, the king, already in his sixties, had to face an operation new to medicine, and with results by no means certain.

With the whole nation hushed from its rejoicings, and on its knees in prayer, the operation was carried out—and successfully. The king who had waited so long for his coronation had to wait a little longer. But he was alive. The country breathed again, and the king's popularity soared even higher.

But to Helen the postponement meant only one thing. She would not see Jack yet. She tried to write to him, but words seemed inadequate for the disappointment she felt: she would come as soon as she could. All her love...all her love... Pen and paper seemed sterile. Better to wait to see him. The postponement would not be for long. The king was already recovering.

Meanwhile Roberts had paid his attention to Helen's own robes and at last announced them restored for her ladyship's use, after weeks of laying them up in lavender to rid them of the smell of cloves put in to disguise the unpleasant odour of moth balls. Even Roberts permitted himself a discreet smile at the spectacle of Helen in the late Lady Gleven's robes. She had been a tall lady, Randolph explained, and her robes trailed over Helen's feet, the huge weight dragging her down, the shoulders dwarfing her tiny figure. Randolph's were a better fit.

Later that evening she looked at the trunk she had insisted be left in her room. Feeling a traitor to Jack she could not resist tiptoeing over to it, almost as though he might hear, and taking out the coronet, silver strawberry leaves now gleaming and bright after hours of loving attention. She took it up gently in her hands, twisting it over and over. Then with sudden resolution she lifted it to her head feeling absurdly like the Sargent portrait of Ellen Terry as Lady Macbeth. She looked at her reflection in the mirror. Just for once it wouldn't matter.

'I've done it,' she crowed. 'Helen, Lady Gleven. A bloomin' peeress.'

Early in August, Helen sat inconspicuously in Duke's stalls and tried to concentrate on the play. Randolph was spending the postponed Coronation Eve at his club, and leaving the children in Miss Wickham's care, scarcely believing her good fortune, she had hurried off to Duke's. She did not dare to get a box in case she was recognized. It had been difficult enough sneaking by old Wilson as he took her ticket. For she had already determined that Jack should not see her; she had so little willpower that she would not be able to resist going back to Hampstead, his glad cries when he saw her, his assumption that she had returned for good. And she could not do that. Not for Randolph's sake, but the children's. This was their time.

And so she sat at the back of the stalls sand watched Jack's profile in his box, watching like a guardian angel over his play. The play was a good choice as a revival Helen knew, but *Lady Castleton's Dilemma* was so familiar to her that his profile was much more exciting. She felt as close to it as in bed and felt she could put out her hand and stroke the lines of his chin, smooth back his hair, pass her hand over that suspicion of a dimple, run her hands over his dear eyes. Shortly before the curtain fell, she hurried out, faint with the effort of leaving, and found herself a cab. She could not risk the linkman, George, recognizing her.

She opened the door, at Hampstead. The familiarity of it almost made her faint with joy. She had not been here for three months. She had to force herself not to take off her coat and rush upstairs, and to remember this was not her home for the moment. She walked—almost tiptoed—into the drawing-room. She did not want Reynolds to hear. There was a cigar left unsmoked on the ashtray.

The fire nearly out. She made it up. He would be cold when he got home. Taking a last look round, she put a letter on the mantelpiece. It was a simple letter, as were all of Helen's. It just said *'I love you'*, in her bold flourishing handwriting. She shut the door quietly behind her again, and returned to the gloom of the Gleven London house.

Jack was tired. The whole of London was rejoicing except for him. After the performance he could not face the thought of returning yet again to Hampstead without Helen. Would she come back? Even Etty seemed to assume she'd gone for good, gone to take up her place as a wife and mother—and peeress—at last. Dispiritedly he took a cab to the Garrick for a late dinner. As he walked into the lobby a familiar figure was descending the steps, John Bladon, a former schoolfriend, now an eminent barrister, and in his pleasure at seeing him Jack did not notice his companion. Suddenly remembering his manners, Bladon swung round with a 'Randolph, I don't believe you've met—'

Confusion overcame him as he recalled too late the club gossip. Randolph walked straight by them to the doors, leaving Bladon red in the face with embarrassment. But centuries of good breeding caught up with Randolph. He turned and went back, back stiff, erect and pokerfaced.

'I beg your pardon. I didn't recognize you at first. Mr Waters, isn't it?'

Jack bowed, hesitated and then with a recklessness usually alien to him asked, 'Do you have time for a drink, Lord Gleven? John, if you'll excuse us—'

Bladon was only too happy to escape, leaving Randolph little option.

In the huge leather armchairs of the upstairs smoking room, Randolph and Jack sat silently over an excellent 1860 Cognac Grande Champagne. It was impossible to tell what Randolph was thinking behind that calm aristocratic brow. But at last Jack spoke: 'Helen,' he said. 'I want to marry her.'

Randolph replied easily, 'But she's married already, my dear fellow. To me.'

'Why do you keep refusing to let her go?' asked Jack bluntly. 'We've given you every opportunity. Is it just the family name?'

Randolph stared at him blankly. 'Refusing what?'

'To divorce her. "No divorces in our family?"—I suppose that's it.'

Randolph leaned forward. 'I don't get you, my dear chap. Helen's a damned good manager. Damned good wife. Energetic. Efficient. No need to divorce her. I'm looked after for—er—that sort of thing.

Helen doesn't mind. Can't say I liked it when you took up living together. Didn't like it at all. Still don't. But wouldn't divorce her unless she wanted it.'

'But she does. She's asked you time and time again.'

Randolph shook his head. 'No reason I shouldn't agree. Lose a manager but you can hire them. Marry my—well, the children get on with her. Better than with Helen. Who can blame them? I say, old chap, are you feeling all right?'

Jack said nothing. He was very pale. It was impossible not to believe Randolph. He was patently sincere—and it was so typical of Helen.

'Helen,' went on Randolph awkwardly, 'dear girl. But complicated person you know. Does things her way.'

Some time later Jack read Helen's letter. Then slowly, deliberately, he tore it into many pieces and threw them into the dying embers of the fire she had so lovingly tended. There they sputtered into life and crumbled under his gaze.

The Archbishop placed the crown of England on Edward's head. A forest of arms swept up through the air, as the peers and peeresses donned their coronets. Helen Jarvis placed the coronet of the Baroness Gleven on her dark hair. 'God save the King' echoed from every quarter. The fanfares pealed as the elders of the church followed by the temporal lords paid homage.

As finally the newly anointed king and queen processed towards the west door of the Abbey, a beautiful Queen Alexandra, clad in shimmering gold Indian gauze, her purple robes trailing behind her, looked up at her peeresses and smiled, as she took her husband's arm. Newly crowned king and emperor Edward VII went to greet his people. Although it was a short ceremony and procession, for the king was still convalescing, the people of London had no such inhibitions.

From their window Robert and Julia looked down with wonder on the crowds revelling in the streets beneath. They had never seen such crowds. So this was London. Where Mother lived. The mother who descended like a princess out of a fairy-tale, thought Robert, all pink and smiling and sweet-smelling. And even Julia thought this; she always longed to throw her arms round her mother like Robert did, but was never able to bring herself to. She wanted to feel her mother's arms go round her like they did round Robert, and yet when her mother did embrace her, she could never respond, never tell her how much she wanted her.

Helen's heart was singing. Just for today she could forget the tug and chain of love that bound her. And it was a glorious day. She was a peeress of the realm. As they alighted from the carriage in front of Gleven House the children and Randolph hurried ahead, but she stopped to watch the crowds a moment in the street. Then fingers plucked at her sleeve.

''Elen. Me lovely daughter. Done up like a barrel of pickled whelks.'

She looked at the dirty hand on her arm and then at the leering face of her father.

'Is this gentleman annoying you, madam?' A burly policeman stepped forward.

Helen swallowed. 'No it's all right, officer—someone I knew once.' He stepped away doubtfully.

With an effort she brought herself to speak to him. 'How are you?' she asked abruptly, 'and George and the rest.'

'George is doing fine. A barrow of his own now. Nice little woman, five kids. You should drop by, madam. See yer little nephews. And the rest, as you kindly call your dear little brothers and sisters.'

'Do you want money?' she said bluntly. She could not, would not, be troubled by conscience over brothers and sisters she had left.

'Money?' he asked. 'Oh Helen what a

question. No I just wanted to speak to me dahling daughter. Though of course if—'

'I ceased to be your daughter over twenty years ago.'

'No, Helen me love. You're my daughter to the day you die, whether you like it or not. You may not think it, but you'll never get away from us, not for all the ermine in the world.' He stroked the fur on her sleeve, till she could have screamed.

His words emblazoned themselves on her mind. Safe back in Devon she could not forget them. 'Not for all the ermine in the world.' But she had position, she had wealth, she had a title. No one, nothing could take them away, send her back to Bethnal Green physically or emotionally.

But what if she gave up that position? What if she asked Randolph for that divorce she knew now he would give quite willingly. She faced social ruin. For living together was one thing. Divorce another. She and Jack were together as firmly as if they were married. Why need they ruin it all? They loved each other. That was the important thing. She would get the estate running, and then she would be free to return—so for nearly two months Helen threw herself heart and soul into organizing the estate. Dan Polryn was plucked from his tenant farm, and installed as manager. After several weeks floundering, her tuition and his good sense contrived to a point where she felt she could soon leave affairs in his hands.

One day after a hard morning's work on the accounts she decided to take the afternoon off. It was a late September day, the air was warm, the trees dappled with brown, the moorland beyond the house assuming its autumn tints. Birds were still singing bravely but with the defiant last cries of those that cannot put off the delaying of autumn and the fall of the year much longer. She wandered down by the stream, and sat on a tree looking at the water rippling by. For the first time in two months she had time to think. And now she couldn't. She had come here to sort out her muddled feelings and emotions, but she was too tired. Jack was so far away. Why not just give in? Stay here, at Monkswater. The children needed her. Even Randolph needed her in a way. It would be so easy.

Her eyes filmed over, as she thought of Jack and her, and a child playing between them on a hillside. Suddenly life was crystal clear. She had been deluding herself for a vain ambition. How could she have been so stupid? Stay here. *Here?* Randolph didn't need her, nor did the children. Jane Wickham was more to all of them than she was. She'd played her part there, fulfilled her duty. Now she was free to go back to Jack. What was being a peeress? And marrying a lord? It was all so pointless. Was she happy here? No. Jack was her lord, their love her security. She had been blind all her life. She jumped to her feet. She'd ask Randolph for a divorce tonight. No, right now. And then she'd go. Back to the stage and Jack's arms.

The door was opened for her—Reynolds had seen her arrival.

'It's only me, Reynolds,' she said gaily. 'I'm back now. Back for good. See to the luggage would you?' She took the shocked look on his face for surprise, until she advanced into the drawing-room, stripping off her gloves.

He followed her in. 'We've nothing ready, ma'am. We didn't know...what was happening...we get our wages of course, but—ma'am—'

But she did not hear him. What had happened? The place was bare, empty. Books were gone, pictures were gone— Jack's Peg Woffington had disappeared. She turned to Reynolds, bewildered, frightened.

'Reynolds, what's happened? Where are Mr Waters' things? Where is he?'

He looked amazed and shook his head in bewilderment. 'I don't know, ma'am.

I thought you—Mr Waters left, ma'am. About a month ago. Didn't say where ma'am.'

She knocked on the door impatiently, fear clutching at her. Where was Jack? What had happened? Was he ill? Had some terrible misfortune overcome him?

Maude James was well advanced in years now and it took her a long time to answer the door, puffing and peering at her visitor.

'Why it's you, dear. Lady Gleven I should say.'

'Maudie, where's Jack?' Helen was crying. 'Where is he?' she burst out as soon as the door was closed. 'I've been to Hampstead and he's not there. Nothing. No clothes. Nothing. What's happened?'

'Why, dearie,' said Maude James, alarmed by the wild look in Helen's eyes. 'Didn't you know? Don't tell me you didn't know.'

'No,' shouted Helen. 'Whatever it is, I don't know. What's happened?'

'He's married, dear. A month ago. We all thought you knew, you being Lady Gleven now, you see.'

'No,' whispered Helen through dry lips, in a voice which no longer seemed to belong to her. 'No, I didn't know. Who to?'

Maude James looked away.

'Who to?' demanded Helen.

'He always did like the slippers and pipe sort, dear,' replied Maude slowly.

'Who to?' shouted Helen again.

'Why, Etty, dear. Your little sister Etty.'

PART THREE

Cynara

Chapter Nine

Even Helen's heart fell as she looked at the drab grey stone exterior, paint and plaster peeling off, grimy with years of neglect from the London dirt. Her enthusiasm evaporated, as spirits dropped. The agent explained that with a dash of paint, a little work here, there would arise from the ashes a phoenix of theatre so glorious as to swamp even Covent Garden in its majesty. Helen glanced at her companion. Ambrose Pearl was looking at her quizzically. He had an uncanny habit of reading her thoughts.

'Well, Helen, my side of the bargain. Your kingdom, my queen. Unless of course you have last minute doubts. I trust not. So plebeian.' He was smug in his grey morning suit, yellow rose in buttonhole, for all it was only March, round and self-satisfied. Fifty years of self-confidence in his own verbal powers, which gave him a power over his fellow human beings that his unattractive face and short physique, rounded by the good things of life, however exquisitely tailored in Savile Row, could never win him. But ugly as he was, had an attraction for women that had made the necessity of a wife superfluous.

'No, I shall have mistresses...' he murmured to himself at the age of twenty, as his father, an embittered solicitor, had railed on the disadvantages of matrimony. And mistresses he had in plenty, from duchesses to dancers. It did his public reputation no harm: his integrity as a critic was unassailable. Essentially he disliked women; a good cigar gave him more intellectual satisfaction, so he claimed. Sex was a mere matter of the body, to be enjoyed, savoured and remembered as one would a particularly good *salmis de faisan* or Château Margaux. Or so he thought, until he met Helen.

Helen amused him—and more than that, intrigued him. Ambrose Pearl was of middle-class origin and the vagaries of society fascinated him. Where had she come from, this Baroness Gleven, Helen Hill? Not of the aristocracy, nor of the gentry, that much was clear. She was too perfect in her attention to etiquette and formalities for that. She had not the ease that came with centuries of breeding, born to the purple. He could detect in her deep sonorous voice when excited the occasional slip into an East London accent.

Where had Randolph met her? A Gala girl. But that told you nothing nowadays.

He'd even had to work hard to find that out. For no girl called Helen Hill had ever worked at the Gala. And having traced Mary May, he was then faced with a further mystery. Where had Mary May come from? There the trail stopped. This mystery about her background, this sharp edge to her personality, gave an extra spice to his feeling for her, and made her twice as desirable in his eyes. Yes, to possess Helen Hill would be an achievement. This he had decided when he first saw her on the stage at Duke's. Something in her bearing made him want to break down that defiance, and more than her body he coveted her spirit. To conquer that, to have her devotion, now that was a diamond for his pin indeed.

'My side of the bargain...' Helen looked at the drab old building in front of her. Perhaps she could be wrong about its potential. It was in the right place, on the opposite side of the street from Duke's, about thirty yards further along the street, but even so was she making a mistake? Suppose she failed...? She pushed the thought away from her. She would not fail. Even though it meant Ambrose Pearl as her backer and lover (another thought she pushed away until it had to become a fact)—but his mind, his alive, sharp malicious eyes, yes she responded to something here. So when he'd first offered to buy this place for her, to establish her as an actor-manageress if she would become his mistress, the idea had not been too repugnant. What did it matter now, now that there was no longer anyone to laugh and make love with?

Jack... The pain had not lessened in nearly three years. Did Etty betray her? Etty, always Etty... For a second Helen was transported back to the little girl who stared out of the grimy window to watch her mother and sister disappearing into some unknown wonderland once a year, drawn together by a bond from which she, Helen, was excluded. Yet Etty seemed to do nothing to court this attention; she was marked out by fate to be a passive victim, to let others look after her. Victim? Who was it that took Mr Hewson away from her... Who was it that inherited all the money from a father she did not even know she had... Who was it who married Jack? Victim? She was as helpless as a polecat.

Her resolution hardened, and Helen took Ambrose's arm. 'Let's go in,' she said.

The building had once been a music hall, many years ago. When that failed, it was used as a warehouse by a paper merchant for ten years, then by a toy manufacturer, then empty for several years.

Now it was on the market again.

Ambrose Pearl was well aware of the reason Helen had been attracted to this particular property—but did not mind. Indeed he was mildly intrigued that Helen still cared enough for her former lover to go to those lengths. After all Waters was safely married; it was no odds to him if he spiced Helen's vindictiveness by pandering to this desire. In fact he rather enjoyed the prospect of the battle. He was a rich man. He could well afford to invest money in what purported to be the drama of his life: Helen Hill in direct competition with Jack Waters.

It was damp inside. What had been the bar and foyer had been roughly converted into a warehouse office, and the broken chairs and furniture, lying on what forty years ago had been a rich red carpet, were mildewed, dirty and worn. A mouse scampered for safety in front of them. The oppressive silence of disuse hung heavy about them. They picked their way along the corridors to the limited backstage accommodation. Ambrose Pearl was busy redesigning in his mind's eye—he knew quite a lot about theatre architecture—and was planning an extension here, extra floor, dressing rooms. Yes, he could see possibilities. But he said nothing, keeping his face straight until Helen should pronounce her verdict. He had faith in her instinct. She would not let her hatred of Waters stand in the way of her own success or failure. Or perhaps she might? It would be interesting to see. The first scene of the new drama.

They went into the auditorium. There was no raked floor, and what had once been comfortable seats had been thrown out for warehousing space, and broken toys lay around in heaps. Here and there an odd doll peeped out perkily from the pile, but most were in broken pieces. In front of them was the stage, or what remained of it. It was not large. There were no curtains left at the proscenium arch. Even the agent had fallen silent now, reconciled to seeing his hopes of a sale collapse. He and Pearl followed Helen who was moving swiftly for the stage. It's hopeless, she was thinking. They mounted the steps at the side of the stage and stood looking about them. No traps, precious little left of the flies, the lighting battens ripped out. Helen stood, back towards the auditorium, looking around her trying to imagine her sophisticated drawing-room comedies here. She couldn't.

Then her eye fell on a lurid illustration hung by one of the warehousemen as a patriotic gesture at the time of the coronation—a picture of Edward VII and the royal arms. For some inexplicable reason hope rose in her heart. If Lillie Langtry can do it, then I can, she thought. She refurbished a theatre, set up her own company, and she was not even much of an actress. I *can* do it, and yes, I will do it and the king will be here. He'll have to come. To see Helen Hill.

She whirled round. 'Ambrose,' she said, her eyes blazing with excitement, 'we'll call it King's—no, Crowns. That's it. Crowns.'

She had not started by wanting vengeance on Jack. Or even Etty. She was too numb. She had returned to Hampstead after seeing Maude James, hurtful though it was, for she had nowhere else to go. Soon she'd have to go back to Devon, she supposed, to pick up the pieces there, rebuild some kind of life, but for the moment she could not think of that. If she went to Hampstead she might understand why the man she had loved so much had married her sister. But the house was full of memories; she could not rest in it, and took long walks to escape its lonely rooms. She had been there a month, when Reynolds reluctantly told her the house was to be sold, the staff leaving in two weeks.

There was no letter to her. Nothing to show that she even existed. Or had ever existed in Jack's life. In a sense it made packing easier. For if it had all been a dream, there was nothing to hurt. No one called. Nothing happened. No one knew she was there. She might just as well have died. Only a dull nagging pain in the pit of her stomach reminded her of what had happened, and resolutely she set out to numb it. But it would not go away.

She had looked out of the window one day to see a cab draw up in front of the door, and watched with cold heart as Etty's familiar figure descended. How could she still look the same? Surely she must have altered, her guilt show on her face, surely the golden hair dimmed—something to show what had happened? But no, her placid face was glancing hesitantly up at the windows, as though bracing herself for the ordeal to come.

Slowly Helen moved away from the window and sat down on the sofa in a room from which most of the objects had already been packed. She sat down stiffly, her arms crossed in front of her on her lap.

Reynolds entered. 'Mrs—Miss Etty, my lady.'

'I am not at home, Reynolds,' said Helen loudly.

'Yes, my lady,' he said stiffly withdrawing. But before the door could close behind him, a figure thrust herself in, pushing him aside.

'Helen, oh Helen. Please.' Etty came into the room, arms outstretched, tears on her face. 'Helen, you must talk to me.'

Helen remained where she was, cold as granite. 'I am—not—at—home,' she said in clipped icy tones.

Etty ran to her and knelt down by her feet, forcing her hands into hers, making Helen look at her. 'Helen, I thought—we thought—'

Helen rose and tore herself away from Etty's clinging hands, backing away, and turning her back.

'We thought you were staying in Devon,' said Etty in agony. 'Jack—'

Only a slight movement of the shoulders betrayed any emotion on Helen's part at the mention of the name. She moved to the bell rope and pulled it.

'Helen, I love you,' cried Etty despairingly. 'You're my sister. You've done everything for me...'

'And how have you repaid it?' asked Helen softly, eyes implacable. 'Ah, Reynolds, Mrs Waters is leaving—'

Stricken, Etty rose and slowly left the room. Only when the cab had borne her away, and the sound of hooves diminished, did Helen relax, then the tears came for the first time, great harsh, angry tears. She fell on the sofa, and pummelled the seat in self-pity. Etty, always bloody Etty. So meek and mild, so lovable. She'd never done anything for herself in her life, always accepted other people looking after her. And now she'd taken Jack, *her* Jack.

She must always have been jealous, and when she lost her own husband she seized on the first chance she could get. It wasn't fair. She, Helen, had striven, had worked for, had fought for Jack, and along came Etty with her sly deceitful ways and taken him from her. But now Jack knew she was back in London, that Etty had come, knew from Etty how upset she was, he'd come to her. He must. Till death us do part, he'd said. He would come, somehow they would find a way.

But he did not come.

At first it was a new part to play: the Baroness Gleven. Randolph had accepted her return to Monkswater philosophically; his visits to Miss Wickham's bedroom went on more or less as before, with Helen taking no notice, and if there was resentment in the nanny's eyes she ignored it. She made it politely clear that whatever went on might continue, provided no jealous eyes were laid on her coronet, and with this Jane Wickham had to be content. She already had the satisfaction of the love of Robert and Julia, who took longer than their father to adjust to their mother's return.

It was yet one more change. From Kent to Devon. From Swithins to Monkswater. But soon the strangeness of their mother's return gave place to more present concerns: the coming of Christmas, the stabling of the new pony for Julia, the new foal for Robert to pet. Julia, older and with all her mother's obstinacy, took longer to adjust than Robert. Helen made no effort to win the children's attention, which was the best thing she could have done. Piqued by the lack of interest Julia took to haunting her like a shadow, on her imperious visits to the kitchen, sweeping into the gardens and greenhouses, and best of all, the long walk through the grounds to Dan Polryn's office.

At first Polryn did not take kindly to her intervention, having just accustomed himself to the job, but Helen, aware of how much she needed him, was at pains to placate him. She took no interest in the animals themselves, but their yield of milk, the price they fetched at Newton Abbot market; why that was a different matter. And it was this brought her to her first clash with her daughter. If the figures were right, it was a prime time to sell.

'They shall go tomorrow,' she told Polryn.

He hesitated. He was a countryman born and bred, with no sentiment in him, but even he paused over this one.

''Tis Miss Julia's favourite, milady.'

'A *cow?* What do you mean?'

'Nursed it as a calf, she did. Proper fond of it, she be.'

Helen frowned. 'But her yield's been down this twelvemonth. She's past her time already. No, my mind's made up.'

Next day, however, attracted by the noise in the yard, she went to investigate and found her daughter in violent argument with Polryn and the cart driver.

'What's all this noise, Julia?' she asked peremptorily.

'He's sending Marigold to market,' she shrieked.

'I ordered it,' said Helen crisply.

Julia's eyes widened. 'But you can't. You can't do it.'

'I can and I shall,' said Helen firmly. 'You're a big girl now. You must understand. She's not earning her keep.'

'I hate you,' said Julia shouting wildly, 'Hate you. Everything was all right before you came back.' She burst into tears and ran screaming into the house.

Helen saw Polryn staring at her and reddened. She hesitated, then said wearily,

'Take her back to the field, Polryn.'

Strangely enough, the episode, instead of losing her respect amongst the staff, gained her some. At the news that milady had a heart after all, Polryn and his men became more co-operative, and gradually a semblance of order was brought into the chaos. By the following autumn the harvest bode well fair to be a bumper yield. The harvesting had been hard work. Helen had insisted on taking part. For the excellent result meant more than just poring over figures; it mean superintending the sowing, of putting her theories into practice, of taking advice, going cap in hand to local farmers and seeking their comments and advice, some of which she took, some she set aside.

Polryn was good but he had no imagination. He could plod along in the old channels, but he had to learn to seek out new methods, new ideas. That was her task. A farmer, she thought to herself bitterly. All this way. From Bethnal Green to being a lady, and finding that it didn't mean a life of ease, of luxury and security, but as hard work as ever a costermonger faced in Bethnal Green. And worse because here one was on one's own.

Clad in only an old cotton gown, for the September sun was still warm, and relieved for once from the constriction of the ridiculous corsets demanded by the day's fashion, she stood in Five Acre field and watched the figures symmetrically engaged in the harvesting, the upwards sweep of the scythes, the rhythmical movement of the bodies, like a chorus line in a Gala show. How far away that seemed. All she possessed now for a stage was the hot sun, the smell of corn in her nostrils and the sight of those hundred men scything a harvest that would set Monkswater on its feet for years to come. By the side of the field the women stood chattering, stooking the hay into bundles, loading it onto the horse wagons; it was hard work though for them it was a holiday, away from the hearth, away from the daily worry of what to eat. This day's work would put food in their stomachs for weeks to come. A holiday indeed.

With a rare sigh of satisfaction she strolled away up to the field harvested yesterday. She loved this particular patch. It was a small one, but it always got most sun and hence was harvested first. Bounded by woodland on three sides, the fourth open to the country around, it was a kingdom on its own. It was here she would walk if she wanted to be alone, walk in the woodland with its bluebells and anemones, and its blackberries in the autumn, the cool lush air almost compensating her for the loss of London's streets fresh after a shower of rain, the smell of wet pavements, and damp trees.

She sat down by a haystack which being incomplete as yet, had a jutting out stook which made a splendid seat, and swung her legs clear of the ground. She lifted up her face to the sun and shutting her eyes to feel its warmth on her face, fell asleep.

'Helen.'

Startled, she sat up, and shielded her eyes against the fierce sun to see who spoke. It was a dim shape against the sun, standing by the trees. It was a trick of the sunlight. As the sun patterns danced in front of her eyes, all colours of the rainbow, it seemed to her that Harlequin stood there, motionless, waiting for her. She stretched out her arms tentatively. Still half asleep—

'Harlequin,' she whispered, 'come to me.'

As the figure detached itself from the trees, her eyes became accustomed to the sun's glare.

'I'm sorry if I startled you, Helen.'

Jack looked at her compassionately. The gentleness in his eyes was because he had been shaken seeing her sleeping there defenceless, her face cleaned of its bitterness and sorrow, as so often he'd watched her sleep on the pillow and would place a kiss on her cheek before dropping back into sleep himself.

Memory made his voice harsh, as he went through the formalities, 'How are you? How are the children?'

She answered briefly, watching him warily. Inside her heart was leaping with joy. He had come to claim her again. Already her mind was racing ahead, planning, plotting. Oh to be in his arms again. Perhaps—even now... He sat beside her on the hay stook and she put her arms round him.

He sat very still, then with a small sigh gently removed them.

'No, Helen, no.'

'No?'

In his city clothes he looked an incongruous figure in that bright field.

'What then?' She was puzzled.

'Etty—' he began.

She turned from him abruptly. 'I don't want to hear of Etty,' she said sharply. 'She has nothing to do with us. *Nothing.*'

'She has everything to do with it, Helen.'

'Yes,' said Helen bitterly. 'She stole you from me.'

He flushed angrily. 'How can you say that, Helen? Your own sister. You love her. If you knew how much you hurt her when you turned her away—'

'Why didn't you come to me, Jack? Why, why, *why?* When you knew I was back in London. I went back for you, to our home, and you weren't there. It was empty. We were going to be married, Jack. How could you; how could she—without a word—'

His face was full of agony. 'You betrayed me again, Helen,' he said dully. *'Again.* Damn you. How could you?'

'Betray you? I don't understand. How did I betray you?'

'You never asked Randolph for a divorce,' he said slowly. 'Never. You lied to me again and again. You didn't want to marry me. Didn't want my child. You wanted your lord, your coronet. Our love meant nothing to you—'

She was white. 'I was coming to you. I left you a note telling you I loved you. Oh, couldn't you have trusted me, darling? I was coming.' There was anguish in her voice. 'It took me a long time to make my decision—all my life I'd been fighting for respectability, and security, and you were asking me to give it all up. I had to think about it, I had to. But you must have known I'd come in the end. I couldn't do without you. I still can't live without you. You're mine. We belong to each other. There's no one else.'

He got up abruptly from her side, and

stood with his back to her, fighting his emotion. Then he turned and faced her. 'Yes there is, Helen. There always will be. Always. We did belong to each other once. But it's over.'

'Then why did you come?' she cried out. 'Why come to torment me?'

'I came to plead with you, to forget the past, come back to London. To us, to the stage, to see Etty again—'

'No.'

'Helen,' he said slowly. 'There's a reason you should come, should be Etty's loving sister again. I came to tell you—'

'What?' Her heart was full of fear.

'We have a daughter, Helen. Your niece.'

She stared at him, grief and jealousy fighting within her. 'No,' she moaned. 'No, no, no.'

He came forward and seized her hands. 'Helen, please try. For all our sakes. We've named her for you—Helen.'

She wrenched her hands away and tears ran uninterruptedly down her cheeks. She could only shake her head in pain. Their daughter. Where was the child of her and Jack's love? Where was that buried hillside?

'Jack,' her voice was choking, 'I realize— if you've a daughter, I know you can't leave Etty now. I know we can't even be lovers. But this you must give me. You owe it to me. Tell me that you still love me.'

He stood very still, looked blindly away and then began to turn from her.

She halted him by the strength in her voice. 'Jack, you never lie. Tell me you no longer love me.'

There was a short pause. Then he said firmly, 'The cock crew three times, Helen. I love Etty now. Only Etty.'

From that moment she forced herself to hate Jack Waters, hate him with all the steadfastness with which she had hitherto loved him, for hate was easier than love to overcome pain. As the sun went down that evening, Helen stood alone in that small field, twisting the strings of her sunbonnet over and over in her hand. And as the sun sank over the green hills, she made a vow. A vow that Helen Hill, not Helen Gleven, would repay the Waters, man and woman, for all the pain they had caused her. That never by word or deed would she acknowledge their presence; that as Helen Hill's star rose so theirs should fall. They were the enemy to be vanquished by whatever means. Devon was no longer her home. Her place was in London, as it had always been. London was where the theatre was—and where Jack Waters was. Already it was easier, as though by telling herself she was repudiating love, it was thereby accomplished now that she was taking action.

And so to the day she had taken Ambrose Pearl's arm and walked into the dilapidated building in Duke Street.

'We'll call it Crowns.' Her eyes were bright and determined.

'A fitting topping for a duke,' murmured Ambrose, his arm around her waist possessively.

Six months later, the theatre was ready, white and gold replacing dingy brown and red, elegant light blue seating, a refurbished stage, with up to date machinery. Helen had been in her element, superintending, discussing, arguing, charming local residents who were alarmed at the thought of yet another theatre. There was not a word from Duke's. Sometimes she had caught sight of a top-hatted figure walking into Duke's stage door. Her heart jumped, though, not so much at the sight of Jack for which she was prepared, but at the other familiar figures—Lights, Props, the wardrobe mistress, from whom she was irrevocably set apart. At first she had determined to ignore everyone from Duke's but wise counsel prevailed. She might need these people. So her vengeance was reserved for Jack Waters—and his wife.

She had studiously kept away from their first nights, determined not to witness that hated carriage arrive and she and he descend—together.

Now her own first production was well under way. She had played safe for this opening play by reviving *The School for Scandal*. As yet she had no playwright, and rather than revive more recent successes, she preferred to play in a field where she would not have to risk following in the footsteps of another living actress who had made a particular part her own.

Let London see that Helen Hill was back, secure and confident in her own right, and then she could afford to branch out and experiment with new playwrights. With Pearl's help she established a reasonably good company around her. Backstage and front of house they were first class. Neither Pearl nor Helen could afford to lose money on this venture. But on stage they were carefully picked neither to compete with nor to be conspicuously deficient beside Helen herself.

'To Crowns, my dear, and its queen.'

Ambrose lifted his glass, looking at Helen covetously, much as he would a Meissen figurine. And indeed her dainty figure would do very well in porcelain, he thought meditatively, save for the eyes.

No figurine could capture the flashing seductiveness of those dark eyes. He had sat in the resplendent box that evening and watched her on stage taking bow after bow as the new theatre of Crowns opened. Not a wild success—but a safe one, that would ensure patrons would return. They felt at home there, they liked the new decor, the new company. They would include it on their theatre-going itinerary. It was enough for the moment.

Helen arched her head coquettishly, aware of her triumph. 'Not tired, Ambrose? Not tired of your conquest? Tired of your bargain?'

He smiled. 'Custom cannot stale your infinite variety, my dear. Nor,' he added, 'age wither you.'

'Hardly tactful, Ambrose,' she said pouting, 'to remind me I am forty.'

'Come, my nightingale,' he whispered placatingly. 'Let me show you how tired I am.'

His voice was curiously caressing, and tired after the long day and too much wine, she responded with more ease than she expected. Making love with Ambrose had not proved the ordeal she had anticipated. At first she had been stiff and unbending with sheer terror as all her former fears swept over her suddenly, but he had proved an expert lover and gradually she had found herself responding. Yet though her body responded, her heart remained numb. She felt gratitude towards him but no other emotion. For his part it was perhaps this very withdrawal that increased her attraction for him. It was a challenge. But something told him that he should not get too close to her—although it might prove dangerously easy with Helen Hill.

'Why, Owen, what a surprise!'

It should not have been, for she had been following him for a good half-hour or more to contrive this accidental meeting.

Owen Orford nervously doffed his hat. 'Miss Hill, that is to say, Lady Gleven.' The years were adding few lines to his face and success seemed not to have laid her mark on him. He still looked the ill at ease young man she had first met at Duke's. 'I am delighted to meet you.' He did not look it. Gossip in the theatre flies on wings, and it had not gone unnoticed that though Crowns was but a stone's throw away, Miss Hill had never returned to Duke's for old times' sake. She was friendly enough, if she met its members outside the theatre, but there was a whisper of a family quarrel, or a quarrel between Mr Waters and Miss Hill, and Owen Orford did not intend to get mixed up in it.

He may not have intended it, but somehow he did. Somehow he found himself at the Piccadilly sitting at a table sandwiched between potted ferns, and Helen Hill smiling at him in the way that had first swept him off his feet—that special smile, that once he had thought meant she was a friend of his; looked on him as a person of importance in her life. And so he listened.

Then. 'Oh no,' he said shocked. 'I couldn't do that.' Indeed he couldn't, he went on to explain... Jack Waters was more than just an employer, a buyer of his plays, he owed to him his whole success in the theatre. As, he reminded himself, did Helen.

'But you also owe it to me,' said Helen winningly. 'I made your first play a success on the stage, didn't I Owen?' And as he looked into her large brown eyes, he realized that yes, that was true. She had brought his heroine to life and given him fame. If he had reflected a moment, he might have realized that she brought his heroine to life because she had been written for her, and round her. But he did not reflect, and before long he was realizing that what Helen said was only too true. He was stuck in a rut at Duke's.

Together they were a team. With her as manager as well as his leading lady they could not fail. Or so they thought.

The Ladies of Glen Carron was a spectacular failure. The speedy writing was not good enough to save the weak plot nor Helen's acting to save the deficiencies of an inadequate cast.

It was not helped by a blistering review in the *London Witness* the following morning. The review was written by Ambrose Pearl.

'How dare you? How *can* you?' stormed Helen. 'Your own theatre.'

'My dear Helen, you must reflect. I have my integrity. It was a bad play. I told you so at the beginning.'

'But you didn't have to ensure that no one will come to see it,' Helen ranted.

'Oh yes,' said Ambrose, softly. 'Yes I did. That way people will trust my judgement when I say something else is a good play.'

'But what about me?' said Helen furiously. 'You might at least have shown some mercy on me.'

'Oh no, Helen. If you can't have a success, if you are faced with a failure then make it a memorable one.'

Chapter Ten

Helen looked out of her office window with satisfaction. Once more the rival pit queues outside the two theatres were embroiled in shouting abuse. Tonight it was particularly boisterous, as it was a first night at Duke's. Not for the first time she wished she could creep out to watch, and not have to wait until Ambrose reported to her. She had her spies planted there of course, but it was difficult to get an all-round picture without being there. She wanted to see Jack fail, she told herself, shutting out pain.

In May this year, 1910, King Edward the Peacemaker had died. Under the umbrella of his enthusiasm the theatre had attained a peak of respectability, but the whole profession benefited. By night London sparkled and the theatres were her jewels. Entertainment and escapism reigned supreme. Ruritanian fantasy swept Britain; in musical operetta, *The Balkan Princess* had England humming; in romantic drama *The Prisoner of Zenda* with the handsome George Alexander in the lead, set many a Holloway heart aflame, lulling Londoners into a panacea that ignored events brewing on the real-life Balkan stage.

Tucked away at the Royal Court, Granville Barker was struggling towards a more immediate form of the drama, and a playwright called George Bernard Shaw remained adamantly convinced of his destiny. But the majority of playgoers remained faithful to the harmless trifles and dramas of drawing-room comedy.

The noise level outside heightened, and Helen looked out again with some alarm. Only two months ago it had come to fisticuffs and policemen had been called. It had been satisfying in one way, but not good for the theatre in another. She could recognize by now the familiar figures in Duke's pit queue. The stout woman with the red face in the old bonnet and trailing red petticoat and the eager youth who always came equipped with a large notepad to record his impressions presumably for the children and grandchildren of a far distant future. There were the entertainers who unlike the pit queues had no allegiances. They travelled the length of the two rival queues oblivious to the taunts raging over their heads. The barrel organ grinder, the double shuffler, the conjuror, the warbler. Helen had watched them so many times before, yet it reassured and heartened her to see the ritual. Seeing her look out, her own loyal pit queue began to sing out lustily and she hastily withdrew.

The rivalry had been building ever since Crowns opened, and the rumours of a feud between the two managers became fact; the theatrical society of London had settled down with interest to see who would win. So far it had been stalemate. Jack Waters' company gained by being a solid all-round company with excellent actors and actresses who balanced each other and who gave a first class evening's entertainment. Helen Hill's plays were essentially a vehicle for Helen Hill. Gone were the days when the limelight followed the leading character round the stage leaving the rest of the cast in semi-darkness, but the consensus was that Helen Hill felt this had been a great loss. Not that her fans minded, for she was Helen Hill; she could do no wrong.

She had an instinct for knowing which roles would suit her, and which required a range beyond her powers. She recalled Ambrose's voice in its clipped nasal tones: 'You lack the gift of tears, my dear,' and was clever enough now to accept the implicit warning. So Helen and Owen Orford clung to the formula that made them famous—the light comedies which demanded polished technique above all. Sometimes she hankered after a more dramatic role but instinct told her that it would be foolish to depart from what her public wanted. For herself she might have dared, but the thought that this might be playing into her enemy's hands—for thus she thought of Jack now—deterred her.

Jack, on the other hand, was venturing into yet uncharted waters. At first she had been triumphant when after Owen's departure he started to vary his programme from drawing-room comedy to take in a wider range; then she became uneasy. If he succeeded in a field remote from Crowns', she would lose her power to rival him.

Tonight was, she knew, no ordinary first night. Her inside source, an assistant props man, had told her that expense on this production had exceeded anything before mounted at Duke's. It was Jack's big gamble, his first excursion into Shakespeare: *As You Like It*. Helen was secretly envious. She had assumed, wrongly, he was doing this because he knew it was an area she could not possibly compete in. She neither knew nor cared about Shakespeare. She had dismissed him as a certain loser. But Jack had apparently set his heart on it, so her source told her. It had always been his ambition.

Always? She could not remember his speaking of it when they had lain close, talking of their plans for life, for their life together. With a pang of bitterness she pulled her thoughts away. Had there been yet one more secret he had kept from her?

She adjusted the final touches to her make-up for Lady Jessica Stirling, heroine of Owen's latest comedy. For all she was forty-five, her figure remained as trim as it had twenty years earlier, and the brightness of her eyes overshadowed the small lines at the corners. With an effort she concentrated on tonight's performance. Time enough to think of Jack Waters when Ambrose came to take her to dinner to tell her all.

Yet he would not do so. 'Wait till you see the notice tomorrow,' was all he would say. Helen knew him well enough by now to know he would not be persuaded, and desisted. Her heart sank, for it must have been a glowing success, otherwise he would have told her now.

Helen was, however, wrong. When she opened the paper the next day, resting in bed, sipping her coffee, it was to read one of the most blistering reviews Ambrose had ever given of a play:

'*As You Like It*—at Duke's
   It was not.
   There was once a genius, a playwright named Shakespeare. One could not recall him last evening. He lives at the Royal

Court, he even lives, a prisoner, at His Majesty's, but he expired before Rosalind had entered Arden on the stage of Duke's last night. *Et ego in Arcadia* to misquote the tag; but I found myself in no Arcadia in Arden last night...'

Helen sat up, astounded, delighted. She raised the telephone which Ambrose had installed from its hook and asked for his number.

'Darling, thank you,' she said. 'Thank you, oh thank you.'

There was a pause. Then Ambrose's voice replied in measured tones: 'My dear Helen, I write as I see. It is not a tribute to you. I am a critic.'

Nevertheless Helen descended the stairs in an unusually good mood. It was such a beautiful day she felt in no hurry to go down to the theatre; its thousand and one managerial problems could wait a little. She might visit Ambrose, lunch with him. Or William Bursdon, her leading man. Such a good-looking boy. It would be pleasant to dine in public with him. Her plans for the day received a sharp setback, however. The door opened and Briggs announced: 'Mrs Waters, madam.'

'Etty!'

The cry was wrenched out of Helen before she had considered. She made to move away, to turn her back, but Briggs had already closed the door. They were alone. Helen turned round, and walked to the far side of the room.

'Helen, look at me please!'

The heart-rending cry in that familiar voice turned Helen slowly round to face her sister. She was rounder now; the golden hair now a light brown, flecked with grey, her face more lined, but despite its current distress the face of one who had not known suffering. Not like Helen's own, where the lines were accentuated.

'Helen, this has got to stop,' burst out Etty. 'Please, please, let us talk.'

Helen remained standing.

'You had better sit down,' she said through stiff lips.

Etty looked round vaguely and quickly sat on the nearest chair. Despite her intention of remaining on her feet and keeping the advantage. Helen suddenly felt her legs weak and she too sat down, gripping the edge of the chair, as though for reassurance.

'You and Jack must stop this ridiculous rivalry,' said Etty quietly. 'You're tearing yourselves to pieces, and all for nothing. At least, you're tearing *yourself* to pieces, and soon Jack will have to start retaliating.'

'Retaliate? That seems to imply that I am at fault.'

'It's not like that at all,' said Etty, wearily. 'But don't you see, Helen? If this rift gets any wider, Jack will be forced into some kind of action. This play—this experiment with Shakespeare—was his last way out, to take his path away from yours, and you've ruined it. What can he do now but fight you, if you go on this way? You are business people, theatre people and whatever private reasons you have for—anger—the theatre should come first.'

Helen seized on just one point: 'I've ruined it, you say. What have I done?'

Etty flushed—and pointed at the newspaper lying on the table. 'That notice. How could you, Helen? How could you get your—get Mr Pearl to write that review. It's so unfair. Jack is ruined by it. He's so unhappy. We've spent so much on the production and now—' She began to cry.

Helen rose to her feet in fury. 'How dare you suggest that *I* had anything to do with that notice—Mr Pearl writes his own notices. He's never influenced.'

'He's your lover isn't he?' said Etty implacably and unconvinced.

The sight of Etty in tears did not move her as once it might. 'I will not be insulted by you, Etty,' she said quietly. 'I've done nothing to you to warrant that.'

'You've insulted my husband,' shouted Etty.

'Your husband,' said Helen trembling. 'Look what he did to me. He swore to love me for life, took me to bed, seduced me—and look what happened. I tell you, Etty, have a care. He's fickle. Who is his leading lady now? You are nearly fifty, after all.'

'Shut up,' Etty shouted, 'you foul mouthed—' They both stopped abruptly and stared at each other. Across the chasm of the years, the spectre of Bethnal Green rose up. Conflicting emotions passed over both their faces, and they were silent. Then:

'You'd better go,' said Helen at last, without expression.

'Yes,' said Etty.

As she reached the door, hand on the knob she turned back quickly, hesitating, with a quick glance at Helen.

In that brief look something hovered, some word to be spoken. Something in Helen cried out to cross those few yards and take Etty in her arms, and comfort her as she had done when she was a child. It would be so easy, so very easy...

But she could not move.

The new king was crowned on a sunny day in June 1911. Forgotten for the moment were the shadows between the countries of the new king and his cousins of Germany and Russia, forgotten the bitterness of the women's suffragism, the parliamentary schisms, the Irish problem and the social unrest. All gathered to do homage to the new monarch on whose empire the sun would never set.

Amongst the peers of the realm present were Lord Gleven, and his wife Helen, in the coronation robes donned for the second time in ten years. Randolph had brought the children up to the London house where Briggs and Mrs Briggs were making fine sport with the children. Robert was now a serious-minded sixteen-year-old declaring his intention of joining his father's old regiment, Julia a rebellious nineteen, here in London much against her will. Helen, unable to spare the time had arranged with someone else to bring her out in society but the season had not gone well. Firstly, after all her careful planning to meet a suitable fellow aristocrat, the one person in whom she had displayed any interest was a young man she met at a public art gallery. Helen had quickly scotched that, but from then on Julia had shown decreasing interest in the social whirl.

There was further cause for anxiety. Randolph was not well at the coronation. He was much thinner, and had a hacking cough that constantly troubled him. He had spent some months the previous winter in Switzerland, but it had done little lasting good.

The gods were not favourable to Helen's plans. In the middle of rehearsals for a new production to open the autumn season, she was summoned to Devon. She immediately sent a message that she would come in a few days. She needed that time to sort out rehearsals, find replacements and postpone the opening of the season.

By the time she got there, Randolph was very weak. He was lying on a daybed in the large drawing-room overlooking the terrace. He was pleased to see her, and Helen's heart smote her for delaying her arrival.

'You're looking better, Randolph,' she lied.

He just smiled and took her hand.

'Glad to see you, old girl,' was all he said, but he kept her hand in his. She had only just arrived in time for the next day she was summoned urgently to his bedroom by the doctor. Jane Wickham, who had been keeping vigil by his bed, rose reluctantly and left the room. His eyes were closed and he was breathing very heavily. Helen leaned over him.

'Randolph,' she whispered in alarm. He couldn't really be dying as the doctor said.

Not Randolph—why Randolph was always there; she needed him—he was part of her life. He couldn't die. Fear stabbed at her as he opened his eyes. For a moment she thought he did not recognize her.

She took his hand in hers. 'Oh, Randolph, I haven't been a very good wife to you.'

He did not seem to understand what she said, and searched her face anxiously.

'Helen,' he said with difficulty. 'Helen— we haven't done badly, old thing, have we?'

'No, Randolph, no,' said Helen choking.

'Robert—' he began. Then his eyes closed. The nurse felt his pulse and looked at Helen.

'It's very near, Lady Gleven,' she said.

Helen's eyes filled with tears. She sat there for a moment, quiet, then with a small sigh put a kiss on his forehead and left the room. Jane Wickham was sitting outside and looked up fearfully, her face swollen with tears. Helen stopped.

'He's waiting for you,' she said quietly.

A quarter of an hour later, her son came into the drawing-room and closed the door behind him. Helen looked at him and he nodded. Helen rose to her feet, crossed to her son, took him in her arms and kissed him.

'Oh, Robert, I promise,' she said, 'that I

304

will be a better helpmeet to the new Lord Gleven than I was to the last.'

Plunged once more into financial affairs, wills, and probate, appeasement of tenants, negotiating with Polryn, inculcating Robert into the ways of the Gleven estate, it was three months before she could return to London, three months when she was forced to rent out Crowns, three months when the theatre was at the back of her mind.

Christmas had passed before Helen was reasonably satisfied that Monkswater could be left under Polryn's management with Robert, and Julia, thankful that her mother had relented on forcing her into London society, running the household.

Julia was a puzzle to Helen. Helen sensed enough of her own brooding restlessness in her daughter's personality to make her sure that she would not long be satisfied with domesticity, or marrying some plodding local squire. The theatre? She had shown no interest in anything —except that painting of hers. Julia was now pestering to be allowed to go to art college of all things, the Slade. The idea was ridiculous as Helen had pointed out.

On New Year's Eve 1911, Helen gazed dispiritedly into the looking glass. Was it tonight—or was it Hallowe'en—where you must gaze in the mirror and see your future? All she could see was the face of a woman who in four months' time would be forty-seven. How long could she go on playing comedy heroines? How long continue as Ambrose Pearl's mistress? Not that she cared for him that much, but it gave an excitement to life. She was a widow now, although still the mistress of Monkswater till Robert married. And what would happen then? She would be the Dowager Lady Gleven. It was a bleak prospect. Monkswater was deserted now. The servants were celebrating in their quarters and the sounds of revelry floated up to her; Robert and Julia were celebrating the arrival of 1912 at a local ball—for young people. All over the estate in their tiny cottages tenants were celebrating. And she, Helen, was alone.

When she awoke the next morning, a pale sun was shining. January 1st. A new year. With new heart she looked in the mirror again. True, there were lines, but there was character. True, she was widowed, but she was a desirable widow. She took a walk through the grounds and her footsteps led her to the field where so many years ago Jack had rejected her. The love she had thought was dead swelled up again in her heart. The pain had not gone away. It was still there, still as sharp.

'Jack,' she whispered. 'Oh, Jack!' What was that poem by Rupert Brooke that Julia had shown her?

'Breathless we flung us on the windy hill,
Laughed in the sun, and kissed the lovely
grass.'

She heard his voice again saying, 'I will love you always, Helen. Till death us do part.'

'And then you suddenly cried and turned
away.'

It hadn't been death that parted them. He'd said he no longer loved her. He'd loved her for twenty years. Could one just stop like that, no matter what happened? Between them now lay a chasm so deep that it could not be breached. She had done great harm to him, but she was forced to admit he had never hit back. Surely that meant something? It was almost thirty years since they first met. Was she the same Helen? She was getting old yes, but Etty was older. Filled with sudden recklessness she knew she must find out if Jack still loved her. She could do nothing, even if he did, she acknowledged.

But just to know, would mean so much. Suppose she tried to heal the rift. After all,

Etty had suggested it...

She considered and rejected the idea of a formal meeting. No, surprise was the thing. She returned to London and began the wearying business of taking over Crowns again. Ambrose was urbanely pleased to see her again, though she doubted much whether he had missed her. It rankled, despite the fact her thoughts were all of Jack now. She picked up her script of Owen's latest play, and, despite herself, a small sigh escaped her as she saw, *'Lady Mary prances skittishly round the room.'* Skittish! She began to suspect that since his marriage Owen's conception of Helen had begun to be intermingled with that of his wife. She had resented his marrying, but being unable to say so openly, had played a gracious hostess to the mousy Mary.

She gathered her company together once more, glad that William Bursdon was available—though this was hardly surprising since she did not pick actors of a calibre that their services were greatly in demand elsewhere.

One day in March, when spring was in the air, and the new production safely established into its run, she knew the time had come. Gathering her yellow parasol and drawing on her cream gloves, she gave one final look at herself in the large dressing-room mirror in which she was accustomed to check every detail of dress meticulously before she went on stage. And that in a sense was where she was going, for the most important role of her life.

The stage doorkeeper at Duke's gaped in astonishment, seemingly wondering whether the door should be slammed in her face. She gave him no chance to consider. With a cool nod and a 'good-day' she swept past him up the well-known corridors. At the end she hesitated—would his office be where once it was? She caught sight of Edwards, her spy, pretending to be busy in the wings and summoned him.

'No, ma'am,' he said in a scared voice. 'Up at top it is now. Quieter you see.' All around people were stopping their work, low growls of inimicable disapproval —mixed with unwilling curiosity as to what Helen Hill was doing in their midst. She swept through the door as she had so often all those years before, a vision in cream and yellow.

This monster villain she had created looked just the same. A little older, a little tireder in the face, but it was Jack, *her* Jack. The curly brown hair was a little sprinkled with grey now. She had seen him in the distance of course over the years, his back view disappearing into the theatre, coming out, clambering into cabs, but there he was a remote figure separated by glass. Now the shock of seeing him face to face almost deflected her from her course.

'Helen.'

She had been right to take him by surprise, for he was not quick enough to hide that sudden flash of emotion that crossed his face. Then the mask fell. He rose to his feet, slowly.

'Lady Gleven. An honour indeed for you to revisit Duke's.'

'Aren't you going to ask me to sit down, Jack?' She removed her gloves. He stiffened but short of throwing her out, there was nothing he could do. Years of social courtesy could not go unheeded.

'Of course.'

There was white around his lips, Helen observed, feeling completely in control of the situation. She sat down, not on the chair he indicated by his desk, but on the sofa so that he must needs sit in the armchair by her. He did not, however, choosing to bring forward an upright chair, so that once again she was forced to look up to him.

He waited, guarded, that small muscle trembling at the corner of his lip. She knew it very well. So well. She wanted to put out her hand and stroke his face, let her hands dwell on the shape as once they had done so frequently, curl his hair round her finger, kiss his eyelids. It seemed ridiculous to her that she could not. Instead:

'It's time we mended this rift, Jack.'

She bent her head towards him so that her perfume would be in his nostrils, for it had been his favourite.

'It takes two for a rift, Lady Gleven. What have I ever done to hurt you?' His voice was remote, polite.

'What have you done to hurt me?' Her eyes were full of indignation.

'Professionally.' The tone was cold. 'That's what we're discussing, aren't we? I created you, I made you into the star you are today. I guided you at every step. And you ask me what I've done to hurt *you?*' Bitterness crept into his voice. 'You use every trick you know, to suborn my cast, my playwrights, my stage staff. I change the kind of plays I put on, only to have you follow suit, and if you can't wreck them by other means, you arrange your very schedule to upset mine. You plant your spies among my staff...'

Involuntarily she jumped. So he knew about that.

'Oh yes.' He turned a cold eye on her. 'Poor Edwards. It's quite amusing to feed him rumours from time to time so that he can carry them off to you like a faithful spaniel. Did you know he had a sick wife?

311

I couldn't sack him, could I? And you certainly wouldn't employ him. Not after his use for you had gone.'

She shivered. 'How can you speak so cruelly to me?'

'Quite easily, Helen.'

Inside her a voice registered that he had called her Helen. He could not be so emotionless as his voice suggested. It gave her confidence.

'Jack,' she said urgently, 'we can stop this feud very easily, but the other rift, the greater one, you and I—can't we—?'

He seemed to freeze, then he said lightly: 'There is no you and I, Helen. I made that clear years ago.'

'But don't you ever think of those days? We *lived* together. Don't you ever remember things—remember the milk jug with the chip you'd never throw away, remember the time we made love before the fire, and found out later Reynolds was in the kitchen all the time, remember when—'

'I remember only that I have a wife I love, Helen, and you have a lover,' he said severely.

She flushed, then shrugged as though his words had not cut her. 'I told you,' she tried to laugh, 'on our hill that day that I should marry a lord and take lovers, now didn't I? Now you must remember that, surely?' She rose and moved towards him pleadingly and he jumped up and moved back as though to ward her off.

But she was too close, and he had to defend himself with words.

'How could you?' he burst out. 'Ambrose Pearl. That paunchy little lecher with no heart, without anything he cares for in the world except his acid tongue, who cares not if he ruins lives for the sake of a joke, and you go to bed with him. You, Helen, you.'

'Jealous, Jack?'

It was out before she stopped to think. Jack covered his face with his hands. Then he raised his head and looked at her, his face flushed.

'God help me,' he whispered slowly. 'God help us all. I think I must be.'

She gave a low cry and ran to him. 'You love me still, don't you? It wasn't true what you said all those years ago.' She realized it with wonder for her stupidity. 'You lied to me, didn't you? You still love me, never stopped loving me?'

'Yes,' he said dully. 'I still love you.' Then a change came over his face. 'Helen, I love you, dear God, I love you so much.'

Then he was seizing her and kissing her, holding so tightly she was crushed against him. Then they were murmuring small

313

broken words, that over twenty years fell away from them, and they were back on their hillside. But now it wasn't a hillside but a sofa, a sofa in an office high above the London traffic that Helen Hill and Jack Waters were reunited.

Afterwards they sat for a long time quite still, holding each other's hand. A great happiness and peace filled her heart, as though nothing outside this small world had power to harm now.

'Nothing can touch us now, can it, Jack?'

'We'll always remember this,' he replied slowly. 'Our hillside wherever it is.'

A faint chill came over her. 'But there'll be so many other times to add to them?' she said questioningly.

He brought her hands up to his face, and buried his face in them. 'Darling,' he said quietly, 'there can't be. You know that. We know now for always what we mean to each other. But it shouldn't have happened. I will always be truly thankful it did. But we can't see each other again.'

She stared at him uncomprehendingly. 'But it's all different now. I'm a widow. I know we can't be married. But you can leave Etty—she could go down to Monkswater, they'll look after her—'

314

He raised a hand in protest but she rushed on.

'Or we could go away, like you suggested before. Go away and live abroad. Anything, just so that we'd be together. For the rest of our lives, Jack.'

He looked at her, his face full of anguish and misery. 'No, Helen. No. I can't leave Etty.'

She couldn't understand what he was saying to her. Then as she took it in, she pleaded. 'If you can't—because of the child—your little girl—then we can still meet, can't we? Like this? No one would ever know. And we'd have each other. I wouldn't mind.'

'But I would. Darling no, you'll never realize what it's costing me to say it, but no. Helen, we've got to forget this. Our lives have parted—we've chosen different paths.'

'But we belong—I love you.'

'And I love you, Helen. But never, never will I say that again.'

Slowly she rose to her feet, picked up her parasol, put on her gloves and hat with infinite care, and walked out of the room without a backward glance.

'But, Helen, I can't do that.' Owen Orford was horrified.

'You can, Owen. You will, or if you

won't I'll find another author to do it.'

'But it's not honourable,' blurted out Owen feebly.

'Honourable?' Helen considered the word and rejected it as having no connection with Duke's theatre, or more particularly its manager. She had offered him all her love and he had refused it. She was bruised and humiliated.

One month later, just one night before Duke's theatre mounted its new lavish costume romance based on the theme of Napoleon and Josephine, Crowns mounted a new surprise production based on the theme of Josephine and Napoleon, Helen Hill playing Josephine. It was a particularly splendid production, a departure for Crowns, with Helen's part more glittering than ever, lavish in every way; Owen had refused to give way and write the script despite Helen's goading—it must be that wife of his, she stormed to Ambrose.

Amused, Ambrose decided to come to Helen's aid. Pearl had no particular quarrel with Waters himself but he had always fancied his hand at writing, and when Owen threw in the sponge he had taken it up with great pleasure.

The Waters' production was the better one, with a good script that would stand the test of time more than the glittering of Ambrose Pearl's gems. But it stood no chance. The laughing stock of London for opening one day later, Jack Waters' production was withdrawn after one week. Across the road Crowns played to full houses. Two months later there was an announcement in *The Times* that the lease of Duke's theatre was available. What plans its manager had were not known. It was a nine day sensation, then the theatre-going public turned their attention elsewhere and forgot Jack Waters.

With Duke's now taken by a musical comedy team much of the zest went out of Helen's life. There seemed little point in work any more. Her enmity with Jack Waters was undiminished, but without his constant presence at Duke's to feed and torment her, it receded to burn as a glowing ember somewhere deep inside her. Her shell of charm became harder, the real Helen more and more removed from it.

In the flush of her success in *The Empress Josephine,* she felt beholden to Ambrose Pearl as never before. What a blow for Jack if she married him now. Let him squirm in anguish at the thought of her married to him. It would give an added spice to the marriage. Unfortunately for Helen, perhaps suspecting the true reason, Ambrose Pearl declined the honour.

'Too charming of you, my dear Helen,

but ageing though I am, I have never considered myself the marrying kind. No, pray do let us continue our—er—friendship if you wish, but marriage, I fear, is not for me.'

It was another rebuff. *If* you wish. He had been coming to her bed less and less often, it was true. She was beginning to age. In fact Pearl was starting to regard Helen critically. Handsome maturity was giving way to definite middle age. It could pass on a stage, but not in a bed. And in bed, as at the table, Ambrose Pearl, despite his own lack of personal attraction, was an epicure.

Too late Helen realized he had never loved her for herself. She was a possession and a convenience. But then, she honestly acknowledged to herself, she hadn't loved him. For once someone had repaid her in her own kind. They continued to make love occasionally, but both cynically now, with the desperation of two lonely people. A shifting rock was better than none.

The bells rang out to welcome 1914. She attended the ball at the Savoy with Ambrose Pearl, who liked to be seen on such occasions, and to have Lady Gleven on his arm was the finishing touch. Outside the bells pealed, trumpets sounded, ornate decorations descended from the ceiling, for the delight of the dancers. That night he came home with her, and they made love.

But he did not stay and she felt more alone than if he had not come. She went to the window to watch his departing cab. It seemed to be an omen, leaving with the New Year. She would not see him again, not as a lover. She decided this with a chilling finality. Perhaps she wanted no more of love. Perhaps she was too old for any kind of emotion now.

Next year she would be fifty. What a contrast, she thought, between the public image of Lady Gleven, a laughing, successful beautiful woman at the top of her profession and a peeress of the realm, and Helen Hill, alone in the world. Had she climbed so hard and so high only for this? Jack gone she knew not where; she had heard no word. Ambrose at the end of their affair, Owen married and no longer her devoted servant. Robert was announcing he was taking a commission in the Guards, Julia was obstinately pursuing her art in Devonshire, the estates were running efficiently without her help. Dear God, what was to become of her? She shook herself impatiently. Something needed to be done. So Helen did it.

Three months later, in a large wedding in St George's Church, Hanover Square, Lady Helen Gleven married her leading man, William Bursdon, fifteen years her junior.

And over Europe the storm clouds of war were gathering.

PART FOUR

The Pilgrim Soul

Chapter Eleven

'You're too old.' Helen Hill spoke dispassionately and not unkindly. At fifty-seven she could still—just—pass as a romantic heroine, but poor William at forty-two was past his days as a romantic lead. 'Look at your face.'

Involuntarily William Bursdon glanced in the mirror. One tended to do things that Helen demanded. A habit like the drink he had taken to so easily.

'What's wrong with it?' he muttered. It was all too clear. Puffy, red and blotchy for continuous drinking had only accentuated the faults that had not been so apparent in his youth. And where his face went his figure followed. It was not so much a paunch as a general thickening of the figure that had once cut so dashing a role in evening dress.

Difficult as Helen was as a wife, she was implacable as a manager. William glared at her. 'Too old—if there's anyone round here who's too old, Helen, it's not me.'

There was an icy silence. Then Helen smiled sweetly. 'Older I might be, William, but a talent for acting can help overcome the problem.'

Nevertheless she acknowledged the truth of his words. She needed to change the emphasis of the plays—she would speak to Owen—the heroines should be more mature, more sophisticated, and she needed an older man to play opposite—a mature interesting man, not an ageing juvenile.

'There'll still be room for you, William,' she explained briskly. 'I shall ask Owen to write in some good character parts.'

'Drunk old colonels, on stage for five minutes, I suppose.'

'Since you ask, it seems to me that might be most applicable,' Helen replied equably. 'Unless you prefer to take a job with another company?'

He was silent, as she knew he would be. There was no room on the stage in 1922 for less than sparkling talent. The pressure was too great. She had won.

The old days of the actor-managers had now passed, together with Edwardian society and all its standards, good and bad. They could no longer compete with the investors, managers who put money in front of quality. Now a brave new world beckoned, full of optimism and daring. Helen adapted well—professionally. The kind of play with which she had become associated fitted neatly into an age which concentrated on daring drawing-room comedy, with an extra element of spicy dialogue. Crowns' programme was ready for the Twenties. So why, she wondered, was this the bleakest time of her life?

It had not been a successful marriage. Had William's age and health allowed him to join up after war broke out, it might have been, but rejected first on the grounds of age, and then on the lack of health that fifteen years on the stage had accustomed him to, he continued as Helen's leading man on the stage, escort off and stooge at home.

Unconsciously she had assimilated him into her plan for her life. She had no need of a heart now. She had a fondness for William—as she had had for Randolph. After all, why otherwise would she have yielded her title to become plain Mrs Bursdon. As Ambrose had asked her cynically on hearing of her marriage. 'Could it be, dearest Helen, that you have expectations of being awarded a title that you have earned otherwise than through the marriage bed?'

Helen flushed. Genevieve Ward had become a dame, so why not Helen Hill? Dame Genevieve was not even English born. Whereas Helen Hill...

'Rather a gamble, is it not, dear Helen?

325

Unless of course young Bursdon's prowess in the marriage bed tempted you.' He paused. 'But hardly likely, I feel. The bed was one of the few kingdoms you never felt impelled to conquer.'

At times she resented Ambrose, because he knew her through and through. Or thought he did. Could he not see her heart, which needed only to be warmed to unfold? Yet the fact that he knew her worst side, and still admired her, made his friendship—or alliance—valuable, and when he had died in 1919 on his sixty-fourth birthday half-way through his second dozen Whitstable oysters, she mourned him deeply and sincerely. Jack was gone, and now Ambrose.

There must be no avenues to her real self, for if she allowed one to open, she might have to think about Jack... Nearly ten years since she'd seen him now, and still he lived on in her heart; she told herself that love was dead, that only work remained—and her children. She'd heard that after Duke's closed, he had emigrated, taking Etty and the children to South Africa where they had built up a successful theatre in Johannesburg. She would never see him again. She clung belatedly but with tenacity to her children. Julia was thirty now, the passionate brooding girl turned into a happy handsome woman, married and living in London with a career of her own. Helen was envious. Thus might *she* have looked, had she and Jack married. Julia had become a nurse during the war, had gone to the western front and while there had painted pictures in her meagre spare time of such intensity and power that by 1917 she was an official war artist in great demand by galleries and magazines. Married now to another artist, Joseph Wantage, she was a recognized artist of social conditions.

It was ironic, Helen reflected, that after all the pains she had taken to remove herself from London's East End, her daughter should now be seeking it out. If she were closer to Julia, she could perhaps explain the fearfulness that had made her what she was. What if Julia came across her own relations...? But Julia had no idea of her mother's background, nor ever would have, resolved Helen. The hideousness must remain buried lest even now it swell up to envelop her once again.

Robert remained her joy. How she had suffered every day of the war while he was in France with the Guards. She had pored over the casualty lists; working out the odds against any officer coming through unscathed. Only the wound at the Ancre saved him. It was severe enough to consign him to a desk for the remaining two years of war, wistfully fingering the colours of his MC, and longing to be back in the fight. But he missed Passchendaele, missed the bitter fighting of 1918 and in 1919 came home, decommissioned, to run the estates of Monkswater.

His rare visits to London were the only occasions softness brightened Helen's eyes. Recently he had been coming more often, three times in as many months. Julia had hinted that there was some attraction, some girl he had met, unusual for serious Robert. She had only known him have one love before—the gamekeeper's daughter, a ridiculous black-haired chit, not at all suitable to become the new Lady Gleven. Not that she didn't want Robert to marry. She did. But to the right person.

The Girl in the Castle had swept London by storm. Its catchy modern lyrics and rhythms had London humming and its feet tapping. The story of a Balkan princess who runs away to become a dancer in a Parisian night club was no new thing—something of the sort might well have kept the stage busy twelve years before—but the modernness of its heroine as played by its charming dynamic star Evelyn Earl was. Her pert impish face framed with golden shingled hair and dancing eyes shone down from every hoarding, and took London into the hectic gaiety of the Twenties.

Half a mile away at Crowns, Helen was busily bringing domestic comedy into the new era of frivolity, with *Two Rings for Mrs Pennington,* a bubble centring on divorce and risqué marital intrigue.

Both plays had been running since the beginning of the year. Both finished in July, as the theatres finished their summer season and prepared to remain dark during August.

And two hundred miles away in Devon the two leading ladies were destined to meet.

'But suppose she doesn't like me?' said Evelyn anxiously.

'Silly goose. As though anybody could not.' And indeed it seemed unlikely, as the staid Lord Gleven looked at her pretty gentle face surrounded by its golden halo.

Monkswater was a-hum awaiting the arrival of her ladyship, for so they still thought of her despite now being Mrs Bursdon. The estates had recovered from the deprivations that war had brought, though in fact it had been comparatively kind to them. While their menfolk were away at war, the women had taken over, determined to preserve the estate and to keep their homes for their men to come home to. Four years later they

329

had come home—some of them. And for those that did not, there were sons to take their places; the estate workers licked their wounds and settled down to making the estate pay its way for their children.

Something had changed, however, and Robert had changed it. No more was it a feudal concern, running itself for the good of the lord of the estate; now there was far more spirit of comradeship, of working together now for the betterment of all. Robert had observed much in his years at the front, and was applying its lessons to the management of the estate. It lacked only a mistress. Hence the excitement when it was known that his lordship had a young lady staying with him—from up Lunnon it was true, but a nice-looking young thing. He hadn't had a young lady since poor Marie, now married and with a family out Torquay way.

And now her ladyship was coming down too. Tongues were wagging as fast as the lawns were trimmed, the hothouses culled for the finest grapes and peaches, the Lagonda given its umpteenth polishing. To the disapproval of the estate the young lady and his lordship had been driving around in the old dog cart, and it made the chauffeur even more determined to do things the proper way when her ladyship came.

Helen rested one hand on the window ledge of the Lagonda. It was a hot enough day for the hood to be down, and for her to bask in the country smells of the hedgerows, and the scent of the hay. Yes, she had been right not to bring William. He was no part of her life here. Here she was still Lady Gleven, not Mrs Bursdon. She sat erect in the car, feeling a sense of homecoming, which was ridiculous since she had been here seldom. Yet each time she came it was as though she experienced anew the ultimate achievement—status as far as possible removed from the Jarvises.

Somewhere, it occurred to her, she had brothers and sisters, perhaps even a father still alive, but they were part of another life. She would not think of them, for it would remind her of Etty... How much Etty would have loved it down here. Helen was impatient with herself. Etty too was no part of her life now. Her future was the theatre—and Robert and his prospective wife. For she was in no doubt that that was why he had been so insistent that she should come to celebrate his birthday. He would have a guest, he said.

She had only seen that look on his face once before, and so she had found out all she could about Miss Evelyn Earl before she came. It was very little. Nobody seemed to know much about her before she arrived like a bombshell on the stage of the Princes Theatre. But what she had heard since then seemed to be good. Determined but pliable, gentle but spirited. But would her taste of stardom make her reluctant to settle down in Devonshire, be the wife Robert needed? She was too young at just nineteen to make that decision, Helen felt.

By the end of the evening her doubts were lulled. By the end of the second day they were entirely dispelled. Or almost entirely. A sixth sense told Helen all was not well. The couple were slightly too much on edge than was justified by their wish that she should approve of them. Very well, she would wait. Whatever it was would emerge.

She sat at the end of the table, toying with her glass of wine. She was playing a part and she knew it. Tonight she was playing Helen, Lady Gleven, stiff and erect as Queen Mary herself in her pearl choker and severe hairstyle. These new straight evening dresses suited her, hid the ravages that time was making with her figure, and the purple satin gave her an imperiousness that suited her role. Evelyn had chosen to wear pale blue. An unwise choice, thought Helen critically. It made her look insipid and she wasn't at all insipid in Helen's view. She must get her into dark green, deep rose, with those eyes, when she and Robert...

'Mother,' began Robert, when they had gathered together for their coffee in the drawing-room before the log fire. 'I—we—have something to tell you.' Helen prepared herself to look surprised, to rise up delightedly and embrace her daughter-in-law to be. 'Evelyn and I wish to marry.'

'My dear children,' replied Helen Hill warmly, a delighted exclamation passing her lips, just as she had practised. She rose to her feet and embraced Robert, then turned to Evelyn. But before she could reach her, Evelyn stepped back.

'No,' she said quickly, 'there is something you must know first.'

Her instincts had been right. Helen glanced at her son. 'Robert?'

'Evelyn Earl is not my real name,' broke in Evelyn, when Robert would not speak. 'I took it when I arrived in this country because I did not want any repercussions from my real name.'

'Which is?' asked Helen. The room seemed chilly.

'Helen Waters,' said the girl.

Helen Hill stood quite still. It was not fair. Inside she was crying out in pain. She was fifty-seven, had she not earned the right to some peace in life? She looked unemotionally at the girl, then at her son, who had turned away and was staring into the fire. Then she bent down, picked up her coffee cup, finished the last few sips, replaced it on the table and walked out of the room.

'Mother, may I come in?'

Helen did not answer. At his second knock, she raised her head wearily and answered, 'Yes.' Robert came in to find her seated on an upright chair, straight-backed and stiff as though sitting in judgement. There he was wrong. She was too shocked by what had happened to sit in judgement. Was she never to be rid of Jack Waters? Must he pursue her everywhere? He had taken her sister, taken her heart, was he now to reach out his rapacious hand and take her son also?

'In the whole wide world, Robert,' she burst out, 'couldn't you have found someone other than a Waters and your cousin?' Etty was only her half-sister but she could not bring herself to tell him so.

'What does that matter? It's nothing to me. Only to you. She's Helen—the girl I love—and the girl you liked only twenty minutes ago, and were going to welcome as your daughter-in-law.'

'Much can happen in twenty minutes.'

'Talk to her, Mother,' pleaded Robert. 'She hated deceiving you. It was me that persuaded her.'

'She comes from parentage well capable of deceit.'

'You don't know her,' Robert retorted angrily. 'This ridiculous feud has made them all so unhappy. When she found out who I was, she would have nothing to do with me in case I brought pain to you.'

'And what exactly has her family told her that she thinks *she* could bring pain to *me*, Helen Hill?' flared Helen. 'Is my private life the subject of jesting in South Africa?'

'Of course not. She just knows there was a family quarrel, that you are her aunt, and thought it would be best if she changed her name in case—' He broke off.

'In case my feud against her father continued to the daughter. In case my influence ruined her career before it had started. Thank you, Robert, for your faith in my character.' She was so convincing in her indignation that Robert had to remind himself that this was exactly what he thought and had good reason so to think—and as was being proved now.

'I shall marry her, Mother, whether you consent or not.'

'You are twenty-seven, Robert. You can

marry without my consent, but you will do so without my blessing. I take it the young lady, being underage, will have no difficulty getting *her* parents' consent. They will be only too delighted to install their daughter as the new Lady Gleven. A typical underhand plan by my dear sister.'

'No, you're wrong as usual, Mother, about Aunt Etty. She won't allow Helen to marry me unless you approve.'

A gleam of triumph lit Helen's eye. 'So there's no more to be said. I wish you good-night, Robert.'

He controlled himself with difficulty. 'We only have to wait two years and we can marry anyway.'

'True, my son—but can you wait two years? Can she? The stage arouses passions, passions that have to be satisfied. New interests come along. Can you trust your Helen?'

'Then we shall live together before then,' shouted Robert, angry beyond control now. 'And the next Lord Gleven can be born out of wedlock—how will that suit you, Mother, with your grand desires for the respectability of the name of Gleven?'

'You have taken leave of your senses, Robert,' said Helen furiously. 'You—the Baron Gleven—to live with a chorus girl—after all you've accomplished here.'

'And didn't you, Mother? What cared you for the name of Gleven, when you lived with Jack Waters in London and left Father on his own here? That's why you hate him so, isn't it? Because he preferred Aunt Etty to you?'

'Robert,' cried Helen in horror. 'No, no, *no*. What have they told her? You don't understand.'

'No, it's *you* who doesn't understand what love is. I love Helen, and if you can't give us your blessing, we'll find a way anyhow.'

With a struggle Helen regained her dignity. There were two spots of colour in her pale cheeks. 'I will never consent to your marrying Jack and Etty's daughter.'

The autumn season at Crowns began with *The Scandalous Mrs Tancred*, a comedy about the arrival of a widow in a small country village society, preceded by rumours of every description, all of which turned out to be far from the truth. In it there was a small but interesting part for William Bursdon, a veteran colonel of the 1914-1918 war, who had taken to the bottle. But opposite to Helen, playing the part of the apparently staid and reclusive owner of the manor house, was an actor of mature years named Percy Summers. Helen threw herself into the production.

337

She had heard no more from Robert since their meeting, and she suppressed the bitterness this gave her by burying herself in work. At least they were not married yet. This gave her some satisfaction. Miss Earl had opened in another play as successful as her last and there, Helen hoped, the matter rested. Toasts of London were too occupied to have much time for a country lord, she reasoned, and for this purpose refrained from sabotaging Miss Earl's career. Indeed she did all she could to make it prosper. Three months later she flattered herself that the ridiculous affair was over.

There, as so often, she was mistaken.

'I'll see myself in.'

Startled, Helen looked up from the escritoire in her drawing-room, where she had been writing letters. The familiar voice had only just registered with her by the time Jack pushed past Briggs and into the room.

She felt an impulse ridiculous in a mature woman of fifty-seven, to cry. His hair, almost completely grey now, was as bouncy and curly as ever. From a face bronzed by the sun, his blue eyes stared out as disconcertingly as ever, though the lines were more deeply etched in his face, so that it was them one looked at first and not the dimples which were still to be seen in the craggy cheeks.

She had not seen him for ten years, but they and other years of separation that had gone before whistled down the wind as she simply said: 'Jack!'

He had come in angry, but the sight of her disarmed him as ever, though he did not display any emotion. She was a year younger than him, a few years short of sixty, yet to him she still looked the same wayward girl he had loved all those years ago. Her hair with very little grey suited her short, made her look younger, vulnerable for all her years. And the familiar gesture—the hand raised in supplication—caught at his heart, and he longed to rush forward to take her in his arms. But too much lay between them.

'Helen, I've come to ask you—plead with you—to end this ridiculous feud. We're too old—'

Plead? It was the wrong word to use to Helen. He realized it instantly. It put her in the position of power. A position of which she took full advantage.

'Why should I?' She gestured to him to sit down. It gave her time to think, to adjust her emotions at seeing him again.

'For our children's sake.'

'And why should I care about your and Etty's daughter?'

'For your son, then? They're in love, Helen. As you and I were once.'

Helen's eyes flickered. 'And look what happened to that love.' She sounded unemotional, but inside her heart wrestled with the words 'were once'. 'You deceived me with my sister.'

'Are you going to go on being bitter for the rest of your life? Etty loves you, Helen. She wants to see you again, for us all to be friends.'

'Friends.' She gave a cynical laugh. 'Can you really see us having jolly family reunions, you and Etty, me and William?'

'Yes, if Helen and Robert were married.'

'As you won't allow Helen to marry Robert unless I give my consent, that means not until she is of age, and then I shan't be present.'

'I've already given them my blessing. When my daughter told me what happened—'

Helen blenched. 'You've—they can get married *now?*'

'I have no right to stand in their way. And Etty agrees.'

'I'm sure she does,' said Helen bitterly. 'Her crowning achievement—take my lover, and now my son.'

Jack rose angrily. 'Do you not remember

you played some part in that, Helen? That you deceived me, time and time again?'

'You should have trusted me,' she shouted, agonized.

'This is ridiculous.' Jack quietened down. 'We're nearly sixty and here we are shouting at each other like a couple of twenty-year-olds.'

She stared at him. 'What went wrong?' she burst out. 'Oh, what went wrong?'

He stiffened. 'We did, Helen. We weren't meant for each other.' He walked over to the window as though he could not bear to see her.

'But we were,' cried Helen. She ran to him. 'How can you say that? Have you forgotten our hillside? Have you forgotten, my Harlequin, how much we loved each other then? Can you have forgotten our home, the four-poster bed, that dreadful picture of St Paul's you won at the fair for me? Can you have forgotten that twelve years ago you said you'd love me always, that you'd never loved anyone else—but that you would not speak of it again? And it's still so, isn't it, Jack? *Isn't* it?' She put her arms round him but he tautened under her embrace, and did not return it.

I loved a different Helen,' he managed to say. 'I loved a Helen who was wild and impetuous and stubborn, but generous and warm-hearted who had love to give as freely as she took it, who burned over with life, energy and warmth. Where is she now, Helen? Where in this elegant, cool, poised remote woman who manipulates people in her professional and private life as though they were marionettes dancing under her fingers? My daughter isn't going to be a marionette dancing to your tune, Helen. She's going to marry the man she loves despite his mother, and she's going to have every help that Etty and I can give her. And this time, Helen you won't succeed. She's going to live in Devon with Robert and you will not be welcome at Monkswater, unless you can bring yourself to embrace her lovingly as your daughter. And Etty and I are coming back to London to live and work—and this time no vendetta will succeed. For this time we are free of you. The Helen I loved is dead.'

She stared at him, shaking her head, weeping quietly because she could not say what was in her heart: *'You don't understand. I'm just the same, but I can't be like that any more.'* She tried, oh how she tried. 'Just give me one word of love, Jack, and I'll let them marry.'

He looked back at her steadily, silently, then walked swiftly across the room and out of the door.

Jack had refused her again; he no longer

loved her. He had been here, now he had gone. This time it was indeed over.

By the time William returned to escort Helen to the theatre for the evening performance she was composed. She was even civil to William. She greeted her dresser briskly, for all the world as though the bottom had not dropped out of her universe.

Mechanically she took off her dress and donned the make-up shawl, seating herself before the mirror. She laid out the greasepaints, the curling irons, arranging the swabs of cotton wool and cream. Then carefully and painstakingly she began to assume the make-up for Mrs Tancred, thinking herself into the part. And as she gazed into the mirror at the unadorned face of Helen Hill and gradually added layer after layer she began to realize that life was not over, for this was real—this assumed identity, this building of another character. This was real, the life of the theatre. It was a world itself created by the individual for the many. Inside it she could hide and protect her wounded heart until it was healed, papering over the wounds with work. What need had she of a family, a lover, a husband, when her world was full of such characters and friends as her art could create? She would soon be an old woman, and old women did not have emotions. Her dreams would be confined to the stage; everything else was mere existence.

One year later she divorced William Bursdon for adultery and cruelty. William was a liability. As her husband she could not allow him to leave the company; as a member of it he caused disruption. Mindful of her reputation she looked after him: she bought him a house, and she saw to it that the housekeeper was comely enough to provide for all his needs. Then she devoted herself entirely to the career of Helen Hill and Crowns Theatre.

Chapter Twelve

'You are a fool, Owen.' The ice in Helen's voice was cutting. Owen held his ground; his round owl-like glasses slightly misted, perhaps from anger, perhaps from emotion. He had written for Helen Hill for nearly thirty years and worked for her for almost twenty of them; he had caused himself to betray old loyalties and he had meekly acquiesced, but this time, however, he was adamant.

'You'll fail—of course you will, at your age. It's quite absurd.'

'But I shall have tried,' said Owen quietly. For many years now he had been hankering to make a break, temporary or permanent, with the kind of drama presented by Helen Hill.

'Bernard Shaw must be trembling in his shoes. I don't see it, Owen.'

'I will write it under a *nom de plume,* if I have to. The important thing is to have it played.'

'Very well,' said Helen. Her small figure was rigid at the window, in silhouette against the light, and with the cloche hat pulled down shielding her face, Owen could not see her expression. 'But why leave Crowns? Can't you just—put this thing on elsewhere, and continue to do your *real* work here?'

'No, Helen. I'm getting on for sixty and I've been your playwright and partner for too many years. I want to do something different and I'm going to.'

It's his wife put him up to this, thought Helen bitterly; I never liked her, so calm, so well-bred, so sweetly smiling whenever she sees me. How could Owen do this to her? They had played together, fought together, come through the war together—why he was part of Crowns. And now, when they were really successful and they had a well established team and audience he wanted to abandon her.

'And what about me?' she asked bleakly.

'You, Helen?' Owen looked surprised as though this was an aspect that had never occurred to him. 'Why, you'll go on, find someone else...'

Go on? Helen looked out of the window at the rainy grey sky of Duke Street. Cars were hooting, people rushing by, eager to get somewhere and nowhere to go. To the left she could see Duke's Theatre, now the home of undistinguished knockabout farce, its day of glory long past. Her eyes blurred over and just for a moment she thought she caught a glimpse of a top-hatted

346

figure passing in through the stage door raising his hat to the flower seller as he always did... She pulled herself together. She was being ridiculous. It was 1927. And she was a woman with a business to run.

'I could recommend someone to take my place as business manager, and as playwright—since we're using other people's work besides mine at the present, that should be no problem. And I won't leave for a month or two.'

'Thank you,' Helen replied stiffly. 'That won't be necessary. I'm quite capable of running Crowns on my own—and choosing my own managers.'

'Are you sure, Helen?'

She reddened with fury. Not capable of running Crowns? Why a child could manage it now. And for Owen, whom she'd always thought her friend, to criticize her...

'Get out,' she said violently, 'go now, Owen. We'll see whether or not I'm capable of managing my theatre.'

Owen sighed. It had not been easy for him. He loved Helen Hill dearly, not with the blind adoration with which once he had worshipped at her feet, but with the deep abiding affection that came of years of working together, laughing together; she was part of his life, and to cut it away was as painful to him as to her. But it had to be done.

'Well, Owen, what are you waiting for?'

'A word of kindness, Helen.'

'*Kindness?* After this, you—you Judas?'

'For the past, Helen. It's all there. We can't just forget it. I'm your only link now with Duke's and with Jack Waters.'

How dared he mention that name again? 'Get out,' she shrieked, her control gone. 'You're a fool, Owen, and your famous life's work, that you've been working on so long, will fail. You need Crowns. You need me. You'll be back.'

But he wasn't. His play didn't fail, and didn't run long, but the notices were good, and respectful. The management of the Jupiter, where it was put on suggested he write another. And then another. Owen had been right about something else too—Helen could not manage the theatre on her own. Where her own career was concerned she lacked the objectivity that had guided her on Randolph's estates. She chose a weak foil as business manager, who lacked Owen's ability to manage simultaneously Crowns and Helen Hill herself. The new man could only manage Helen by giving her the flattery and the deference she required. Within two years, through inept financial and artistic control, the theatre was teetering on the brink of bankruptcy.

Even the pull of Helen's name was insufficient to draw people in to inferior plays. In 1929 when her lease came to an end she was in no position to renew. After twenty-three years of management Helen Hill was out of a job.

On the other side of London's theatre-land, in Holborn, Jack Waters was filling the Victoria Theatre with a series of revues that captured the spirit of the Twenties. Occasionally they starred Evelyn Earl, whenever she could spare time from Monkswater and her young family. Robert and Helen had two children now, a boy, Randolph, now five years old, and baby Helen, who was eighteen months. Helen was a grandmother. She had received a photograph of the children last Christmas, looked at it once, her face impassive, and forced herself to toss it into a drawer.

The Glevens were nothing to do with her any more than were the Waters, she told herself. She herself was no longer a Gleven. Moreover she had been disappointed that Ellen Terry had been made a Dame, but Helen Hill went unrecognized yet.

She had nightmares. She was fifteen again, seventeen, beating on doors that remained firmly closed. Managers loomed over her, sneering, turning her away, laughing in her face. Swains gloated, reaching out a lecherous hand towards her as if to say 'I've won'. And then it changed to her father's face whispering, 'You'll never escape, dahlin' daughter mine. Never escape. Never, never—never—'

She woke up crying, as she had not wept for many years. The shock made her come to a decision.

She dressed in lavender. All in lavender, save for the triple row of chunky pearls. It made her look fragile, complementing her greying hair, giving a soft look to the face that close up revealed hardness.

Mary Orford's eyes detected at once that it might be a Chanel jersey suit but it was last year's model, and Helen knew it, though her stance gave nothing away. With a slight but impeccable sniff Mary withdrew, leaving Helen in no doubt that she was the victor. Helen for once, did not care.

'I need your help, Owen,' she began dictatorially. No point in creeping along cap in hand.

A slight smile crossed his lips, not in triumph, but at the thought that Helen Hill could have come for any other reason. But the bond was still there between them, still unbroken.

'You were right, Owen, about your play. And I was wrong.' Owen nodded his head in acknowledgement, and waited. 'You have heard about Crowns?'

'Yes.'

'I can't find a job, Owen.' When Helen took down the barricades, they always came down in one fell swoop. It was one of her most endearing qualities, and disarmed Owen at once.

'I find that hard to believe.'

'I think perhaps I frighten them, Owen.' She looked at him pleadingly. She was right, of course, he thought. Her reputation had gone before. Stickler for discipline, for punctuality, intolerant of failure, imperious, professional to her fingertips—any manager would be proud to be able to bill Helen Hill, but hesitate to employ her. For she had another label inexorably pinned on her—'difficult to work with.'

'Perhaps,' was all he replied.

Helen sighed. It had been pointless coming. She reached for her handbag. He saw the movement.

'Don't be so impatient, Helen. I can't produce an answer for you out of a top hat. Give me time.'

She gave him time. And more time. And all the while she fumed in her Mayfair home, driving her small staff crazy. It was better to have Mrs Bursdon rushing in and out like a whirlwind than to have her constantly and impatiently around the house. They sighed for her to work again. Then at last the telephone rang.

'Helen? Owen. Could you come round to luncheon tomorrow? There is someone I'd like you to meet.'

His name was Jacob Charles. He had a mop of black curly hair and intense dark eyes. He was tall, gangly and instantly engaging. He did not shake her hand, but bent over and kissed it with an enthusiasm that shook Helen from her pose of gracious condescension.

'Miss Hill, you have the most fascinating hand. Has no one told you that?'

'Not on such short acquaintance,' remarked Helen coldly. She saw Owen flinch in the background.

Jacob Charles was not deterred. 'Your lifeline is remarkable, deep and strong—but the heart line! Oh what heart you have.' He glanced up at her suddenly from under dark lashes and the twinkle was so like Jack's that she quite forgot the stinging remark she had been going to make, and found herself laughing.

'Mr Charles, unless you release my hand I shall be quite unable to partake of Owen's undoubtedly excellent sherry.'

Throughout the luncheon that followed he both flattered and mystified her. She cursed the ridiculous convention of waiting till luncheon was over to discuss the business of the day; she had no idea who this young man was, but she wanted to find out. Meanwhile she felt younger than she had for many years, and to her own amazement found herself relating anecdotes from her early stage life that had dwelt in cupboards for many a long year. Her pre-London career was previously known to only a few people, but here she was chatting about music hall and her days as a *femme suspendue* and even as Columbine. Though here she faltered for a moment as she had a vision of Harlequin shooting up through the star trap...

Owen marvelled, as he glimpsed a Helen Hill he had never seen before, seen her as she must have appeared as a girl, before the years froze softness from her eyes.

At last Helen was unable to contain her impatience. 'You are an actor, Mr Charles?'

He shook his head. 'Manager, Miss Hill.'

'Manager?' Her eyebrows shot up. 'But you can't be more than—'

'Twenty-five, Miss Hill.'

'Twenty-five,' she said disbelievingly. 'But you can't be a manager at that age.'

'Jack Waters was,' said Jacob easily. Owen studied his wine glass intently.

Helen fixed Jacob with a steely glance.

353

Had he heard gossip or was that an innocuous remark? She studied his guileless face and hypnotic eyes. 'True.' Owen breathed again.

'And where are you in management, Mr Charles?' She reverted to her grand manner.

'Nowhere yet,' he replied cheerfully.

'Nowhere,' she echoed in resignation. 'You are either a very confident, or a very arrogant young man, Mr Charles.'

'Confident,' he said. 'Now that I have met you.'

'Me? May I ask how I enter your plans?'

'I want you as my heavyweight.'

Helen rose from her chair with dignity. 'I am not a pugilist, Mr Charles.'

He leapt up and grabbed her hand. 'Oh, now I've offended you. My dreadful tongue. That's what comes of being in management and not an actor. I don't have all the graces at my touch.' (This Owen doubted.) 'But you must know what I mean, Miss Hill. Now do forgive me.'

One glance at his contrite face, and she sat down again with equal dignity. 'Very well then, Mr Charles. Continue with your plans for my—er—heavyweight role, in a non-existent theatre, and I presume non-existent company?'

He nodded. 'I'm Jewish, Miss Hill,

or my family is. And they're also very rich. And they want to invest in the theatre. I've got the money. I've been waiting for the right inspiration to start off—the right theatre. Now I've found the inspiration—you.'

'So you're from the Jewish aristocracy,' murmured Helen.

'No.' He shook his head vigorously. 'My parents were born in poverty—they scrimped and saved and had just established a kosher store when the war came—and the riots. Their shop was burned down and they lost everything. They started again, in textiles this time—and this time they didn't lose it. They wanted to put their money into something they thought worthwhile—and they said that what gave them the greatest pleasure while they were so poor was the theatre—the music halls of the old East End—'

'East End?'

'Yes, I was brought up in Hoxton. That's where they lived. Near the old Britannia.'

'Hoxton,' repeated Helen softly. 'Did you know—?' She caught herself abruptly. No, she wouldn't talk of Swains', not with this stranger, however charming. But the thought of those days swept over her—Mr Hewson, Etty, those evenings round the piano. Herself at sixteen in that dreadful dress with the spangles. A lump formed in her throat. This young man was of Hoxton.

'Mr Charles,' said Helen Hill crisply, 'you have your heavyweight.'

Crowns had passed into other hands, leased to an American, but there were other theatres in London. The Regency was a new theatre in Shaftesbury Avenue, and its opening production under the Charles management, *Teacups for Two,* established itself as a West End theatre of note. Helen became once more the established grande dame of the London stage. However, no amount of bullying, wheedling or cajolery would persuade Jacob to give Helen her way and allow piano and song to have a part in a play. That, he said, was the old Helen Hill, not the new Jacob Charles model. Her roles were not as large as she would like but they were clever, displaying her talents to the full and allowing her to dress at Hartnell or Chanel.

Nor had there been the difficulties with the rest of the company that Owen had foreseen. Jacob Charles seemed to exert some uncanny magic; Helen was regarded as a rather strict but kind maiden aunt with quaint eccentricities—though this was not how she herself saw it. Her arrival at rehearsal impeccably dressed, and strictly on the dot of the appointed time, peeling off her long white gloves, and bidding her gracious good mornings created a family feeling in the company unknown to her before. Devotion yes, loyalty yes, admiration yes, but this warmth, this sense of belonging was new.

She had been working at the Regency for about six months when something happened to prick the new found security and happiness of her position. *Teacups for Two* was still playing to good houses, but its successor was in rehearsal. It was hard work rehearsing in the morning, and playing in the evening, but Helen had never resented hard work, and nowadays time spent at the theatre passed with more ease and less strain than the lonely hours passed in the tranquillity of her home. It was at home one afternoon that she received an unexpected visitor.

Her daughter-in-law arrived, with her baby daughter. Helen received her graciously, but coolly. No one should say that her manners were not perfect. Inside she was longing for news of her son. She had heard nothing of him; she had not even seen Julia.

'I've come,' said the younger Helen awkwardly, 'to ask you...'

Helen waited impassively, but watchful.

'I haven't come here for myself.'

'Robert?' Helen's voice was like a whiplash.

'No. Robert's well. It's—Mother, she's not well. Her chest—you know she's always had a weak chest.'

Helen's eyes flickered. Yes, Etty had always had a weak chest. Etty tall and pale, bravely saying, *I'll see Mrs Blades. I don't mind.* 'No, Etty, I'll lift that. It's *too heavy for you.* 'No, Etty, you do the *sewing. You can't go out to work. I'll look after you, don't worry. I'll always look after you.*' Her own childish voice echoed back down the years. Two girls, Etty and Helen Jarvis.

'I remember.'

'The doctors are afraid that—she's had bronchitis so badly; they think it's turned to pneumonia and then...oh Aunt Helen, couldn't you come to see her? She wants to see you again so much, they both do.'

'Both?' Helen doubted that.

She felt no animosity now towards her daughter-in-law, but she couldn't go. It was all too long ago. How could she stir up the painful embers of her heart?

'Please come, please do.'

Helen thought of her present happiness discovered so unexpectedly. She didn't want anything to disrupt this haven of security she'd found. Least of all Etty—and Jack. She didn't want to have to think about it. It was too painful. But how could she explain all that to Robert's wife? She was too young to understand. Helen didn't even feel animosity towards Etty any more, now that she'd found Jacob. She didn't feel anything at all except her excitement every time she entered the Regency; as she dressed for her part, rehearsed. That was her family now.

'I'll think about it,' she said at last.

'Telegram for Mrs Bursdon.' The telegraph boy stuck his hand out hopefully and went off whistling but disappointed. All the same these theatres.

The stage doorkeeper, new that week, looked at the telegram in puzzlement. He put it on the shelf in his cubbyhole. Never heard of her. Must be someone coming to the first night. He'd give it to Mr Naylor, the front-of-house manager, later on. There were other things to think about tonight. A first night. Already the theatre was a-hum, flowers were arriving for Helen Hill, flowers for young Miss Wilson, new to a leading role, flowers for everyone it seemed, and a stack of telegrams a mile high. All his life he'd queued up in pit and gallery queues. Now he could push them around for a change. It was going to be a good 'un, this new play—*The Disenchantment of Mrs Gorrindge.* As the time wore on, the cast started arriving, more telegrams of good wishes, more flowers, and in the excitement he quite forgot the telegram for Mrs Bursdon whoever she was.

'I shall feast you with ostrich's eyes, with pearls from the choicest plovers' eggs and treacle pudding,' said Jacob Charles, whirling Helen round on stage after the fifteenth curtain call and the house lights had come up. 'I shall feast you on ambrosia; I shall feast you *all* on ambrosia.'

And so he did. It was three o'clock before Helen returned to her bed.

'I'm too old for all this,' she murmured to herself, wearily creaming her face. But the smile on her lips belied the words. She was not too old, not too old at all.

The telegram was brought round the next morning; it reached her at almost the same time as the newspapers with their congratulatory notices. It read simply: 'Please come. Etty dying. Jack.' But it was eighteen hours late in delivery.

Helen Hill, grande dame of the stage, was a child again. Etty with the great big sad eyes and the bewildered look. Etty, whom she had vowed always to look after. All the years in between were swept away, and she saw only the child, and then the girl, the songs, Mr Hewson. What had happened to Helen Jarvis? And what had happened to her love for Etty?

She hurried to her Davenport. Tucked away at the back she found the photograph she sought: two girls in a seaside photographer's studio, hair wind-swept, arms round each other's shoulders, hope shining out of their eyes. She wept.

She was eighteen hours late—what might have happened? Her car was ready at the front door fifteen minutes later. It only took a further fifteen minutes to reach the house in St John's Wood, where Jack and Etty lived. As the butler opened the door, the atmosphere of grief was heavy. Silently he showed her into the drawing-room. Jack was sitting there in an armchair, his grey head back to her. He looked round as he heard her enter, but did not get up. There was recognition but neither welcome nor condemnation in his face.

'You're too late, Helen. Etty died last night.'

Helen stared at him, numbed and white. 'Oh, Jack.' Her heart was crying out for his grief. And then for her own. 'I only heard just now. Your telegram—it only just arrived.'

There was no comprehension on his

face. 'It was your first night, Helen. How could you—'

She rushed to him and knelt by his side. 'Jack, I'd have come. But I didn't know. Don't you believe me?' Her voice was agonized. Surely he couldn't believe she was so cold-hearted as to ignore that summons? He must know that she loved Etty. She always had. Always—only so much had come between them.

'What does it matter, Helen? What does anything matter, any more?'

She would not go to the funeral. She could not face her own son, let alone Jack. Afterwards she went to the church where the funeral had taken place, and walked to the front, not noticing another mourner sitting in the shadows of the side chapel. It seemed to have little to do with Etty, this huge empty building. She tried painfully to examine her conscience; had she behaved so badly to Etty, misjudged her? Had she genuinely thought Helen had abandoned Jack and thought her, Helen, as cruel and heartless then as later Helen did her? But she could not answer these questions and with a sigh abandoned them as irrelevant. What was more important is what she would have said if she had seen Etty again that last time. Perhaps nothing. There would have

362

been no need. She would just have caught her in her arms, embraced her, and then they would have been laughing just as they did all those years ago.

With a sigh Helen left the church. Jack, in the chapel, watched her, and wondered.

She went slowly to the churchyard. She gazed at the flowers, huge numbers of them, edges beginning to curl in the harsh wind. Then she looked at the little posy in her hand and placed it on the grave, whispering:

'Sweets to the sweet.
There's rosemary—that's for remembrance...'

'Remembrance. Do you remember, Etty? Mr Hewson taught us that bit? Do you remember him dancing around looking so soulful, those old carrots in his hand for flowers? He couldn't do Hamlet he said, but he could do Ophelia. Do you remember, Etty? Do you?'

Helen Hill had been fifty years upon the stage. (She always omitted the music hall years.)

Only a few days before she had heard that in the honours list she was to be made a Dame of the British Empire. At last she was a lady in her own right. Shortly she would go to the palace to have the decoration pinned on by her monarch. She had won Helen's Gold at last. It was the culmination of all her ambitions. But yet now she had the honour, her life seemed empty—now there was little else to attain. Yet how Etty would have gloried in it for her. If only Mr Hewson could see his pupil now.

Tonight she was celebrating her Golden Jubilee. It made her feel like Queen Victoria. She thought of that small round figure dressed in black, decorated with fine white lace in the open carriage—or was that the Diamond Jubilee she was thinking of? She sighed. It was all so hard to remember clearly now. And now she was having her own Jubilee. Surprise had been her first emotion when dear Jacob told her what was being planned, surprise that the London stage folk thought enough of her to want to celebrate her fifty years upon the stage.

It needed a much larger stage than the Regency to do justice to the hundreds of players who wanted to pay tribute to her. The programme had been kept from her, and Jacob had arranged for her to have lunch elsewhere. She was not allowed at the Princess of Wales till half an hour before curtain up, and when she saw the programme, presented in red covers embossed and threaded with gold, she gasped. It seemed the whole of the London stage was represented in its pages.

As the performance began, she watched from the royal box until it was time to take the stage herself, enthralled as stars from the past mixed with those of the present. Goodness me, who was that portly woman in the tight black dress—Margaret Cunningham, yes, it must be, her theatre life well behind her, even Rosie Ellis from her Gala days—the list went on and on.

Yet even more than old friends, the youngsters moved her; there was young Mr Eldon who had been a bit part actor in her first production for Jacob, making a speech now recalling some small pearl of wisdom she had unconsciously dropped his way, and that timid girl who crept around like a mouse and three years later had blossomed into a leading lady. There were faces from Duke's days even, and many from Crowns. They had not forgotten their 'school' nor their teacher. She was still with a humble astonishment.

At last Jacob came to escort her to perform her own contribution. As he came into the box she managed to say: 'All these people, Jacob. Do they—*love* me, do you think?'

He raised her hand to his lips. 'Oh yes, Helen. They love you.'

She did not rebuke him for calling her Helen. She was too happy. Despite everything, they loved her. They liked her. She wondered why, and then dismissed the thought. The reason did not matter. She smiled at Jacob. 'Come, Jacob, I mustn't miss my cue. Not tonight.'

Tonight she was allowed her piano again for the excerpt from Owen's most popular play, *A Swallow in Summer*. After her scene was over, she sat at the piano and ran her fingers over the keys, and softly began to sing. 'For my heart is yours'. It seemed as though she was in that great vast theatre, alone with Jack.

She was a small figure in her silver lace evening dress on that vast stage. Laughter and tears... She had tried now to give them both. Had she succeeded? She held her hand up for silence and the applause died away. She didn't know, yet, quite what she was going to say. She had prepared a speech, but as she stood there looking at the row upon row of her friends—for such all the audience seemed to her—she found herself saying something completely different, saying what lay deep in her heart.

'When I was on the halls—the music halls, you know—they said to me, you'll be dead by the time you're forty, you'll burn yourself out. But the theatre, the real theatre, isn't like that. It's a family. With all the squabbles and love that a family have. It took me a long time to learn that, for as a child I never had that family love, and I had to learn what it could mean. Now I know that it takes your love, your devotion, your travail, and rarely gives you a word of thanks. But it enfolds you in a tide of love between audience and performers when it works right, and when it doesn't—well it's just like ordinary families—you go off disgruntled, but you know you've time to put it right for next time. I've had fifty years now of my family life and I want to thank you. I wouldn't change it for the world. Thank you all for coming to my party.'

The applause seemed to recede and eyes were misted as she bowed her thanks. She knew Robert was out there, with his wife and children. Julia too. She knew Owen was out there. And tonight, just for tonight, perhaps Jack was there; she could imagine him so clearly, by her side, holding her hand, giving her strength, old woman that she was, to face the world.

There was one last thing: 'No one in a family stands alone; they are strengthened and enriched by the other members. And in my life I have been lucky enough to have three people without whose help I might still have been a worn out music hall singer. Firstly dear Owen Orford, who writes from his heart and who wrote so often for me; then there is Jacob Charles, my present manager—and friend—and there is—was—most of all, Jack Waters.'

Her voice trembled, but she had said it, and there were tears in the eyes of her audience.

Late that year, 1932, Jacob married his new young star, an auburn-haired girl named Norma Sweeting, who promptly retired from the stage and devoted herself to building a home and a lineage. She was not Jewish. Bitterly disappointed, Jacob's parents withdrew to the fastnesses of the family enclave, excluding Jacob, and into their place as favourite visitor and surrogate mother stepped Helen Hill. In their baby girl born in September 1933 she found all the delights of grandmotherhood she had denied herself with her own family. On her she poured all the love that she had to give, and still could not bring herself to bestow nor was offered the opportunity of bestowing, on her own. Julia and her three children were so intellectually inclined that on the rare times she met them she found them bewildering. Robert's and Helen's children she saw but once a year, on a formal visit that gave little pleasure to anyone, and instead lavished her love and attention where she knew there was no danger of rejection.

Jacob and Norma had another child, a boy this time, in whom Helen delighted even more than the first. Then once again clouds gathered over Helen's life without her noticing. She had quite understood when Jacob explained to her that he had long wanted to produce a Restoration comedy, and now had the opportunity, but there was no part for her. However, it wouldn't be a long run. She had said she needed a holiday in any case. She would visit Swithins, perhaps even visit Robert and Helen in Devon.

The holiday did her good, and made her all the more eager to recommence work. Jacob had promised her that after the end of the present run, she could try Lady Bracknell. She was looking forward to it. What better part after all? She had had to talk him into it, but he'd come round in the end. She'd been so tired before she went on holiday, she hadn't been at her best, but he would see now what she could do.

Rehearsals began well. Jacob had promised to direct this one himself, which pleased her. She wasn't used to all these new young producers and responded only to Jacob. The readings and early rehearsals went very well. Really, she thought with contentment, this will be the happiest production I've ever been in. The young men playing Jack and Algernon were perfect foils for each other; dear Norma was playing Gwendolen, and a perfectly enchanting child Cicely.

She did not know that Jacob had pleaded with Norma to be in it, much against her will with two small children to look after. But for Helen's sake she had agreed.

'The old girl sees this as the high spot of her career,' he said to her. 'You've got to be there, look after her, see nothing—goes wrong.'

'What could go wrong?' asked Norma puzzled. 'And when did Helen become an old girl?'

He avoided her eye. 'She's seventy this year, my honey child. She can't go on for ever.'

But it seemed as if Helen was set to do just that. The rehearsals continued and her reading improved. Already as she moved around the stage she was getting the right feel to the walk, the all important thing. The words could come later. The rest of the cast were dropping their books by now, but she knew she had to concentrate on character first.

Three weeks away from the opening night, Helen was still on the book. He quelled his own misgivings, but then Jacob began to notice the signs of uneasiness in the company; he had a quiet word with Helen.

'Dear boy,' she said charmingly. 'How silly to worry about such a trifle. I'll learn them this weekend and I'll be word perfect—at least for the first two acts on Monday.'

But when Monday came she wasn't. She stumbled her way but so haltingly and slowly and with so many mistakes that Jacob suggested that for that morning she used the book again. On Tuesday it was little different.

'Oh my dear boy,' came Helen's contrite voice. 'I'm so sorry. By tomorrow it will be all right.'

But it wasn't. Jacob could not bear to watch.

'You've got to do something, Jacob,' said Norma sombrely later. 'I've done my best. I've sat with her, gone through them, but I think she's so confident, she just doesn't realize.'

'And we open in two weeks' time,' said Jacob despairingly.

All that evening Norma sat with Helen who was completely mystified. Why was Norma making such fuss about nothing?

Of course she knew the words; did they think she was an amateur? She grew quite angry. Only when dear Norma became upset did she soften. She could not bear to see Norma upset.

'Don't worry, my dear,' she said, engagingly. 'It will be all right. It always is, isn't it?' she said brightly.

And looking at her confidence Norma wondered if it would indeed be all right. The theatre gods always smiled on Helen Hill.

Helen faltered, and looked winningly at Jacob who was somewhere in the darkness there, the darkness that looked so alien. 'If I might have a break, Jacob dear?'

'Certainly, Miss Hill,' he replied formally. 'Fifteen minutes everyone.'

As she turned to leave the stage he bounded up the side steps and took her hand. 'Come with me, Miss Hill,' he said quietly. 'Let's go somewhere quiet where we can talk.'

She allowed herself to be escorted up the stairs that led to the royal box, and he seated her gently in the tall high chair. Then he moved his chair in front of her and took both her hands in his.

'Helen,' he said gently, 'it's no good, is it, my dear?'

'I can learn them, I can,' she said

hurriedly, nervously.

'It's less than two weeks to the opening night,' he said. 'Dearest, you can't remember them, can you?'

'They're coming. I've never had any trouble before. It's just a matter of concentration.'

'But you have had trouble before, haven't you?' he said gently. 'I've seen the little notes left here and there on the stage, in your costume, on the props. The cast are loyal, Helen. They love you, and so do the stage staff, but they couldn't keep it from me for ever. And now it's worse, isn't it?'

'Yes.' In the dimness he thought he saw a tear trickling down her cheek. 'What can I do?'

'Helen dear, I can't take the risk, you must see that? It's not fair to the rest of the cast.'

He felt the conflict in her, the desire to plead with him to trust in her, give her another chance. But Helen Hill was a professional. And the professional in her won.

'You have no choice,' she told him briskly. 'Have you a replacement?'

Jacob nodded miserably. 'Ah,' said Helen. 'You will make my apologies to the cast?'

She stood up, fragile and lost in the

ornate box, and felt round blindly for her hat.

'I wonder,' she said, 'I wonder, dear Jacob if I might ask for your arm down to my car. It is waiting, I suppose?'

'Yes,' he said humbly. 'Norma is seeing to it.' (And pray God, something else as well.)

'Then let us go,' said Dame Helen Hill. She talked quite brightly as they walked down the stairs, of the parts she had played for him, of her watching first nights, of spending more time with his children.

As they reached the foyer, he looked round as though searching for something or someone. But it was empty.

'Thank you, Jacob. Now return to your rehearsal. I would prefer to leave the Regency alone.' He leaned forward and kissed her on the cheek, something he had never had the temerity to do before. She tried hard to appear disapproving. 'That will do, Jacob. This is rehearsal, not a first night orgy.'

Helen Hill went out alone through the heavy doors of the Regency and they swung closed behind her. Ahead of her was the Daimler to take her back into solitude, her chauffeur standing ready by the door. Helen paused on the steps. It seemed a long way to walk. Six or seven paces into the unknown, into an unknown and empty future. Seven paces that had to be taken, as she had taken so many before. Resolutely she began to walk forward.

Into the sunlight, came a figure, an elderly man with grey hair but a light and a love in his eyes that the years could not extinguish. Then a familiar hand was under her elbow guiding her, helping her down the steps. A great peace enveloped Helen and enfolded her safe for ever. She was going home with Jack.

Epilogue

Dame Helen Hill walked slowly to the piano, and forced herself to look straight at Etty's picture. Not at the one of the two girls at Scarborough, but at the large full-faced picture taken not long after the First World War; a mature, placid, content Etty. It stood there for Jack's sake. She could never confess, even to herself, that it still caused her pain.

'But one man loved the pilgrim soul in you
And loved the sorrows of your changing face...'

'But our love, has not fled?' she had asked Jack last night when he read the poem to her. 'Not changed to kindliness?'

He had taken her hand. 'No, Helen.'

With a rush of love, she picked up the photograph, and put it at the front beside the photograph of Robert and Helen.

'There, Etty,' she whispered. 'The family we began.' She grimaced at herself for being a sentimental old fool.

Behind her she heard the door close.

Jack had come in. He must have seen her. He put his hands gently on her shoulders, and she turned to smile at her husband.

The publishers hope that this book has given you enjoyable reading. Large Print Books are especially designed to be as easy to see and hold as possible. If you wish a complete list of our books, please ask at your local library or write directly to: Magna Large Print Books, Long Preston, North Yorkshire, BD23 4ND, England

This Large Print Book for the Partially sighted, who cannot read normal print, is published under the auspices of

THE ULVERSCROFT FOUNDATION

Other MAGNA Romance Titles In Large Print

ROSE BOUCHERON
The Massinghams

VIRGINIA COFFMAN
The Royles

RUTH HAMILTON
Nest Of Sorrows

SHEILA JANSEN
Mary Maddison

NANCY LIVINGSTON
Never Were Such Times

GENEVIEVE LYONS
The Palucci Vendetta

MARY MINTON
Every Street

1	21	41	61	81	101	121	141	161	181
2	22	42	62	82	102	122	142	162	182
3	23	43	63	83	103	123	143	163	183
4	24	44	64	84	104	124	144	164	184
5	25	45	65	85	105	125	145	165	185
6	26	46	66	86	106	126	146	166	186
7	27	47	67	87	107	127	147	167	187
8	28	48	68	88	108	128	148	168	188
9	29	49	69	89	109	129	149	169	189
10	30	50	70	90	110	130	150	170	190
11	31	51	71	91	111	131	151	171	191
12	32	52	72	92	112	132	152	172	192
13	33	53	73	93	113	133	153	173	193
14	34	54	74	94	114	134	154	174	194
15	35	55	75	95	115	135	155	175	195
16	36	56	76	96	116	136	156	176	196
17	37	57	77	97	117	137	157	177	197
18	38	58	78	98	118	138	158	178	198
19	39	59	79	99	119	139	159	179	199
20	40	60	80	100	120	140	160	180	200

201	211	221	231	241	251	261	271	281	291
202	212	222	232	242	252	262	272	282	292
203	213	223	233	243	253	263	273	283	293
204	214	224	234	244	254	264	274	284	294
205	215	225	235	245	255	265	275	285	295
206	216	226	236	246	256	266	276	286	296
207	217	227	237	247	257	267	277	287	297
208	218	228	238	248	258	268	278	288	298
209	219	229	239	249	259	269	279	289	299
210	220	230	240	250	260	270	280	290	300

301	310	319	328	337	346
302	311	320	329	338	347
303	312	321	330	339	348
304	313	322	331	340	349
305	314	323	332	341	350
306	315	324	333	342	
307	316	325	334	343	
308	317	326	335	344	
309	318	327	336	345	